SWANNSONG

SWANNSONG

ANN BLAIR KLOMAN

This book was printed in the United States of America.

This book is published by Seawrack Press, Inc., 61 Ely's Ferry Road, Lyme, CT 06371 USA.

To order additional copies of this book, contact:
Xlibris Corporation
1-888-795-4274
www.Xlibris.com
Orders@Xlibris.com
28132

The places exist,
the people and events are only in the author's imagination.

PROLOGUE

BOSTON 1958

In the dimmed room, the doctor watched the young girl rise awkwardly on her elbows.

"Make it stop," she said thickly.

He pressed her gently down onto the sweat soaked pillow and smoothed her matted hair.

"I can't give you more sedatives. It would slow things down and you need to work harder."

She pushed his hand away.

"I can't. Please, just get it out of me"

He watched a new contraction stiffen her body. Her back arched and he gently massaged the taut, hard mound of her belly. He felt helpless, unprofessional and angry at being coerced by the Swann family to manage this clandestine business. What man had gotten her into this mess? She refused to tell. He regretted that he was unable to relieve her futile pain. When the spasm subsided, she rolled away from his touch.

He sat for a moment, fingers pressed to his eyes. Then he switched off the overhead light, leaving only the bedside lamp to cast soft shadows over them. When she finally slept, he stood and stretched. The room smelled of stale sweat. He raised the blinds, opened the window, and let the rising sun stain them with its hellish redness.

"Je-sus," the girl woke and groaned. Her face contorted and she gripped the bed sheets as involuntary muscles lifted her hips. Again exhausted, she sank back onto the tangled bed sheet.

"Please, do something before it comes again."

In a decisive voice, he said grimly, "More sedation would be dangerous for both you and—"

"I hate you. All of you want me to die."

He knew she was wrong. They did not want her to die. But she might if he risked waiting much longer. He hadn't the skill or experience needed, but he knew she was not going to propel this captive baby into the world on her own. They had wasted enough miserable hours, physically and emotionally. He saw her hand rise to strike him and he grasped it mid-air.

"You're not going to die," he said calmly, "but your baby's not coming without help."

The young doctor looked around the completely equipped delivery room of this small, very private clinic. He must gather himself and keep calm. He had never done a Cesarean section alone.

Her baby was born on that cerulean morning in early June. Neither a happy nor celebrated event, it was a misfortune for any unmarried sixteen-year-old. But this descent from grace by the only daughter of a venerable and unforgiving Boston Back Bay family proved grievous.

Her thoughts were woozy as she drifted back from the limbo of anesthesia. Her hand stroked the dressing covering her aching, but now flattened belly, and cautiously stretched. With childish disappointment, she mused that her baby, a week late, had the common pearl, instead of emeralds, for its birthstone.

They had not yet told her that the baby had been stillborn.

CHAPTER 1

ELMORE HARBOR 1985

Hannah Packwood smiled. Under the cover of mist blowing in from the ocean, she watched Emily Parrish trying to sneak out discreetly from a night spent with Phil at the Rectory. The black lab, Emperor, jogging at her side, recognized a familiar body and took off toward the church, barking his throaty greeting. Emp's enthusiasm foiled Emily's furtive escape and Hannah waited as Em maneuvered her antique three-speed from behind Phil's woodshed.

"Call off your dog," said Emily with mock ill humor.

"Getting a little religion on the side?" teased Hannah.

"Yes, dear, but as I am generally admired in the village as a 'nice' middle aged woman, past all carnal pleasure, maybe God will turn the other cheek."

"Go for it! I doubt whether HE cares a rat's ass about illicit sex on earth."

Though Hannah was more than fifteen years younger, she had befriended Emily, one of the nicer members of the large Swann family whose homes dominated the southern side of the harbor. And she was less odd than most of them.

The once substantial income inherited from the Swann sea captain's shipping fortunes had suffered in past years from bad investments, and no longer supported the maintenance of the grand old houses anchored to the cliffs above the ocean. Despite the family's misgivings, Emily was the one most supportive of Hannah's coming from Australia to expand and rejuvenate the faltering Swann Greenhouse business. But beneath Hannah's enthusiasm for starting a new life in this strange new country, she had her own moments of doubt. Her first bit of luck was to hire Thea Morgan, after just one interview, to be her assistant. They had connected immediately. Hannah respected that Thea, only one year out of college, had considerable botanical skills. She also admired her guts in the face of her handicap. Thea was blind.

Emily leaned over her handlebars. "I hear you and Thea are invited to Bea's birthday dinner on Saturday."

"Bea's been very good to both of us," she said of the woman who was the Swann family's domineering matriarch. "As for Saturday's invitation, I think she wants us there to diffuse the family foments."

"The fact is," said Emily, "Bea likes you. She was skeptical at first, especially over hiring Thea. But she has come to approve of your efforts. However, you're right. There might be some bombs to be defused that night."

Hannah shared Emily's amazement at how easily she had adjusted, considering their volatile personalities, to find her place within the Swann family. She'd also found little trouble adapting to Thea's blindness. With comfortable camaraderie, the two of them shared the cottage below the greenhouse.

Emily pushed off to gather speed for the short steep hill up from the church. She called out over her shoulder, "Race you home! I'm feeling rather fit."

Starting after her, Hannah admitted that Emily was indeed trim and wrinkle-free for a woman in her forties. She had also managed to snag Phil Vaughn—the rector, and the town's only attractive bachelor-widower. Hannah stifled a jab of disloyalty and imagined enjoying a lustful romp in Phil's bed. Despite her own healthy good looks, there had been a sad lack of lustful romps for too long. Or any romps at all. She found that the harbor was no haven for attractive men. Most of them were comfortably settled with families. The single bozos that hung together in front of Strait's Market on summer evenings, whistling and making rude gestures, were too much like the cowboys she'd left Down Under. She lied to herself that it didn't matter. Besides, she was too busy in the greenhouse and too tired by the end of the day to venture out for the long drive to the singles nightspots in Camden or Rockland.

Hannah and Emp passed the huffing Emily halfway up the hill, then waited by the ramshackle tier of mailboxes that marked the head of Neck Road, the dead end leading out to the Swann compound

Emily stopped, gasping. "It's this old bicycle, Hannah, not me."

The two women turned at the sound of the postal van chugging up the hill behind them. It stopped in front of the row of the Swann's mailboxes and a grim, accusing face—not the regular deliverer, jolly Mrs. Hobie—leaned out the open side. He held up a large pile of mail and gestured at the weathered and sagging shelf that held their mailboxes.

"Mornin' ladies." He pushed back his cap. "You two any of these people? Mostly named Swann?"

Emily answered. "Yes, I mean no. Actually I'm one of the non-Swanns—Emily Parrish." She smiled bleakly. "I know our boxes aren't up to postal standards, but Mrs. Hobie has had this route for so long that it never mattered. Is she ill?"

"Broke her hip," he answered with no apparent sympathy. "I'll be delivering 'til she's mended." He scratched under his blue U.S. Mail visor, and studied the two women. Hannah watched the old goat's wandering gaze and was annoyed by Emily's guilty fluster.

"Well now," Hannah spoke up sharply, "if you've got a pencil, maybe you could take a minute and jot this down. The blue box is for Colin Swann and his mother, Beatrice Swann, and Miss Emily Parrish here. The red one belongs to Ian and Grace Swann. The one marked Studio is Graham Viero's, and the big green one is for the Nursery Greenhouse. I'm Hannah Packwood, its manager, and Thea Morgan is my assistant. That's easy now isn't it? Green for greenhouse." Before he could answer, she took the entire packet of mail from his hands and dropped it into Emily's bicycle basket.

Emily, still penitent, said, "We'll put our names on the boxes by tomorrow. Sorry."

Hannah called the dog to her side and watched the postman lean out of his van to better appreciate the motion of Emily's nicely lobed bottom as she disappeared beyond the canopy of firs. Before Hannah started down the road after her, she heard him mutter under his breath.

"Easy, ayuh, green for greenhouse." Hannah gave him a sour look as he turned his van and drove back down the hill. She followed Emily down the Neck Road and watched her labor her bicycle onto the semi-circle of packed gravel that fronted the big Swann house. Emily had lived there with her Aunt Bea and her aunt's eldest son, Colin, for most of her life. That would never change.

Or would it?

The fog had receded beyond the harbor, and the pale June sun shone on the white clapboards, dark green shutters and its trim, symmetrical squareness. The whole look was completed by the low-railed captain's walk centered on the roof.

Hannah crunched onto the gravel and puffed to a stop beside Emily. The older woman hauled the bundle of mail from her basket before dropping her bike onto the grass. Hannah saw her face tighten and frown.

"You can work off a lot of aggro, Em, with a pitchfork, she suggested. "These beds need some mulching."

"I'm not aggressed, Hannah, just apprehensive. And I'm not the only one nervous about Saturday. Bea's grand birthday dinner will test everyone's humor." She added wryly, "Not to mention tempers. Most of us are expecting another of Bea's unpleasant surprises." She shrugged. "Oh, well, nothing as good as a family roast." She gave Hannah a wicked grin. "Actually, I can hardly wait."

Hannah grinned back. "I shall have to rehearse my role as diplomat. Bea scares me a little. However, we're not family and it was nice of her to include Thea and me."

"Don't be silly. Bea Swann can be sharp tongued, but she

probably likes you better than her own children. Come on in and we'll sort this mail."

Hannah clapped her hands. "Go find Thea, Emperor." Despite the agency's rules regarding dogs trained for the blind, Emp suffered no ill effects from joining Hannah on her morning jogs, and for the remainder of the day would be Thea's adoring and obedient eyes. She watched the sleek animal take off for the greenhouse cottage.

She followed Emily inside and they crossed to the small desk tucked into an alcove off the library. The bow window behind it overlooked the front borders that were now a soft carpet of bluebells, *aubrietia*, and yellow *primulas*. Emily sorted through the mail, most of which was greenhouse business.

"Give Grace, Ian's, and Viero's to me," said Hannah. "It's a fine morning. I'll walk around by the sea wall and deliver it. Maybe one of them will give me a cup of coffee."

"Stay a bit," said Emily, "I've not had breakfast myself. Phil left the rectory at dawn to go fishing and when I came down, his kitchen was such a disgusting mess that I didn't want to fix any. He'd packed his usual drooling fried egg sandwiches that he'll eat after they've congealed out there on the ocean along with the rest of the brownies he burned for our dessert last night. God must personally oversee his digestion."

"At least you didn't clean up for him." She paused. "You didn't, did you?"

Emily sighed. "You're the eternal feminist, Hannah."

"Not really. I just think grown men can wash their own dishes."

Before either of them could settle the question of kitchen fealty, Emily's house phone rang, and Bea's voice came from the speaker.

"Em, are you at your desk? Come up with the mail when you're free. We must talk about Saturday evening."

"Right Bea," she answered. "I'll be up in a minute." Emily dropped the receiver back with a thud. "She who must be obeyed. There goes breakfast. I promise you a rain check."

Hannah laughed. "Maine in June, you'll get it."

After Hannah left, Emily picked up a legal sized manila envelope addressed to Beatrice Swann. She tapped it idly with the tip of her ivory letter opener. The return label identified it as being from Hobart and Hobart, Attorneys. The stuffy appellation didn't suit the young Stuart Hobart, who had grown up as a friend of the Swann family. Stu assumed the ceremonious role of family lawyer only when he solemnly attended to family business in the Rockland offices inherited from his father.

She drew the sharp point of the opener lightly across the envelope addressed to her aunt and, for a moment, rationalized that it was not marked personal. Did she dare? It wouldn't be the first time. After only slight hesitation, she slit it open, shook out the contents, and began to read. Slowly, disbelieving, she re-aligned the pages and slid them back into their wrapper. Arms resting on her elbows she let an amused smile form behind her palms. She spoke softly through her fingers and gazed out at the blue and yellow blur beyond the window.

"Holy shit, Bea. It's going to be some birthday party!"

CHAPTER 2

Hannah hunched her shoulders beneath her sweater. The damp mist permeated the path along the cliff top and a chill ocean wind soughed overhead through the fir trees. Spongy mats of resinous needles, compacted over seasons, had crept across the narrow ledge, and dangerously hid its edges. She tightened the bundle of mail against her hip and stepped carefully. Beyond the narrow wood separating the twin mansions of the founding Swann sea captains, the cliff path dropped away and merged gently onto a crescent of white sand. Any sand beach on this rocky stretch of coast was a rare treat, but not in her running shoes. She squelched through the rubbery slick band of bladder wrack, scurrying the little crabs that hid under the rocks above low water. At the far end of the beach, the silvery gray boathouse stood empty of its winter collection. The children's daysailers, and the varnished, lap-straked motorboat had been launched and now swung on their summer moorings in the harbor.

From the beach, she climbed up the rough path through a field of meadow grass and negotiated the snags of blackberry brambles that, in August, would hang heavy with berries. At its rise, Ian had mown tidy strips of lawn to tame the wild *rugosa* that threatened the flagstone patio where he and Grace now sat with their newspapers amid the remains of breakfast. Grace looked up and waggled her pen at Hannah.

"Just the clever person I need. What's a five letter word for a plant disease?" She looked at her watch. "Quick!" She allowed herself only ten minutes for the New York Times daily crossword.

"Edema or ergot."

"Right," she said, finishing off the puzzle. "Monday through Thursday are walk-throughs, then Friday and Saturday impossible." With disgust, she tossed the folded paper aside.

Ian stood effortlessly to pull out a chair for Hannah while Grace poured her a cup of coffee. He was a lanky, handsome man in his mid forties, whose movements around women seemed naively intimate. He pushed across the basket of buns and pastries and gestured to the bundle in front of her.

"Is our mail now to be delivered by beautiful women risen from the sea?" he mused.

Hannah laughed. She always felt slightly uneasy under his attentions. "Hardly. I went out for an early run with the dog and suffered some digressions. Mrs. Hobie's broken her hip and we have a new mailman. He's a sour old coot, and Emily and I met him grousing in front of our boxes. He cowed us into promising to assign them our proper names by tomorrow. If I can scoff up some paint and a brush, I'll try my hand at it."

"I'm sure Colin has everything you need in the studio," said Grace. "Ask him to do it himself." She glanced at Hannah and bit her lip. "Or might such a mundane task insult his 'creative muse'?"

Ian sat up in his chair and snorted. "My brother's an arty ass who turns out stuff that would embarrass a blind monkey." He frowned, unsure of his analogy. "Anyway, this annual show of his is always a polite farce. Of those two, Graham Viero is the real artist. Colin indulges our mother who supports him financially and pats him on the head. Behind his back, even she admits his stuff is rubbish."

Grace agreed with her mother-in-law, but said quietly, "That's a bit harsh, Ian. Some of his paintings aren't so bad. And we're all glad it keeps him safely away from your family's business. He proved a disaster at that. Colin's, ah, intimate friendship shall we call it, with Graham has lasted for years. Different, but harmless. Be glad Viero keeps Colin and your mother happy."

And off your back Ian, thought Hannah. She rose and said, "Thanks for the breakfast."

Grace buttered another pastry and licked the flaky crumbs from her lips. She frowned at her husband and Hannah.

"How do you two so effortlessly keep your figures? Why did God handicap me with these latent fat cells, ever ready to fill and billow? I shall pay for this indulgence with no lunch. In fact I'll starve myself until Saturday. Colin may not be a first rate painter, but he's an incredibly good cook. Carrie's awed by his menu for Bea's dinner."

Hannah gathered up the rest of the mail. She knew that Carrie, their dramatic fourteen-year-old daughter, was enamored of her Uncle Colin.

"I can believe it. He's a wonderful cook," she agreed. "I told Emily how kind it was of Bea to include Thea and me."

Grace raised her brows. "It's no kindness, my dear. We need you both to dilute the family combat. You're doing us a favor by accepting."

Hannah sighed. "It will be a relief from our microwave specials. I'll drop their mail at the studio and ask Colin, diplomatically, if he'll distinguish our mail boxes."

After Hannah left, Grace watched Ian open his mail as she pondered the creamy dregs of her coffee cup. She knew her husband realized how much she dreaded Bea's birthday party, and thought it unlikely that Ian's newest fling would be civil and not come. The woman was a houseguest of summer people Bea liked, and it would be inhospitable not to include her. Bad enough having to suffer through the family dinner, prolonged by birthday gifts and toasts; she'd also have to cope with the tedious cocktail party beforehand. 'Entertainments,' Bea coyly called them. The big front room would echo with people mouthing noises. The endless routine of summer parties gave Grace a pounding headache and, despite her closets of clothes, she never wore the right dress. Or it just never looked right on her.

Brooding on her wardrobe, Grace tugged at the knotted belt of her daughter's cast-off robe. She knew that the ingénue pattern of little red bugs didn't suit her and felt its tight stretch under her arms. She'd get serious about a diet. Her features had blurred over the years to become frumpy. It was definitely time for a trip to Camden to try on bathing suits. The resulting self disgust would inspire several days of Spartan meals; worth it, even if it made her grumpy and forced Ian to hungrily prowl the kitchen after dinner.

She looked across at her husband, who was staring absently beyond her. She reached over and nudged his arm.

"Ian, whose invitation is that soaking into your butter?

He started at her voice, and in reflex, crumpled the card held in his fist. Grace raised her brows.

"Well, er," he stuttered, "ah, not really. Someone's made up some strange kind of, um, something."

Grace regarded him skeptically. Her husband was not a glib liar and the ease of quick subterfuge was beyond him. It had hampered the concealment of what she called his 'games' and allowed her to be woefully aware of the philandering he'd begun early in their marriage.

She had no fond memories of their hasty marriage, a Boston Brahmin affair. Her family had arranged it and she, having proved a socially disappointing debutante, had been too spineless and naive to confront the domination of her elegant mother who failed to hide her dissatisfaction at not having a beautiful, polished daughter. They'd mis-named her Grace, and she'd not been allowed to forget it.

Behind that well-contained misery where it hurt so to probe, Grace understood Ian's boredom. He'd married her for the money that had allowed him to outwit his family. His notorious liaisons had displeased the conservative Swanns, and they had threatened him financially. Grace had been swept up by his good looks and the social ease that she lacked. But if her money was so necessary to his lifestyle, why did he continue to jeopardize it?

She was disgusted by her own weakness and wondered why she stayed with him and continued to be hurt and humiliated. Because she was a doormat and he knew it. And pity? His peccadilloes—now that word she thought grimly, was as coy as Bea's 'entertainments'—were always discreet and never lasting, but they embarrassed her. She wanted to protect their children from the misery of a marriage that had become unstitched. But she had not been able to muster the strength or resolve to divorce him. Until now! This time, with his newest fling—the athletic goddess Nan—right here, under her nose, he'd stretched the limits of her humiliation. She witnessed their children's knowing sighs as Carrie and twelve-year-old Clay raised brows over her explanations of their father's 'lady friends.' She was tired of it.

She roused herself. "Give it to me," she said to Ian and took the note from his hand. At least it wasn't from Nan. He would have slipped that out of sight.

"I'm afraid it's unpleasant," he sounded confused. "Some person is having a bad joke." His eyes avoided hers.

Powered by new resolve, Grace pushed away the remains of her buttered croissant, and pressed at the creases of the crumpled card. As she focused on it, her anger faded. Its front was a hand-printed invitation to Bea's sixtieth birthday dinner: Saturday, June 8th at 8:30, etc.

She looked up, puzzled.

"This is ridiculous," she said. "Why would someone send us an invitation the day before the party? It's a family party and we're all invited."

"Open it."

Inside, it read:

GRACE

Here's a puzzle too easy for an expert like you.
Match these clues so that when you are through
You will have information, some old and some new.
Take quick action now or it all may prove true.

MIX AND MATCH

Wife	Out of Will
Clay	Infidelity
Graham	New Venture
Colin	Out of Luck
Ian	Divorce
Nan	Police

Grace flushed. "Ian, this is bizarre. Where's the envelope?"

He shrugged and shook his head.

"It was mailed from the village." He scraped back his chair and its metal leg caught in the flagging. He cursed, caught himself upright and strode over to one of the Italianate terra cotta tubs of salmon geraniums edging the terrace. He began jerking out small weeds. "I can't imagine who sent it." He flung a green tangle onto the lawn. "Who would be so malicious?"

Grace said nothing. His voice was genuinely confused, and Ian, though blind to the fruits of his own offenses, was seldom rancorous. She was sure he honestly couldn't imagine who had thought up this embarrassing prank.

The screen of the sliding door leading from the kitchen squealed on its rollers and Carrie emerged onto the terrace like a circus performer in slow motion. She balanced her toast plate on her cereal bowl with one hand and held her tea mug in the other. A plastic glass of orange juice was clamped between her teeth. No one spoke until she made it to the table where her father relieved her of the juice.

Under a cover of exasperation, Grace slid the folded card into the pocket of her robe.

"Carrie, why not simply use a tray? That could have been a disaster."

Carrie shrugged off the suggestion and stared at her mother.

"Mom, why are you wearing that yucky preppy robe? I put it in the Goodwill basket."

Grace had rescued it the day after Christmas, unable to discard it unworn, even for charity. It was an expensive present from a relative who didn't understand a fourteen-year-old's idea of couture, even in the bedroom. Their adolescent daughter's postures and gestures amused them now, but Grace knew that the straight dark hair, green eyes, and the slim athletic build augured a brewing Circe and some rollicking years ahead. Ironically, with a skip in generation, she'd produced the graceful and elegant daughter her own mother had wanted.

"It's a perfectly good robe, Carrie. You can't give things away just because . . ." She broke off defeated by the bemused looks of her husband and daughter. They had long since consigned her to frump-hood.

Grace watched Carrie slather jam on her toast and considered the casual odds against them producing such decent kids. Despite Ian proving himself a dubious role model, most of the time Carrie and Clay were normal and agreeable. Drugs, motorcycles, unsavory peers, and unplanned pregnancy had so far eluded them.

Over her toast, Carrie threw prim darts of disapproval at the objectionable robe. "Mom, Gran has tons of dressing gowns. She'd be glad to give you one."

"That's very kind of you Carrie, but we're not exactly the same size and I would never carry off Bea's suave élan, or, any of her dressing gowns."

Carrie's shrug conceded this truth, and Grace passed off the jab of hurt. Just as she'd never competed with her own mother, she avoided contention with the voguish and adored grandmother who allowed Carrie entrée to the walk-in closets and jewel cases in her dressing room. Grace recalled a past dress-up fashion show where she'd watched her daughter and her bosom friend Lucy slink about in front of the long mirrored wardrobe doors, mimicking the postures of professional models.

Ian bent over his daughter, took a large bite of her jam laden toast, wiped his mouth, and pecked her on the cheek.

"I'm going to play a little hooky on this beautiful morning and take a couple of sets before I go to the office. I'll see you both later."

Carrie examined her leftover crust and cried in mock anguish, "Dad!" She watched him leave the patio and turned, rolling her eyes at her mother.

"He's gone to play tennis with that Nan person. I think she's hot for his body." She leaned forward conspiratorially. "They say she's after any man's body."

Her daughter seemed to find no topic, however explicit, too embarrassing for conversation, yet Grace supposed she should be thankful. Her direct approach was better than the aloof and prickly self-centeredness common to the age of Carrie's friends. Touching the sharp edges of the taunting card in her robe pocket, she was not going to discuss Ian's infidelities.

Getting no response at this teasing, Carrie broached her newest plan for the summer.

"Mom, I've changed my mind about the sailing program."

Grace looked up, surprised. "I thought you hated sailing? Last week you said you'd have nothing to do with anyone down at the town dock."

"I know, but Lucy's going to be in California for two entire months and I'm getting too old to spend another summer stranded with my brother. Besides, I've decided I'm ready to get serious about boys."

Grace hid her amusement over this unlikely commitment.

"Carrie dear, if you've decided to try out some of the actions in those trashy romance novels you've been devouring lately, please forget it. The boys you know would find it all beyond them."

"Mom," she said with disgust. "I don't mean to hang with any of the dips from school. I saw a very interesting new guy down on the dock rigging his boat. Besides, Dad would love it if I joined the program. He always goes on about my learning to sail. As if living in Maine and not being a sailor is some sort of crime."

"Dad doesn't know your true motives."

Carrie drained her tea mug and rolled her eyes in an exaggerated arc.

"Stop doing that," said Grace. "You'll injure your eyes."

"Not true. Thea does it. They're part of the special exercises she does to keep her eyeballs from rolling up, so when she takes off her glasses she won't look so scary."

Grace agonized over her daughter's frankness, but she was glad Thea Morgan had come into their lives. Carrie now spent most of her spare time helping in the greenhouse and Thea was her idol. The calm advice that the older girl offered on Carrie's assorted crises had to be better than any given by her grandmother.

Carrie jumped up, clumsily rocking the table.

"I've got to go. Uncle Colin said I could help him with Saturday's party. When his cookbook is published, he says he'll dedicate it to me. Dinner's going to be a French feast!"

"I can well imagine." Grace watched Carrie stack the dishes, ready to repeat the juggling act back to the kitchen.

"Either leave them on the table or get a tray," she said. "I can't watch that again."

"I'll send out Clay. Mom, he's getting so creepy. He was in his room staring at himself in the mirror as if his skin was rotting. I think he's having an identity crisis."

She sighed. Too often lately Grace was reminded of her son's despair over his bad eyesight and un-macho physique. Before he appeared, bearing this morning's troubles and complaints, she resolutely filled her cup with the last of the coffee—black. The card in her pocket had upset her, and oral gratification was her downfall. Since childhood, unhappiness had been succored by food. But no more. She shunned the cream, and stretched back to savor the sun's peaceful warmth. She would plan some changes.

CHAPTER 3

Bea Swann crossed the pale carpet of the sitting room that was her private aerie. Puffy blue, green and white linen cushions reflected the colors of the sea and softened the wicker chairs arranged in the bay of the window overlooking the ocean. It was a serene, tranquil room—a room she knew belied her true nature.

As she stood in front of her Cheval glass mirror and slightly tilted its mahogany frame, she smiled with deserved gratification at her trim reflection. Silver blond hair swept back from her temples and was held in place by tortoise shell combs. The chic linen dress came from a shopping trip to her favorite Boston boutique. She had an air of confidence bred by background, and a sufficient income from her late husband to free her from life's wrinkles. She stroked the firm line of her jaw, musing that perhaps good bones came from generations of having your own way and not just lineage.

Bea would have preferred to forget this birthday and the fast advance of years. Today she felt and looked ten years younger. Tomorrow night, she would make dutiful exclamations over her son's elegant dinner, while discretely eating as little as possible. Colin resented and chided her energetic regimen and stringent diet, and it annoyed him when she thwarted his lavish cooking. She ran her hands over her slim hips, justified that sacrifice proved its rewards. Bea enjoyed the role of matriarch, directing her family's affairs—managed in their best interests of course. Her fingers twisted the gold links circling her neck and she turned to stare at the fog hanging gray above the horizon.

Perhaps, she conceded, she *was* a little domineering—even bossy, as her sons chided. But they spoke warily, as they should.

Over the years since their father died, she had eased their lives considerably. They were wise enough to not complain about living free in her houses and enjoying the rare porcelains and antiques that filled them. Nor did they protest receiving the monthly checks Stuart mailed them.

Her dear, short-lived husband had left the distribution of the Swann estate to her option, and her children depended on the trusts she had arranged long ago with Stuart's father to provide them with substantial allowances. She smiled, satisfied that tomorrow night, after Colin's dinner. After the champagne and cake she would announce her newest plans.

She moved across to the solid teak desk brought back from China long ago on one of the family's Clipper ships. It dominated the otherwise feminine room and confirmed the more forbidding, business side of her temperament. She was pleased that she'd inherited both her grandfathers' vigor. They'd been ambitious and enterprising men who had profited by their affiliation with the *Sons of The Cincinnati*. That elite and powerful society gave them the advantages during the 1850 China trade that had made their fortunes. On the polished desktop, a delicate Nanking porcelain cup held her pens and pencils and a lattice-bordered bowl patterned with a rare river scene held a forced branch of dogwood. She reached for her intercom phone and pressed Emily's number.

Bea ceased her musings when her niece entered the room and angrily dropped the sorted letters and bills on her desk. Emily held out the large envelope from Stuart Hobart.

"I opened this," she said without apology. "I read the copy of your letter and also his reply. You're going to be an unpopular birthday girl. I'd open your presents first."

Bea's nostrils flared and she stiffened. "Emily," her voice was icy. "That was not meant for your eyes."

"Come off it Bea, you are manipulating us again and making drastic changes. Do you think that, in the name of some admirable social justice, you have a divine right to interfere in our lives?"

She dropped the lawyer's envelope on the desk.

"Stuart says here that he's tracked down Robin and bribed the spoiled brat to come 'home' from Australia. Has the useless Aussie boyfriend finally run through all your daughter's money?"

Bea reddened and looked wary. Her stomach tightened.

"Emily, it's to be a surprise for everyone tomorrow. Robin hasn't been home for—"

Emily cut her off. "It'll be a surprise all right! Bea, why do you take such pleasure in antagonizing people? You want your prosaic son Colin to give up his 'artless daubs' and join his brother in some impossible position in the family business. God, Ian's useless enough and Colin will destroy what's left of it! He knows nothing and cares less about any business."

"Emily, wait."

"You wait, I'm not through." She stabbed a finger at the manila folder. "It says here that you and Stu have discussed how you plan to keep your roving son Ian away from the likes of Nan. We know Grace is a doormat, but she needs Ian, and twenty years ago she vowed to take him—for better or for worse."

Bea broke into the tirade with unconcealed impatience. Their conversation bored her. They'd had it too many times.

"Just calm down Emily. More often this summer, I've seen Carrie and Clay embarrassed by their father's behavior. I am glad to hear, whether she needs him or not, that Grace seems to be running out of her sublime submission. The gossip around here over Ian's affairs is humiliating us all. We've chatted lately, and she appeared to listen to my advice."

"You and Grace—chatted?"

Bea flushed and ignored Emily's incredulous look.

"Great," said Emily. "And after you punch down Ian, tomorrow night, you're planning to anger Colin by expanding the nursery into his studio. Graham, the misogynist, will manage our resulting new greenhouse business, all generated by Hannah and Thea. But of course Hannah and Thea will do the real work because he knows nothing about plants except how to draw them!"

Emily gripped the back of the chaise, working up a rage.

"What you've arranged for me, after all these years doing and fetching for you, I can't imagine! After you're dead, am I to be retired to some little cottage in the village so Robin can sell this house out from under us? If she comes back, it will only be to pry loose enough cash to escape again. Bea, how can you be so naïve about the real, calculating Robin?"

Emily slumped, upset at her loss of control, and the hostility drained away. She curled her shaking hands into fists to quiet them. "I'm sorry, Bea. That was cruel."

They had weathered verbal storms through the years, but this was a savage attack and Bea thought it wise to speak gently. She came from behind the massive desk and put an arm around her niece.

Emily pulled away and sank down onto the chaise cushions.

"How could you and my mother have been sisters? She was so patient and delicate. She never fought with me."

"Em, please," Bea soothed. "After your father died, Diana just gave up. Your mother drifted into her big feather bed and welcomed that vague neurasthenia that killed her. I'm sorry, but I found it hard to forgive her that passive indulgence."

She reached across to touch the younger woman's cheek. "You only remember your mother as the good fairy, Em, because Diana left the practical side of your raising to me." She quickly held up her hand to cut off more protest.

"As for tomorrow night, if my plans prove too disturbing, I won't force them on anyone. I miss Robin. So many years have passed with all that ill feeling between us." Bea regarded her slim ankle, but when she looked at her niece, her vivid green eyes dulled to gooseberry.

"You're partly right about Robin. Stuart and I have traced her and she's not lost, but she is poor. That boyfriend Keith and his rock band fell apart, and she's been working as a bar hostess in some dingy hotel in Sydney. She's had a bad patch and became desperate enough to look up the Packwoods. That's how we found her. They are generous, sweet people. You never knew them, but Hannah's mother, Jane Packwood, was my closest school friend. Some innate modicum of good manners remained under all Robin's rebellion, because they wrote and said how much they'd enjoyed meeting her. When Stuart and I answered their letter, we mentioned our new nursery venture and they wrote back and said their daughter, Hannah, had just graduated from Sydney University with a degree in botany and was eager for a change. We all hoped something might work out."

"It has," said Emily, now calmer. "I'm very fond of Hannah. We all are. She's a treasure."

Bea smoothed the soft cashmere sleeve of her sweater.

"I want to see Robin again." Her voice brightened. "Maybe we can smooth things over. Perhaps we've both tempered." This time she confronted the wry look. "No, Emily, I'm serious. I'm sure these changes can work out for us all if handled diplomatically, and Stuart with his charm and tact will help me." She moved over to the bay window, her back to Emily. "I admit I lack those two those character traits." Out on the ocean, a swirl of gulls screeched and scavenging wheeled in the wake of a lobsterman hauling pots.

"Don't worry about your future," she continued. "You and Colin will always be welcome to live in this house. I just wish my son was more independent and less reliant on Graham."

"Come on, Bea. Admit that Colin is a dependent man. He doesn't *want* to be free of Graham. He's a hedonist and inherited the noble Swann bones but not the power genes."

Bea ignored the reference to her son's homosexuality, and that his long alliance with Graham was a commitment not easily dissolved. She turned, and with perfectly manicured nails, continued to tick off her litany of censures. "Ian can't philander forever. My grandchildren need a more responsible father. They're running wild. Clay spends his free time with that odious man Luther on his fishing boat. And I know Luther's involved somehow with the volatile trouble brewing in the village, and it could become dangerous."

Emily sighed in disgust. "Be reasonable. Clay's only trying to earn summer money, and lobstering is decent, hard work. And

Carrie hardly runs wild. If you're referring to her befriending Angela, I think it's more of a social cause than an intimacy."

Bea brushed aside this latest unpleasantness and changed the subject.

"Hannah and Thea are an even match for Graham, and I appreciate the marketing sense he brings to the business." Bea folded her arms and began to pace. "To keep the nursery business successful, we must expand into Colin's studio space." She smiled and rested her forearms on the back of the chaise. "I also have a special surprise for you, Emily."

"I hate surprises. When Robin walks in on your birthday party, that will be stunning enough."

"Em," she cajoled. "Pease don't sulk. She flew from Sydney to California and now is staying a few days with some friends in Boston. Her flight arrives here tomorrow evening at seven. I'm the birthday girl and can't leave my own party, so I'm asking if you would slip away and pick her up at the Rockland airport. You'll be back before the family dinner. Would you do that for me? It will be a marvelous surprise."

Emily gave an ironic snort. "And in case it is not so marvelous, you have enough other guests coming for drinks to buffer your bombshell." She raised her arms in defeat. "I have bad feelings about tomorrow, but you've made up your mind. Let the games begin."

CHAPTER 4

Hannah found Colin in his studio soothing the agitated sounds coming from the phone pressed between his shoulder and ear.

"Don't worry dear, everything's arranged and in order. You have no responsibilities except to enjoy the evening."

He arched his eyebrows at Hannah, mouthed an exaggerated 'mother,' and motioned her to sit. She put down the studio mail. There was a lengthy pause in his end of the conversation while she watched him consider two watercolor renditions called *Harbor Fog* balanced before him on the floor.

"Mother, my love, Carrie knows exactly what to do. I've taped up lists for her and we've gone over everything together. She'll be fine if we leave her alone. She is a very mature young lady. Don't worry. No, mother, we will be extremely careful not to hurt Doris's feelings. Doris can put her feet up or bustle off and polish the silver, boil the tea towels, anything. Don't fuss. Carrie's perfectly capable, more so than either Doris or Stella. Those two village women have been helping us out for years, but they're getting old and when they start gossiping—"

A burst of protest came from the receiver.

"Relax now," he soothed. "Take a nice nap; you have a big day tomorrow. Of course mother, you don't *need* a nap, but it's your birthday, so why not indulge yourself. I'll be there in plenty of time to take charge of the kitchen before dinner. Mother, sweet, I must hang up now, Hannah's just comes by. Ta."

He dropped the receiver back on its cradle and tucked at the disarray it had caused to his paisley neckerchief.

"God, she irritates me."

Colin was not a complete piece of wet, thought Hannah, but he affected a manner of dress more suitable to an English country house than the Maine woods. She admitted, however, that his languorous style suited the tall, slim build bestowed by the Swann's fortuitous genes. His longish blond hair was swept artfully above the lineage bones and after several whiskeys, he'd often confessed they were what kept at bay his sag into middle age.

She gestured around the skylit room whose walls displayed his 'painterly' renditions of tumultuous seascapes, vast landscapes and smaller, less frenetic renderings of the local shores and harbors. Hannah thought the difficulties of the watercolor media required a more delicate touch and were not kindly achieved by Colin's harsh brushwork.

She indicated the scores of canvases. "You've had a busy year," she said with diplomacy.

Colin continued sorting through the canvases stacked along the walls.

"I really look forward to my little annual show," he said, rejecting a particularly muddy perception of Owl's Head. "But I'm not vain enough to think people rally round each July just to see my work. The Grange Hall supper is our summer social event, and I'm lucky they let me share it."

"I hear you sell most of your local scenes," said Hannah. "Especially to the B & B owners and their guests." Her voice stretched a little for enthusiasm and Colin gave her a sardonic smile.

He laughed and arched his brows. "I understand the paintings relieve their guest rooms' 'earth tones' décor, and the innkeeper's around here find no need to nail them to the wall."

"Nonsense," said Hannah. "The villagers love it when you paint something they can recognize." She realized her remark could be taken amiss and was saved from sinking deeper into the mire by Graham's appearance. He stopped just inside the doorway, holding a small, square card.

"Enter," said Colin. "Hannah's been flogging my ego."

Graham seemed preoccupied and offered only a vague nod. "There was no mail, only this bizarre invitation."

"I'm sorry," said Hannah. "I collected yours with the rest from our new mailman this morning. Actually, that's why I'm here. He's the summer's grumpy replacement for Mrs. Hobie, who's had an accident. He insisted we must distinguish our boxes with proper names, and I was hoping to entice one of you to do the duty. I would myself, but I don't have any paints or brushes and the results would be messy and horrid."

Before either could refuse, she gestured to the small envelope that Graham held. "I must have missed that."

Colin held out his hand, but Graham paused and eyed Hannah. "It's rather personal Colin, you may want to read it later."

"Nonsense," said Colin "I'm always game for an invite." He reached for the folded card. "If it's 'de trop', we can always refuse."

He took the card from Graham and after reading the formal invitation to Bea's dinner party; he looked up, puzzled, and read it again.

"What's wrong?" asked Hannah.

Frowning, Colin read aloud the short verse:

> "You Are Invited To
> A Gala occasion—or a Deathly event?
> Gourmet touches for a Life Ill Spent.
> Your Just Desserts will revenge years of hurts.
> This delicious Repast
> May well be your Last."

"I opened it," said Graham. "It was addressed to 'The Studio.' No names. I don't think we should take the message too seriously."

In spite of his words, Hannah saw that the dark eyes, whose long lashes were wasted on any male over five, remained solemn. Graham Viero was a compact, muscular, olive skinned man who carried off his flourishing mustache with aplomb. This, combined with high cheekbones evoked more of a *pistolero*, a vigilante, than the recognized painter of exquisitely accurate botanicals. She'd become wary of his chameleon personality. '*Il est sortable*,' quiet and moody, with that facile ability to charm.

Bemused, but perturbed, Colin passed her the card.

"Pretty venomous little threat," she said. "Who do you think sent it?"

Colin turned to Graham. "Rumor says mother has some wild, new plans. Is this some joke concocted between the two of you?"

Graham stopped sorting through the letters Hannah had left on the desk. "I don't take sides in your family, Colin," he said stiffly, "if that's what you mean. And I sure as hell could write better verse." Then to mollify his vehemence, he indicated the lofty room around them and forced a more affable voice. "The only alliance I have with your mother concerns the better management of the nursery business. Bea's ideas for remodeling the greenhouse are sensible. In the short time Hannah has been here, we've seen her hybridizing talents create a stock of unusual plants whose quality and variety the summer people have noticed. The mail order business she's generated can't be handled in that antiquated crowded space."

He spoke seriously, and Hannah looked at him in surprise. His sudden concern and knowledge of their business problems distracted her from the odd and threatening card.

He saw her confused, but pleased, look. "I've been talking to Thea," he explained.

Hannah considered that his motives might be questionable, but for the moment they needed any ally. She turned to Colin.

"Can't we compromise, somehow, on sharing some space?" She gestured over her shoulder. "Graham's right, we're struggling back there."

The studio, and Graham's apartment above it, were part of the original carriage house that had once stabled horses, then later the Swann's grand old automobiles. Now, a badly lit potting shed connected the greenhouse, and served as a cramped nursery office. Soaring above the greenhouse were three cupolas, quaint designs of arched glass supported by ribs of rusting iron gingerbread. She had been told that in better years, the family kept a staff of gardeners to coddle the fruit trees, hot house grapes, and out-of-season delectables grown to tempt the captains' palates after their months of deprivations at sea.

Hannah pleaded. "Colin, apart from leaking vents, decayed staging, and the rest of its rusting Gothic ills, the foundations over there are so rotten that even Ugly Joyce, can't keep up with the invasions of our resident rodents."

"Joyce?" asked Colin. "Is that what you call that whack-faced coon cat that slinks around the place? Not only ugly, he's monstrous."

"His scars are from battles. He patrols," she defended, "and U. J. enjoys the innards of beasts and fowl."

Colin shuddered, but Hannah was implacable. "Of course," she added wickedly, "when the rats become really ravenous, they will travel over here, next door."

Graham intervened, getting back to business. "I'd like to help you and Thea develop your marketing. Your local seasonal sales are icing on the cake of what should be a more profitable venture. I have a good head for management, and could free you to concentrate on horticulture. You can give me a quick course in enough of your jargon to get started." His serious determination to become their mentor made him oblivious to her tight smile.

"Jargon?" She kept her temper.

Colin intercepted the warming conflict. "Why don't you both fetch Thea and go over to Daily's for lunch. Discuss it in the sea air on the dock over a basket of fried clams. I've got to go pacify Doris and Stella. My French menu for tomorrow night has rippled their meat, veg, and potatoes regimen."

He frowned and took the white card from Hannah. "I'm still confused as to the point of this nasty poetic invite. The sender has not made it clear which one of us might fall poisoned onto their dinner plate, or who's to do the dirty deed, but I'm absolving those two village ladies."

"We should ask if anyone else got one," suggested Hannah. "Perhaps it's only someone's nasty joke. However," she paused, "I'd watch what you eat tomorrow."

She turned and spoke coolly to Graham. "I'll leave our mailbox identification problem in your very competent hands."

"You've pissed her," said Colin, as the door closed behind her.

Graham realigned the fan of gallery catalogs spread on the refectory table behind the couch.

"Promoting your art career, Colin, doesn't support me. Nor do my contracts for freelance botanical illustrating. You've spoiled me to the good life, and I could never return to the subsistence level if serious changes in your most tacit generosity forced me onto the streets."

Colin was uncomfortable. They rarely spoke of the particulars that held their agreeable partnership together. None of the family did. Most of them refused to acknowledge any relationship at all, even after ten years.

"Graham, I would never do that. You are well aware that you are the buffer that makes living with my mother bearable." Colin turned away and shrugged into his painting smock. His embarrassment evaporated quickly, as did most of his bad moods, and he regained his altruistic composure. He liked his life to remain free of unpleasant entanglements. He sought the innate goodness in people and chose not to make enemies.

"Don't worry about Hannah," he spoke affably. "We'll work something out that will satisfy us all."

CHAPTER 5

'Rustic' would be a wily realtor's description of the bungalow Hannah and Thea shared. But it was a short walk from the greenhouse and they found it more comfortable than the grander Swann houses. Its shingled siding was weathered to a silvery gray, and in summer it became a rose-covered storybook cottage amid beds of tumultuous perennials.

Lying off-duty under the high-legged stove, Emperor, Thea's traveling eyes, slept with his nose on his paws. This morning, after his long run with Hannah, Thea had not wakened him for their familiar walk up to the greenhouse. Instead, she let her feet, more confident and better than hands, reach out into the dark. The angle of the sun and the soft movement of air on her face guided her.

When she entered the glass house, she stood for a moment to savor the warm moist smells of loam and peat mixed with the tangy pong of dried manure.

"Hannah," she called. No answer. The office was open, but she sensed it was empty. It didn't matter; she liked being alone and quiet here.

She pulled her stool close to the high staging bench and deftly began to fill small fiber pots with transplants. Most tools were no good without sight. Rather, her fingers felt their need for water and distinguished the subtle differences between the species' leaves, stems, and flowers. She'd read somewhere that the seedlings sent out from most nurseries have a survival rate equal to infant mortality in the Middle Ages. She smiled and patted her tray of pots. There would be no such statistics for her carefully nurtured babies.

The big commercial greenhouse in Portland, where she'd worked before the accident, had taught her the horticultural skills she needed, and with patient effort, she was adapting them to her disability. She had conquered the new spaces here at Swann's. Fewer bruises on her shins attested to it.

She heard a soft knock against the greenhouse door, and Carrie's voice.

"Thea?"

"Come in, honey. Grab a stool."

"I feel terrible." The girl spoke apologetically, and learned over to touch Thea's arm to place her, as Thea had taught her to do.

"I know that I promised to help you pot up all those orders this morning, but I have to go down to the sailing dock and sign up for the summer program. I'll be back as soon as I can."

"Carrie, a week ago you—"

"I know, I know. I hate sailing. Everyone's reminding me, but with Lucy gone, I've got to do something this summer beside hang around with my little brother." She rushed on. "And I saw this gorgeous guy down there yesterday rigging his boat and— well anyway, it'll make Dad happy, and with Lucy in California and Angie working everyday at the drugstore, I'd be stuck out here with nobody but Clay, and well, you know." Carrie trailed off and Thea understood her adolescent despair over a looming, friendless summer. She sympathized even more because she missed her own friends left behind in Portland after the accident.

"No trouble, Carrie. There's plenty to do here with any time you can spare."

"I'll be back right after lunch." Carrie gave a deep sigh. "There's a big problem I've got to talk to you and Hannah about."

Thea turned quickly toward her, and Carrie watched the dark points of her bobbed hair swing against her chin.

"No," Carrie reassured. "It's not about me. A friend of mine is in trouble and I need to help her. It's sort of illegal and I don't know where to start. Mom and Dad, even Gran, don't understand why she's my friend so I want to talk to you two first."

"Sure." Thea's voice remained cool, but the 'sort of illegal' part alarmed her. "Hannah's not come in yet. We can work while we talk, after you've checked out your potential new conquests." The energy of Carrie's parting kiss almost unseated her.

She acknowledged how the pleasurable company of Carrie and Clay was one of the reasons that her personal horror film rewound itself less often now. The last thing she'd seen was the grill of the huge truck, out of control and filling her rear-view mirror. Then came the realization of her unfastened seat belt and eerie recall of breaking glass, followed by her body flying through the windshield. She remembered the blood, sticky and warm, but no pain.

"A miracle," the doctor had told her. "Only the one permanent injury."

From her point of view it was a limited miracle. Her face was unscarred, but that one permanent injury had been to the occipital lobe of her brain, the source of vision. She still woke sometimes in the dark and for a moment forgot what had happened to her. Then the night became night again forever. Aware that she had become too fiercely independent, she knew she must try to meet new people without such a load of defense. The circle of friends she had left in Portland was too far away to keep in touch and she particularly missed the company of a good male friend. She and Hannah had both commiserated over the lack of local prospects.

Thea gave a bitter laugh at her self-indulgent pity and returned to filling pots. Still, she thought, it's hard to check out eligible prospects when you can't see them—and then find a find a man who isn't daunted by dating a blind woman. However, at twenty-five, she was hardly a spinster and knew she still had her looks. Thea rested her slim wrists on the redwood edge of the potting bench. The rote filling and tucking in of the little plants soothed and helped smother her bitterness. She sang softly to her seedlings.

The impatient plateau of rehabilitation during recovery—what doctors call the mending point of body and psyche—had come for Thea when she left the hospital to live with her parents in Portland. Suddenly she'd had enough of support agencies and everyone's over-anxious attentions. If only people would realize that she was not helpless, miserable, inferior, maladjusted or in possession of enhanced other senses. It was just that her eyes didn't work.

Her father had discovered the Swann's ad for the greenhouse position in the Portland newspaper, and with the freedom provided by Emperor, her wonder dog, she'd begun a new life. Not great, but acceptable.

There was no knock this time before the door burst open. It was Hannah.

"I don't believe it. Who does he think he is—Jesus reborn?"

"Graham?" Thea guessed.

"Who else. Our new Savior," she scowled. "Do you think he's bi? He sure exudes something musky around me. Then bam," she snapped her fingers, "he suddenly puts his knickers in the fridge and becomes a complete pig misogynist!"

"Hannah," Thea groaned.

"I'm sorry." Hannah laughed. "I'm sexually frustrated. I ran into Emily early this morning, sneaking out from a night with Phil at the Rectory. I bet she's the only one of us getting a regular dose."

"You're probably right," said Thea. The timbre of a person's voice and cadence of speech reveal more than physical description. Thea understood Hannah's character more by her inflections than from the brief self-accounting of medium height, brown hair, and hazel eyes. The addition of 'trim but messy' had made Thea smile.

Thea heard her friend pacing the aisle between the benches.

"You wouldn't believe the unreal conversation I just had with Colin and Graham," Hannah went on. "We are to lunch today on Daily's dock over fried clams, and the three of us are going to discuss how easily Graham will solve all our business dilemmas."

"Hannah, relax. I've talked to Graham and he seems genuinely supportive. I think you're exaggerating his motives. Managing Colin's 'artwork' isn't enough. He's bored."

She slid a filled tray of pots onto the trolley shelving beside her stool.

"Besides, he's sharp, despite his arrogant manner and if he really wants to help us," she pointed towards Hannah's office, "we're loaded with more new orders than you and I can handle. Even Bea agrees that we're understaffed."

"Understaffed!" The pacing stopped and she heard the anger in Hannah's voice. "*What* staff? Haven't you noticed it's just you and me, honey?"

"Well," Thea paused. "So far we've managed, in spite of it all, to begin a successful business from nothing. It's time we had some help. I'm sorry. I know how hard you work. Even with unskilled part-time help for the heavy labor, we need someone who knows what they are doing and with muscle for digging and transplanting to the outside frames."

"I'm sorry I'm so impatient," said Hannah. She gave a rueful smile that she knew her friend could not see. "Everything you do, Thea, seems so under control. I'm frustrated by our working conditions. And you're right. Aside from the office work, it's become too much to handle by ourselves." She touched Thea's arm. "I'm wrong to complain about any offer of help, but Graham's patronizing manner got to me. He simply assumes that in a few days he can master taxonomy, plant physiology, hybridization, and then maybe in a weekend pick up genetics and polyploids. We're talking of study that I barely covered in four years at University! 'Jargon', he called it."

"Hannah, you must realize that Graham has a quirky sense if humor. He likes pushing your buttons. He wants to know just enough to understand the basic terminology to decipher our records and handle our bookkeeping. If Bea will invest in some electronics and Graham becomes our computer whiz, we should try to be politic. You didn't travel 12, 000 miles to be stuck in that box of an office pushing paper."

"You're right that our quirky Graham's got Bea's sympathies, and something's in the wind. I guess we'd better be agreeable and go eat clams down on the dock with our new partner," said Hannah.

Thea laughed. "Something's in the wind all right. It's Bea's foul night blooming *Cereus*." She wrinkled her nose in disgust. She found its heavy smell sickly overwhelming. From its thick waxy leaves, Bea's prize possession had sprouted a pendulous, pink shaggy flower that drooped, lengthening daily. It had its place on a high shelf in a far corner of the greenhouse. It rarely produced its display, but this spring, pot bound, and spurred by some primal trigger of feeding and warmth, it was ready to flare open, after dark, putting out lengthening dark blue and then cream-colored stamens.

Hannah went into the office to search out the nursery logbook, a three-ring binder in which she recorded their work in progress. For Thea, she carefully duplicated them on tape cassettes. The blue binder was usually jammed tightly among catalogs, reference texts, and the ledgers overflowing the shelves of the makeshift bookcase they jokingly called their 'library.' This morning it slid out easily. Along with it came a wrinkled invoice, long lost behind the thick, mildewed horticultural bible, 'Exotica'.

"Damn it!" She flipped through the lost order. It was a lengthy one that she'd spent hours searching for and tried to duplicate by memory. Another example of their Dark Ages management. Puzzled, she ran a finger across the dusty shelf trying to remember what was missing to create the space. It bothered her, but she couldn't pin it down, and the sight of the stack of orders piled accusingly on her desk put it out of mind. She carried the work log into the greenhouse and balanced it on the staging next to Thea.

"The red spider and mites on the cyclamens were not checked by foliar spray or the predatory mite control. Much as I hate using poison, I think that they've become bad enough to warrant setting off smoke bombs. And the god awful *Cereus* will probably decide to bloom tomorrow night."

"I know," said Thea smugly, "I've been feeding it up. It will be our birthday present. We'll invite Bea over to watch it open after the party and light the smokers after she leaves."

CHAPTER 6

In the kitchen of the big house, on the day of the birthday dinner, Doris and Stella gossiped as they worked. For years, the two village women had helped out at the Swann's parties and moved easily around the big kitchen. With a grin that displayed her pearly dentures, Doris steadied the platter of hors d'oeuvres on the shelf of her bosom.

"Now tell me, Stell, ain't this gawjus?"

Stella curved her narrow shoulders, wrapped her hands around her skinny upper arms and nodded wordlessly. She wouldn't hurt her friend's feelings, but to her mind, a radish should look like a radish. She considered that Doris's diligent attendance at the food-garnishing course she had taken over at the Domestic Institute had rewarded her a too lavish hand with flowered and animalized vegetables. Tortured looking, some of them.

Doris nestled a rosy petal cut from a tomato between a round of Brie neighbored by frosted grapes.

"Nice and colorful," said Stella, who wiped her hands on the tea towel stuck through the ample waistband of her apron and patted her netted hair. The chemical combination that had produced its dense matte blackness gave off peculiar green glints under the kitchen's lights.

Stella tugged at the over-large cardigan she'd knit herself out of some brown stringy wool she had found at a yard sale. It bunched up under the wrap-around apron knotted across her front. She looked over a plate of tea marbled quail eggs and shook her pointed chin.

"I don't know Doris, these don't look healthy. Nothing I'd trust ta' eat."

Covering the surrounding counter space were baskets of crackers and breads, plates of crab-stuffed endive nestled on ruby lettuce, and dill-flecked gravlax that Colin had pressed under bricks cushioned by vodka-doused juniper berries. Wooden trays of blanched vegetables were embellished by seashells filled with herbed dips for the dieters.

At the stove, Doris prodded a kettle of plump Long Cove mussels, steamed open and cooling in a broth of garlic, parsley and wine. The mixture scented the kitchen with its briny sea smell.

"Your Anson, Stell, he would like ta' add something awful ta' these little devils hmm?"

"Poison 'em if he was standing here," Stella answered bluntly. "Mad as hell he is. Anson's been too good to them mussel folk. Even plowed out their road this winter. We tried being neighborly and then these fellows sneak up ta' Augusta behind our backs and lease out the whole Cove bottom."

Doris clicked her tongue against her formidable teeth. Stella's husband. Anson, square built and stubborn, was one of the harbor lobstermen losing their grounds to the mussel draggers. The volatile Swede increasingly provoked ugly confrontations over territory and the unwritten bottom rights to the seabeds that were their living. The humble *Mytilus*, once ignored except as bait, had risen from its ooze to become a fashionable gourmet item, and Anson and the other lobstermen fumed They felt exploited by the sophisticated entrepreneurs.

"Trash fish," Stella hissed. "Them and those skate wings Mr. Colin ate for supper t'other night. I tasted them and, even all sauced up with onions and tomatoes, I told him they need a lawge dose of A-1. He told me I had the palate of a Philistine. I told him right back that I'm not ashamed of being a religious woman and that he had the taste buds of a billy-goat." She cackled at her own wit. She got on well with Colin. Not much of a painter, in her opinion, and *that* she never hesitated to offer in spite of total ignorance on the subject. But she thought him a nice fellow. He and his friend Graham might be a little too friendly, but not hers to worry. None of her business.

The birthday cake decorated by Colin and Carrie stood majestically waiting for its entrance after dinner on the tea trolley in the pantry. One tactful candle was centered in the swirls of lemon icing. The cake, to be served with champagne after dinner, was a tiered creation of piped frosted shells nestled with candied violets. Doris heard the crackle of gravel and peered through the window just as Emily's car disappeared down the drive.

"Now where's she going? She promised to help me set up the dinner table."

"Where's who going?" asked Hannah, coming into the pantry with an armful of tulips and lupines she'd cut from the garden.

"Miss Parrish," Doris answered and nodded toward the driveway. "With all them people coming for cocktails and then the fancy dinner party after, she told me she'd help us set up the dinner table."

Hannah wiped her hands on her smock. "I'll take care of it Doris, after I do the flowers. Emily seems to have a mind full of worries tonight and she probably forgot. Ladies, you're marvelous, everything looks delicious."

Doris beamed at her handiwork. "I'll not be modest about it deah, it surely does, but flower arranging—I'm afraid it's zinnias in a jam jar for me. I'll leave fancy bouquets to you. Go to it."

Hannah got to it. She let the salmon tulips arch over round glass bowls and in an old copper bucket arranged branches of lilac, stripped of their wilt prone leaves, to support stalks of blue lupines. She stuffed any offending holes with tidy stems of boxwood. For the center of the dinner table she filled a low round basket with primroses, hiding their pots under layers of wood moss. No one would have to peek through a distracting "arrangement."

Satisfied with her creations, she lifted the plastic film from a tray of feta and spinach morsels and popped one in her mouth. She was re-arranging its neighbors to fill the gap when she heard Clay and Carrie's voices. When Clay came into the pantry, she saw that he'd been coerced into jacket and tie and, except for the heavy horn-rimmed glasses held together with hockey tape, he looked remarkably neat.

He held out an ashtray. "Where'll I put it?"

"Just one?"

"Gran's orders," said Carrie, coming in behind him. "She says anyone who smokes is disgusting and once this is full, they'll have to use their trouser cuffs or go outside."

Hannah shrugged. Few people smoked nowadays, and even fewer sported trouser cuffs. The die-hards were likely to do more damage dropping ashes on the carpet than coating their lungs.

"Stick it on the drinks table," she said. She carried the basket of primroses into the dining room and centered it among the array of candles whose soft light Bea insisted produced the flattering ambiance necessary to the mature woman. The round table was expanded for tonight by intricately fitted pie-shaped wedges and covered with heirloom double damask.

Hannah pondered the flatware storage box on the sideboard next to the stack of Coalport plates. Beside them Emily had left a printed card with Colin's menu as a guide to the needed serving pieces. She soldiered up the required cutlery around the dinner plates and added crystal wine and water goblets. The champagne flutes would come later with the cake. Everything sparkled and glittered, and the pink and white primroses poking through the soft green mounds of moss looked lovely.

Except the table seemed crowded. She hadn't counted the plates as she'd placed them around, and now she made a quick check in her head. Bea's sons, Colin and Ian would sit on either side of her. Emily between Ian and Phil, and Thea between herself and Clay. Hannah knew that Thea's *bete noire* was eating in public and had simplified her place setting. Graham was seated opposite Bea, then Grace, Clay, Stuart, across from Phil, and completing the circle, Carrie next to Colin. Twelve of us. The crowding was the thirteenth place. For whom? Should she leave it?

Stella pushed into the room through the swing door from the kitchen. The tiny woman stopped short and pulled up her apron to cover her eyes. "Lord prepare us, the Queen must be coming to supper!"

Hannah smiled. "Could be, Stella. There's an extra place set for her. Pretty dazzling, hmm?"

"Looks like a night at the palace. But that Mrs. Beatrice is pretty dazzling herself. Some folks are older than they look," she cocked her head, "but sad for most of us—it's mostly the other way round."

The evening stayed warm and as the guests arrived, they wandered through the house to gather outside along the length of the wide porch overlooking the ocean. They drank and nibbled, and offered what Grace called 'conversational snacking.' She heard husbands warned, in low asides, to make this lavish spread of food their dinner. Colin and Ian did their duty as hosts for the first round of drinks, then announced 'summer rules' and joined the crowd on the porch to watch the evening parade of cruising boats enter the harbor. As the Mount Gay flowed, the hum of conversation swelled to a gentle roar. At dusk, the insidious onslaught of mosquitoes drove the guests inside.

Grace's head began to buzz. All these people talking without saying anything. She watched with envy as Bea effortlessly introduced guests who were strangers to each other. Her simple ivory silk dress and strands of pearls emphasized her sleek blondness tonight. Grace stood next to their neighbor, Bunny Watson. She felt a small one-up on Bunny, who bulged hip and belly in one of her garish polyester combinations.

"Grace dear," Midge Branch's gush pierced the room. Grace hadn't seen her come up beside her. She tried to move away but the odious woman grabbed her arm. Midge took a large helping of crab mayonnaise from a passing tray, and stuffed it in her smug, narrow mouth. "Thin as one o'clock and I never gain a pound. Well now, I hear your son Clay has been out setting traps with Luther. I hope he doesn't get mixed up in those nasty village squabbles. Do you know there were actually fisticuffs outside

Strait's Market the other morning!" She paused, distracted by the toast point pinched between her fingers. "I love raw steak mince, dear, but are you sure there are no ground up glands in this meat? A friend of mine spent weeks recovering from peculiar symptoms before they diagnosed it was caused by ground up thyroid bits in her hamburger."

She saw Midge looking suspiciously at the sirloin tartare topped with capers spread on the triangle of toast.

"I can guarantee its purity," Grace assured her. No additives to the canapés would make Midge more bizarre. The woman's remarks about Luther had upset her, though, and she felt the need to defend him.

"Clay enjoys helping Luther. It's unfortunate that the man's speech is a little hard to follow and his gait's sometimes alarming, but he manages all right and works hard at his fishing. He's been kind to Clay. Luther isn't allowed to drive, so Clay runs errands for him on his bike and, in return, Luther's taught him to fish and trap. Right now, Clay's having a little trouble with his pubescent image and working for Luther boosts his ego."

Midge fastened on Grace's flushed face with skeptical eyes. "I don't know about boys. We never had any. Which is just as well, as Herb is no great shakes as a father figure, either. Most of the time he's useless as a catdoor on a sub."

Grace turned away, rankled at the snide reference to Ian. She saw that Hannah had kept to the edges of the room and excused herself from Midge's nastiness to join the young Australian girl. Together, they edged toward the bar. Grace knew liquor was not on her diet, and though her headache might be eased by rum, she re-filled her glass with soda.

She saw her son Clay standing beside Hannah, frowning at his slim face reflected in the mirror above the drinks table. With spit-wet finger, he tried to smooth his errant red cowlick. Hannah had told Grace how he had confided his adolescent woes while helping her in the garden. They all knew how much the boy mourned his lack of physique, the meager promise of his ever reaching his father's stature, and the fact that his skin never tanned but only compacted its freckles. But his constant woe was broken eyeglasses. He couldn't manage without them, and tonight's stopgap solution had failed. The black hockey tape he'd wound around the frame had lost its grip. The sidepiece dangled loose, and Clay ripped it off. "I hate them. I wear these heavy duty jobs and they still break."

"Wait here," said Hannah. "I have a safety pin in my purse that might do the trick." She returned in time to rescued the glasses he'd been about to fling in a wastebasket. She fastened the pin through the broken hinges and secured the thick frame behind his ears.

"I've tried not wearing them and almost crashed my bike," he said. "Anyway, I'll make enough money working for Luther this summer to buy some cool looking frames." He checked out his face in the mirror again. "Something French or Italian. If I pay for them myself they can't say no. Right?"

"Right."

He saw his mother standing forlorn and alone, and gave Hannah a plaintive look. "Could you rescue my mama? She hates these parties."

"Gladly, Clay."

Hannah went over to Grace who had retreated to the edge of the room and was now held captive by slim, slinky Kikki Baldwin.

"Grace, darling, did you see that palazzo motor cruiser moored in the harbor last night? Straight from the Adriatic. Probably moving drugs. My God, First, I heard the ex-CIA have settled in Rockport, now that the Iranians are buying up the Camden waterfront. Let's hope our little harbor's not attracting the Mafia set!"

As Hannah approached, Kikki directed her fashion conscious eyes at her to make a quick approval of the creamy gauze blouse belted into cord knickers. Under her scrutiny, Hannah was glad she had made an effort for Bea's party. Tonight, for a change, she felt put together.

"Of course Australia is the 'in' place now," she said and gazed at Hannah as concern briefly wrinkled her brow. "Darling, you must be horribly homesick? It all sounds like paradise—all those crescent miles of white sand, limpid blue green water, the romance of the outback, tangles of bizarre tropical flowers rising from arid earth."

Momentarily exhausted by such excess, she pressed her empty wine glass against the ropes of beads that sloped down her breasts. Her voice dropped. "So much easier than that passé China rage. At least in Australia they do speak a kind of English. Our travel agency in Camden is going to raffle tickets off during the Art Show Supper at the Grange Hall—'Win an Adventure Down Under! As far from Maine as you can get!' Don't you love it? I've bought a dozen tickets. Those gorgeous blond men in their tight little shorts. God, life here is so boring!"

Hannah smiled. She knew all about those men. Most of them 'ockers—only after women for sex and a night on the town. And the chain link nets to keep off the sharks patrolling the "limpid green waters." Poisonous spiders like the Funnelweb, *Atrax robusta*. Robusta indeed—they're the size of doorknobs lurking under the ledges of swimming pools and leaping four feet to sink their fangs into you. Then comes the winter season when sticky flies walk across your eyeballs between blinks. And the real outback—back of Bourke—was still mostly an untracked and waterless waste of 110-degree desert.

"Sometimes it's about as romantic as death," offered Hannah. "I'm not homesick, not yet anyway, but I'll buy some raffle tickets the next time I'm in Camden. What I do miss is the daily swimming, despite the blue bottle jellyfish. The water temperature here is life threatening."

"My dear, she called him weasel penis."

The three of them turned and smiled at this anonymous revelation that wafted up from the crowd.

"Doesn't anyone here speak kindly?" asked Grace. From a passing tray, she snatched up a succulent piece of smoked eel. "I promised myself nothing but vegetables until dinner, but this eel is my favorite treat. I am serious about my diet, but I have lived today on one sliced tomato and some cottage cheese."

Hannah followed Grace over to the wide doors leading out onto the dusky porch. The fish treat she carried was left uneaten. They both saw Ian's head bowed over Nan's. The woman's tan, mobile breasts were exposed at the cleavage of a black jersey dress that must have cost a year's groceries. Grace's own solid breasts rose on an unhappy sigh.

Feeling guilty, but unable to offer comfort in the awkward moment, Hannah left Grace to her misery and went back to the bar where she filled a glass with vodka and ice for Thea. An agitated Bea diverted her.

"Hannah, have you seen Emily? She left on an errand for me ages ago and hasn't come back. Our guests are beginning to leave. And where on earth is Stuart? We had business to discuss and he promised to come early. We were to meet before cocktails."

Hannah was astonished. Bea's nail tips were marking her cheek. She had never seen her so flustered.

"I'm sorry, I heard her leave earlier while I was in the pantry arranging the flowers, but haven't seen her since. Where did you send her?"

Bea shook her head, but didn't answer. "I'm more concerned over Stuart's desertion. He knows that he's expected to be here for this party, but I've called and there's no answer; just his machine saying that he's out of town. I don't understand it. Stuart's always been so reliable and he knew how important this evening was to me. To us all. He never makes this kind of mistake. I'm worried, Hannah." She drew a breath and composed herself. "I hear you and Stuart have become rather chummy," she paused, "I thought you might know if something had changed his plans."

Hannah raised both her shoulders and eyebrows, but before she could comment on Stuart's defection—about which she knew nothing—Bea muttered something inarticulate and swiveled away. Hannah was not surprised at Bea's familiarity with her private life. Bea was like a spider centered in its web with her filaments leading out to all of them. Hannah shrugged. The woman was insidious.

She carried Thea's drink out to the porch where she saw the immediate need to rescue her friend from the onslaught of blue-haired Mrs. Roach. The old lady, leaning over her silver knobbed cane, equated blindness with deafness, and Thea was pressed dangerously over the porch railing in an attempt to avoid the assault on her ears.

Back in the library off the hall, Grace collected her purse. She was desperate to escape for a few minutes peace and more aspirin before dinner. She startled guiltily when Bea appeared abruptly beside her.

"Grace, have you seen Emily? She's not back yet and everything is ruined!" Her mother-in-law's aloof calm had deserted her. She twisted and threatened the pearl necklace around a throat flushed by agitation. They turned together at the crunch of tires on gravel and Bea, in a swirl of silk pleats, almost ran from the room. By now Grace's head throbbed, but she was checked again by the last departing guests and, with Bea's sudden absence, had to cope alone with good-byes and the requisite kissing of cheeks.

When she closed the closed the door on the last of them, she leaned and rested her head against the cool wood panel. Something brushed her mind. Something unpleasant. The nasty dinner invitation? She must ask Colin about that. With all his elaborate preparations, tonight's party seemed more Colin's than Bea's. A sudden frisson made her shiver. Apart from Bea's uncharacteristic fussing and having to witness Ian's blatant attention toward Nan, something else disturbed her. Maybe her biorhythms were out of sync. More likely it was hunger.

The spring evening had cooled. The cocktail guests were gone and Hannah settled Thea with Emperor before the low burning fire in the living room. She loaded a tray with party debris and carried it back to the pantry where she was relieved to hear Emily's tires crunch to a stop in the driveway. She still felt uneasy over Bea's concern. Why all this fuss?

Someone had opened the dining room windows and, through the thin curtains, she saw them standing together in the drive. Fragments of raised voices drifted up to her, and congenitally curious, she eavesdropped.

" . . . not at the airport, Bea—I waited—she probably stopped for a drink—got cold feet—maybe went back to Boston—took a taxi—arrive . . ."

These disjointed words came from Emily, but Hannah saw that the hand comforting Bea's shoulder was shrugged away angrily as they walked together out of sight.

She wondered what disturbed the stalwart birthday girl enough to have made her neglect her departing guests. She continued clearing up from the cocktail party then turned to make a final check on the dinner table. Someone had lit the candles. The silver and crystal shone and glittered, but it looked less crowded. She counted. The place settings had been reduced to eleven.

Who now, besides Stuart, wasn't coming to dinner?

CHAPTER 7

The mellow wood patina of the dining room's paneling reflected the candlelight, and, as relief from the cocktail party's earlier din, the thick Persian carpet underfoot muted conversation. Immersed in their own thoughts, the family waited for Doris and Stella to begin serving. At the round table, they sat under the dour scrutiny of ancestral Swanns. From the wall, the two brass-buttoned naval commanders paired in ornate gilt frames, with their equally forbidding wives, stared down on them.

Seated between Hannah and Clay, Thea enjoyed the flow of familiar voices commending themselves on the success of the cocktail party and cooperation of the weather. Colin's wicked parodies of their guest's idiocies made her smile. But she sadly missed the best part of his meal. She found her taste was diminished without color and form; without the sight of food, she had lost the joy of eating. And tonight she was tired.

Beside her, she felt Clay fidget and thought he must be bored by the long hours trapped with adults. She heard his finger squeak around the rim of his water filled wine glass until it rang with rubbery vibrations.

"Stop it," she heard say Grace sharply. Then she apologized to her son. "Sorry," she whispered. "It's been a long day."

Clay eyed his mother in silent agreement and transferred his energy to drowning the fishy tasting pellets floating in his soup. He submerged the last anchovy crouton and glared at his great-grandfather on the wall across from him. Above a shrub of pale gingery side-whiskers, the captain's prideful eyes glared back from a head held stiff above narrow, sloping shoulders. Freckled fingers pressed a thick monocle against his slender chest.

"It's not fair," Thea heard Clay mutter. "Why did those wimpy genes by-pass Dad and land in me?"

Beside him, Grace sympathized and privately regretted her own genetic inheritance as she watched Graham, with ectomorphic unconcern, lavish rich wine sauce over his duck filet. Tonight she'd begun her new regime. Mentally as well as physically.

Grace noticed that Bea had relaxed some as a result of Colin's attention to her battery of wineglasses. Bea had also seen Ian's overt dalliance with Nan out on the porch and turned to her offending son.

"You didn't mingle much this evening, Ian."

Grace saw her husband flush and quickly turn away to refill Emily's wineglass. Grace too wanted to find solace in wine, but not tonight. The new regime forbade it. She was satisfied that Ian chose to ignore Bea's barb. Her own dependence on him made her as angry as his kow-towing to his mother, but this was not the place for the scene she was planning. Another part of her new regime. When they got home this evening she'd begin her attack.

Doris and Stella served Colin's elegant dinner and Grace was pleased to see that they'd taken care to arrange Thea's plate, food cut to fork size and in accustomed clockwise order. Beside her, Grace heard Hannah quietly explain each course. Stella had removed her apron and the tatty brown cardigan, but Grace knew she'd never submit to role-playing in any maid's uniform. She remembered hearing Stella's disgust at the cleaner, Mrs. Pink, who 'did' for the big houses on the Neck. "Stuffs her fat body into that green trouser suit and calls herself a cleaning consultant."

The dinner plates were cleared and they ate small salads of red lettuce topped with slivers of runny Brie. Carrie's coin-sized buttermilk biscuits were passed with pots of dark clover honey combed from their own hives.

Colin brushed the crumbs from his lap and observed that his family had eaten fearlessly well. When his first tentative mouthfuls provided no poisonous effects, he had relaxed and enjoyed the meal. He considered good food to be as sensual a pleasure as good sex and the intricacies of its preparation as enjoyable as the eating. He was feeling content and avoided Hannah's earlier suggestion to question the others about his strange invitation.

His gaze shifted to his mother. Throughout the meal she had frowned over her plate, rejecting its fat, sugar, and health threatening constituents. He could not resign himself to her rebuff of his culinary efforts, but admitted the success of her diet strictures. She did not look the septuagenarian.

He caught Carrie's eye and gave her a thumbs up sign. The girl had the natural instincts of a talented cook. Her light hand had produced the flaky biscuits and the dressing for the duck, and she was roundly praised.

He was aware, however, that despite the excellent food, there ran unpleasant undercurrents. The birthday dinner was not going well. Perhaps two parties on the same evening had been a bad idea. Around the table, awkward lapses hung between bursts of conversation, and not even the prodigious amount of wine they'd consumed erased the subtle tensions. He watched Emily and Phil murmur quietly to each other. Even Phil was subdued tonight. The man possessed a good parson's ease of rhetoric and could usually be counted on for politic and amusing conversation. He found Phil's weathered face attractive; he had certainly charmed the gamut of village women, old and young. His angular hooked nose and dark eyes under those fire and brimstone brows captivated his congregation, but Colin wondered if such a rough sexuality might be a slippery aura for a man of the cloth in a small rumor prone village.

He eyed his cousin Emily, and wondered how the town gossips explained the nights she spent at the rectory. And why did she keep refusing Phil's offers to become the parson's chatelaine? She had lived with this family like an older sister since her mother died. He could understand her outbursts of vitriol and antagonism toward Bea, but she alarmed him sometimes with her fierce independence. In turn, he sensed her tacit disapproval of his own lack of spine. He thought Phil was just the kind of calming influence Em needed.

He raised his glass and savored the last of the mellow burgundy, watching his mother absently tap her empty wineglass with a painted carmine nail. She looked decidedly un-jolly for a birthday girl.

From the pantry, came the tremulous beginnings of Happy Birthday, and Doris held open the swinging door for Stella, who ceremoniously pushed through the tea trolley bearing the cake. The rest of them joined in the impossibly keyed song while Ian attended to the champagne, pouring half glasses for Carrie and Clay.

"Wow," said Clay. "We might pass out on all that."

Carrie punched his arm. "Don't be an animal."

Bea took a dainty breath and blew out the single flickering candle, and when the wish making and congratulations died away, Colin stood.

"Speech, mother," he insisted.

With a grimace, Bea rose and raised her champagne flute to them.

"In the sanctity of my family, but never beyond these doors, I admit I've become a bona fide senior citizen."

The Moët flowed and they truthfully assured her that this would not be believed. Bea opened the gifts piled on a small table beside her chair and went through the ritual of gracious and admiring thanks. When the phone rang in the kitchen, Hannah watched her hesitant rise and saw her strain to hear the muffled conversation. Was she still expecting some message from Stuart or her missing guest?

They finished the last forkfuls of cake and laid aside their napkins, expecting Bea to begin the pronouncements revealing her newest manipulations. They wondered if she would dare suggest any momentous reshuffling of their lives without consulting Stuart. Where was he?

Carrie fidgeted, head down over the linen napkin in her lap, and hoped no one would spoil her Gran's party.

But Bea didn't speak. When the silence around the table became strained, Colin rose to his feet, champagne in hand, and gestured to them. The metallic fibers in his silk vest glinted in the candlelight. "I think tonight we all should . . . ." They waited, smiling expectantly, then looked at each other, embarrassed as his words died away. With a deflated exhalation, he simply shrugged and raised his glass to his mother in a silent salute.

Bea's shoulder's slumped, as if suddenly overwhelmed, and she pushed back her chair, signaling the end of the party. Murmuring, perhaps more relieved than disappointed at the abrupt and unexpected end to the strange evening, they got to their feet and moved away from the table.

During the ritual goodnight brushing of cheeks, Hannah remembered the *Cereus* and turned to her hostess.

"Bea, please promise to come over to the greenhouse tonight before you go to bed and witness your treasure's grand opening. Thea and I think it's ready, but we'll check in on our way down to the cottage and call you."

Bea dipped her chin in amusement at Hannah's forced enthusiasm.

"Thank you dear, I realize my pet plant is not your favorite, but I raised the beast from a cutting and I feel like the mother of a particularly ugly child—very liable. You can hide it away after tonight."

"I'll come back up after you're gone and light the smokers," said Thea. "We've had an infestation." She silently hoped the treasure might pass away during the fumigation.

Colin took his mother's arm more as a gesture of dignity than support.

"I'll try again to phone Stu," he told her. "Come sit by the fire and I'll bring you a nightcap."

CHAPTER 8

Thea had sensed Emp's reproachful eyes on this quiet Sunday morning when she left without him, but she couldn't risk subjecting her precious dog to any residual poison from the deficiencies of the greenhouse's ancient exhaust system. She opened the door and sniffed cautiously. The moist air still held only a slight acrid trace of the deadly nicotine fumigant from last night's smokers, but she felt the draft from the open roof vents and heard the humming of the big exhaust fans.

It was peaceful to be alone under the sun-warmed glass. She slipped a cassette into the recorder above her workbench and settled on her stool. Hannah's metallic voice intoned the new orders, and she began to pot them up.

Working steadily, she cursed when her hand swept the bin below and felt the last of the fiber pots.

"Damn!" The supplies cupboard was a rickety metal cabinet jammed beside the cramped office where Hannah now should be grumbling over the deskwork that kept her from her pet projects. They'd decided to work weekends to catch up, but Thea hadn't heard her come in and there were no sounds from behind the closed door. Then she remembered Hannah had gone to the studio to bring back Graham's drawings of the new greenhouse plans.

"We'll hassle the details later," she had said after their lunch together yesterday. "First, let's see what he's designed."

Thea had been surprised at the success of their session on Daily's dock. They had eaten fried clams from paper cartons, lathering on ketchup and tartar sauce. Coleslaw, onion rings and glasses of jug wine completed the ultimate Maine junk meal.

Gathering up their mess of plastic forks and paper napkins, Hannah had mollified her stubbornness and Graham, tactfully, convinced her he was ally, not a foe, and everything hung on Bea's generosity with her checkbook.

Thea's thoughts returned to her work, and lugging the empty bin to refill with peat pots, she navigated the staging rails to the storage cupboard. In that dim part of the greenhouse, the stone path's mossy coating was slick under her rubber thongs.

Something caught at her ankle and her bare foot twisted in the flimsy shoe. She lost her balance, lost hold of the plastic bin, and fell awkwardly onto the gravel. Sharp stones tore into her skin, but the pain that stabbed at her wrenched foot hurt far less than the lapse of dignity.

"So what," she spoke aloud crossly. "People do occasionally fall down."

She groped about for the sandal, but instead her hand brushed something soft and lumpy. She was suddenly aware that she was holding cold, rubbery flesh.

Fighting nausea, she realized she was not alone after all.

CHAPTER 9

Hannah entered her office from Colin's studio and dropped the roll of drawings on the jumble of paperwork that covered her desk. She looked at the open door leading into the greenhouse.

"Thea?"

No answer. Strange, she thought. She swatted and missed a black fly buzzing over the remains of yesterday's chocolate doughnut.

"Vicious maggot breeding blood-sucker!" She swatted again. "Nasty enough biter to be an Aussie."

Maybe Thea was in the loo. She stared in dismay at the pile of new orders that came in last week's mail and lay still unrecorded. And today that mailman would deliver a bloody new load. She groaned aloud. How did all these people hear of us?

Hannah slumped into her desk chair. She realized she could no longer keep up with the relentless paper work. Graham, persuasive and tactful at lunch yesterday had convinced them they could not survive with their cottage industry mentality.

She scratched absently at the itching welt raised by the fly and noticed the state of her hands. She'd stopped on her way up to the studio to grub in the soil. A creeping infiltration of *Stellara,* the local kudzu, had infiltrated one of the cold frames. Scraping under her nails with the letter opener wasn't enough and she vowed to schedule a weekly professional manicure. She'd call it a business perk. She would also become, like Thea, a neat, organized, well groomed person. Right, she thought. Like I still believe in the tooth fairy.

She went to wash away the worst of the grime at the tiny corner sink and reflected that, when he was away from Colin's companionship, Graham's masculinity confused her. She sensed his sexuality focused on her as a woman. This puzzled her, and in her male deprived state, she regretted the waste of any handsome man. Forget it. She remembered, then quickly put from her mind, the indulgences of her past Sydney nightlife. There was too much work here to even think about party times.

On her arrival in the village, she'd been amused by the attention of the muscle proud men who leaned against their pickups in the lot outside the market making appreciative comments. They seemed to subsist on a diet of wooden toothpicks rolled around lips that were barely visible under the pulled down visors of their Gimmee caps. On her trips to town, she was tempted to accept one of their invitations just to witness a cowardly retreat.

Her social life wasn't entirely without diversion. As Bea had remarked, Stuart Hobart was being nicely attentive, and because the local eatery began serving breakfast at five a.m. and closed early, she'd invited him to a more civil dinner at the cottage. She enjoyed cooking, and the alternative was a long drive to the nearest decent restaurant. Later that night, they had sipped Armagnac in front of the fire and she'd detected his appraisal of her wifely possibilities. Agreeably flattering, yes, but she was not ready to become any man's little sheila. She'd come halfway around the world to make a success of this nursery business.

The pile of orders facing her waited, accusing and rousing guilt. This was no time to cultivate a new love life. More frustrating, all this garbage on her desk was keeping her from her real passion—the exacting and patient work required for tissue culture of the *Gerbera* that was so difficult to propagate reliably from seed.

She dried her hands on her jeans and clicked on the coffee machine. The onslaught of gurgling dribbles made her wonder why she bothered. It made vile coffee.

She froze at the sound of pained mewling coming from the greenhouse. My God! Had Ugly Joyce been trapped in there last night? The aloof yellow cat had become her friend after his first raid on her lunch when she found they shared a liking for cantaloupe. The shaggy beast now appeared regularly at midday to cruise her ankles before settling his twenty-pound mound on her desktop. When he was tucked up and comfortable, he'd narrow his wedge-shaped eyes in anticipation of goodies to be offered from the day's brown bag. She could not face the sight of his body contorted in nicotine-poisoned agony.

"Hann . . . nahh." The mewling cry became pleading. Though clever and demanding, the cat had never called her by name. She pushed through the greenhouse door, nearly stepping on Thea, who was sprawled on the gravel path and clutching Bea's forearm.

It was the older woman's body, not the cat's that lay twisted on the greenhouse stones. The silk collar of her dressing gown was stained red from the pool of congealed blood that had seeped from the deep gash in her temple.

Hannah helped Thea to sit, and watched her face contort in horror as she rubbed at the gluey wetness of Bea's blood on her palms. She shuddered with revulsion and wiped them on her apron. Thea tried to pull herself to her feet, but cried out when the pain caught at her ankle and made her sink back onto the gravel.

"Hannah," her hands covered her mouth. "Who is it?"

CHAPTER 10

"Mac!" Dr. Hastings snapped his fingers at the young man.

Detective Mackintosh MacNeill started, then reddened. He'd been staring at Thea like a smitten teenager. She reminded him of the costumed storybook dolls that his sister had collected, and like them, this lovely woman now sat still and doll-like on her high work stool. Mac sensed her discomfort and wanted to touch her to let her know his presence was more than an anonymous and official questioning voice.

Though Mac grew up in Rockland, and heard tales about the Swann's that included some wicked gossip, he was sure that none of the family was ever involved with the police. He was sorry that his first encounter with them was in his official capacity and might prove painful.

Doc Hastings, locus for the Maine state medical examiner, was a tidy, taciturn man. He was competent at delivering babies, patching up bloody bodies pulled from wrecked cars, and, when needed, not above responding to a neighboring farmer's veterinary emergency. He prodded and wrapped Thea's ankle then raised it to rest on a work stool.

After an assessing examination of Bea, Hastings pushed hard on his thighs and rose stiffly from his squat beside her body. He turned to Watty. "Rigor's well set. She's been dead at least seven or eight hours."

Watty, MacNeill's detail officer, licked his pencil.

Hastings scowled at him. "That's bad for you, always sucking on graphite."

Watty ignored him and scribbled in his notebook.

"I hate ballpoints. They write sleazy."

Mac depended on his Sergeant's precise note taking. The observations and sketches Watty made while the rest of them talked often recalled case breaking details. Especially helpful on a day like this with his attention skewed by the attractive blind woman.

Hastings peeled off the papery surgical gloves and brushed non-existent dust from his trousers. He sniffed the air.

"What's that stink?"

Mac pointed to the ruined Moonflower. The twine that had supported it was torn from the shelving and the pearly, deflated bloom lay in a tangle of golden stamens that hung from its limp, silky pouch.

Hastings picked out the plant tag embedded in the soil that had spilled from the fallen pot.

"*Selenicereus grandiflora*," he pronounced. "Looks like it belongs in the jungle." The doctor shook his head. "Why spend your time growing something so ugly?"

"The night blooming cereus is a botanical oddity—and a challenge to make bloom," said Hannah. "Sometimes it won't flower for three or four years. You have to cosset it."

Mac saw her bite hard on her lip and avoided looking at the shape of Bea's body under a hastily found covering.

"Well," said Hastings, "it looks like the flower killed her."

He pointed to the stepladder pulled close to the bench where the cactus had climbed. "Maybe while she was trying to get a closer look at the thing, she slipped off the stool. She must have hit her head on the sharp corner of that bench when she fell; there's blood on it."

"The flower didn't kill her," Thea spoke in a disoriented voice. "I did."

She spoke with an odd lack of emotion. "I came up here alone last night, and if I had seen her body, I'd have never lit those bombs. If I had brought Emperor with me, he'd have found her in time for me to call a doctor. If she was only unconscious from striking her head, I might have saved her life. She covered her face with her hands. "Instead," she sobbed, "I poisoned her."

Mac looked puzzled. "Poison?"

Hannah turned to Mac and explained. "We use nicotine smoke bombs as seldom as possible, but this was a big new commercial venture and the *cyclamen* mite was spreading. We've made a large investment in this project and it had to be quickly controlled."

Thea sat rigid on the high stool. Mac felt a rush of compassion and wanted to comfort her against him. He controlled this unprofessional emotion and instead moved toward her to gently take her arm. Both women's shock and revulsion were plain on their faces and he saw their need to get away from the mound of Bea's body. Mac helped Thea down, turned toward Hannah, and nodded to the office.

"Let's talk in there while we wait for the ambulance."

Hannah put an arm around the girl and with Mac's assistance helped her hobble along between the benches.

"Thea," she insisted, "you did not poison Bea."

After they settled her with her foot raised on the only other chair in the cramped space, Hastings used their phone to make his official calls. Watty settled a hip onto the corner of the desk and flipped to a fresh page in his notebook. Hannah picked off the dead fly she'd left amid the doughnut crumbs.

"Could we begin with last night, Miss Packwood?" said Mac.

Hannah composed herself and took a deep breath.

"Bea—Mrs. Swann," she began, "seemed exhausted by the evening's parties, but this odd plant, the night-bloomer, meant something special to her, and she didn't want to miss its opening. I told her after dinner that we thought tonight might be its debut and, after checking the greenhouse on our way home, we called to tell her to come over as it looked ready to bloom."

"We'll check with the others," Mac said, "but did she go directly to her room after dinner?"

"No, her son Colin settled her with a brandy by the living room fire. That's where I saw her last. Ian, Grace and the children were getting their coats. Graham, Phil and Emily—I don't remember exactly, but we were all milling around, saying goodnight. It had been a very long day and everyone was tired."

She nodded toward the glasshouse beyond. "She must have taken our call after she went up to her bedroom, because she came down to the greenhouse in her dressing gown."

Mac saw her lip tremble, and thought she was not so tough and controlled as she tried to appear.

"Thanks, that's enough for now," he said, quickly. "We'll talk to everyone tomorrow. One more question. Did you and Thea leave the dinner party together?"

"Yes, just as I said. We checked in here on our way to the cottage and saw that the Moonflower was beginning to open. It takes a while. I called her from this office—it was around eleven o'clock—and she said she would be right down. We waited here for her and when she came in, we left her alone with her treasure. I told her we would come back later and light the fumigant."

Thea gave Mac a brief smile. "Along with too much wine, topped off by champagne, we were both ready for bed. But Hannah had helped with the party that afternoon, so I insisted she go to bed. I said I would come back and light the cone bombs after Bea left. I know the way so well and it only takes a few minutes. I didn't bring my dog." Thea continued in her soft voice. "When I came back up here, just before midnight, I heard nothing and felt sure I was alone. It's hard to explain, but I can usually sense people's presence, even if they don't speak. I didn't *feel* anyone was here. I called out but no one answered. I assumed Bea had left." Thea stopped and swallowed. "She must have fallen, over in that corner, yet I thought I was alone, so I lit the smoke cones, closed the vents, and left her lying there—to be poisoned by twenty minutes of deadly nicotine sulfate smoke." She stopped speaking, covered her eyes with her hands, and began to shake.

Hastings wrapped a cup of water into the blind girl's palms. She drank, and her voice grew calmer but still full of self-reproach. "If only I'd wakened Emperor and not come alone, Bea would still be alive. Emperor would have found her immediately. I just couldn't risk the dog ingesting any of the fumigant. She shook her head and the dark bob of hair swung across her chin to hide her face. "I wanted to come up here anyway because I'd forgotten my tape recorder and a book on tape I was listening to. It helps me fall asleep at night." Her voice trailed away. "I still have trouble sleeping."

Mac touched her shoulder. "Hey, you didn't kill her," he said gently. "It's dark in that corner at night. She probably fell, just as you did. The stones back there are slick with moss. As Hastings said, the stool must have tipped under her, and when she fell, she struck her head on that sharp corner. It was unlucky that she hit that soft place on her temple. Bleeding into her brain could have caused her death before you got here. An autopsy will check all that. It was probably just a terrible accident." He spoke earnestly, wanting it to be so. Mac looked over at Hastings, hoping for confirmation, but the doctor wouldn't meet his eye.

Hastings opened his bag, fumbled through its compartments, and spoke firmly to Thea. "Your ankle will be all right. It's only strained. We'll help you home where you can put ice on it. However, I would like to give you a mild sedative, Miss Morgan. You have had a terrible shock."

Thea shook her head, vehemently. "No more pills. I'm through with all that. I'll be fine."

Hastings shrugged but didn't argue. They helped escort the two women down to their cottage, and then left them to wait for the ambulance to come for Bea's body. Outside the cottage, the men breathed deep of the salty morning air. Watty grinned up at his partner and nugied a schoolboy fist into his shoulder.

"Tall, handsome policeman loses his heart to beautiful suspect. Good thing your Rosie wasn't there, Mac, she'd 'a thrown a ree-all jealous fit. The girls told my wife that Rosie's been filling one of them trousseau chests and it has your name on it."

Mac slid his lanky frame into the front seat and gave his partner a steady look. "Just drive, Watty."

Inside their cottage, Hannah settled Thea on the sitting room sofa with a knit-cosied teapot and an ice bag on her ankle. Emperor pushed his nose as close as he could and Thea stroked the dog's black head.

"Rest, Thea, I'm going to walk over to the big house. They must all be in shock."

Hannah avoided the path to the closed off greenhouse where the police had stretched their yellow tape. Despite the warm morning, she shivered in the cotton tee shirt that read "Eat Mussels" across her chest with the details of their nutritional benefits listed down her back.

She found the adult Swanns, along with Graham and Emily, huddled in sober contrast to the sun-filled living room. Except for the flowers that still scented the room, all evidence of last night's party, including its marginal cheer, was gone. The family gathered in glum silence, sunk in the squashy cushions that covered Bea's tasteful mis-match of chairs and sofas. Amid the overflow of Sunday papers on the low rubbed-pine table in front of the fire was a coffee pot and a plate of sandwiches.

The sweet scent of tulips and narcissus were losing battle to Ian's chain smoking. Despite his promises to quit, they all understood this morning's relapse. His smoking and the way Grace was eating methodically through the plate of food, clarified their collective anxiety.

Emily, looking ill and gray, slumped into the embrace of an oversize rocker and Graham, his back to them, stood staring out over the harbor. Colin hunched over a balloon of brandy cradled between his knees. They looked up as she entered, nodded, but none of them spoke.

Grace gestured vaguely as Hannah dropped into the rocker across from her.

"Coffee, Hannah?"

She refused and Grace absently offered her the plate, now empty, of sandwiches. Seeing Hannah's puzzled expression, she frowned.

"I'm sorry, I'll go make some more." Grace started toward the kitchen, then stopped and turned. "Hannah, what can I tell the children? Carrie spent the night with Lucy and Clay left early to fish with Luther. Neither of them has heard of their grandmother's accident."

Their anxious, expectant faces annoyed Hannah. Where in hell was Stuart? Toiling away in Chancery? And why should they suddenly rely on her to act as family guru? She'd anticipated Colin would be dazed and drained by his mother's death, but she was surprised by Ian's lack of presence.

"Have you called Stuart?" she asked them. "Why isn't he here when you need him?"

Ian reddened and tossed his cigarette into the fire. They shifted in their chairs, waiting and hopeful, Hannah thought, for someone to take charge, rally and protect their clan.

"We can't reach Stuart," Ian said. "I've tried his house, the Rockland office, even called the home of that girl Jenny who works for him. That young Detective MacNeill just left here. He said he'd already spoken to you and Thea, and asked us polite questions about who was who, and where and how we live. He seems an atypical policeman, quite the gentleman. His little sergeant flapped his ears over in the corner and scribbled down everything we said. MacNeill assured us that it's only routine, but tactfully insists we stay put." Ian sucked in a lungful of smoke from a fresh cigarette, then looked perplexed by its magical appearance between his fingers. He muttered to himself. "Fire at one end, fool at the other," and tossed the crumpled package into the fire.

"It was a ghastly accident, no question about it." Emily spoke for the first time. "I'm sure that Stuart will cope with the depressing practical arrangements as soon as we find him." She pulled herself from the depths of the rocker to pour more coffee. "MacNeill may be quiet," she said, "but he seems keener than most local deputies." She spooned brown sugar crystals into her cup and stirred.

"No doubt he has had experience with felonious expertise," mused Colin as he roused to eddy his brandy glass. The words were slurred. "A different breed of cop, our urbane MacNeill. I'm sure he heard more from us than we'd planned to say. Not that we have anything to hide," he added. His conceit expressed the Swanns dictum of closing ranks against any invasion of their privacy, and Hannah saw Graham turn, amused, from the window. He stroked his mustache and she wondered if he also questioned the family's innate lack of candor.

The front door slammed and they heard abrupt footsteps along the hall. Stuart Hobart stopped in the doorway to stare at the grim assemblage. He looked around the room. "Hey, where's the birthday girl?"

They stared at him, speechless.

"What's up?" he asked. "Bea and I were to meet this afternoon before the party. I should have called first. I'm sorry, but I've been gone since Friday and the red-eye back from the coast was late. I've come straight from the airport." He bent to help himself to coffee. "Where *is* Bea?"

Still no one spoke.

He sank into an armchair and rested the bulging canvas satchel he used as a briefcase on the floor beside him. He rubbed his eyes, and pushed up the overlarge horn rims that, like Clay's, constantly slid down his narrow nose. He stretched his hands behind his head and leaned wearily against the high back of the rocker.

"I'm beat," he said. "Those airline seats don't comfort my length. Someone tell Bea I'm here, and we'll get to work." He yawned. "I'll need a nap before tonight's parties."

He drained his coffee cup then looked at them over its rim, finally aware of their strained silence. Hannah saw Stuart's puzzled frown. Ian's authority had deserted him, and as no one else offered to explain, she got up, went over to him and rested her hand on his shoulder.

"Stu, where have you been? There's been a terrible accident," she said bluntly, "Bea's dead."

He stared up at her in disbelief.

Emily spoke. "We tried to reach you all day yesterday. There's been some awful mix up." She rushed on. "Stuart, the parties were last night. Bea was very upset when you never showed up."

"But it's Sunday," his voice broke. "Today is her birthday. I was invited for Sunday. I'm sure of it because I rushed through my meetings and flew all night, so I'd be back by this morning." The young lawyer ran both hands through his brown curly hair. "I can't believe this. Bea was perfectly well when I left. What happened?"

Graham turned from the window and leaned against its wide sill. "Who invited you for Sunday, Stuart?"

The boyish face turned thoughtful. "I'm sure it was Bea. I assumed when she phoned, that the party was on her birthday. I can't recall that she mentioned another day. No, wait, I swear Jenny said someone called and confirmed a meeting here with Bea before drinks on Sunday. Jenny's off camping for the weekend but I can check in the morning."

They knew Stuart's capricious secretary-cum law clerk. She dressed like a flake, sported tattoos and body piercings, but her steel-trap mind would never have goofed an appointment with their most prestigious client.

"Bea waited for you before the cocktail party and through dinner," said Hannah. "She was really upset when you didn't arrive." She briefly recounted the accident in the greenhouse and Thea's grim discovery only hours ago. "The police have been here and are trying to get in touch with you. Bea's body has been taken away." She sank down in the rocker. The retelling vividly recalled the body lying beside Thea on the greenhouse stones.

Stuart brushed aside his jet lag confusion and let his professional gears begin to function. Bea's children sighed audibly as he took charge. With relief, Hannah escaped and left them to discuss the details of the grisly and sudden death of the head of the family.

She stopped at the entrance road leading to the greenhouse, to put up a notice warding off any Sunday trade. Back at the cottage, Thea sat at the kitchen table eating a large dripping cheeseburger. Hannah knew that a hand-held messy sandwich was easier than meals requiring fork and knife and that Thea now dealt with the world on tactile terms.

She looked at Thea's burger and was suddenly starving. She should be too saddened to eat, but Bea's death seemed unreal. This awful morning was over, but tomorrow, going back to work in the greenhouse would be worse.

"I know this is gross," said Thea wiping her chin, "but I was so hungry. Shock doesn't affect my appetite. How are things holding up at the Swann's?"

"Stuart finally arrived. He insists he was told that the parties were tonight. There are some real ball ups somewhere. How's your ankle?"

"Hmm. The ice and aspirins helped."

Hannah rummaged in the refrigerator and after stuffing a warm pita pocket with cold turkey, tomatoes and sprouts, all lathered with mustard, chutney, and mayo, she poured herself a large glass of good Australian red. Wirra Wirra Church Block found at the Liquorette in Camden—incredible. Yet maybe not, Australian wine was finally receiving its just notoriety.

"Thea, maybe it's untimely to discuss this, but our tidy future plans may be in serious trouble without Bea's financial support. I'll talk to Stu, but I don't know what he can or will tell us. What arrangement did she make for the new nursery business? I'm selfish, I suppose, but I don't want to go back to Sydney."

Thea gave an unladylike belch and patted her stomach. "Very acceptable Chinese custom," she said defensively. Hannah was always relieved by this delicate creature's human lapses.

"I still feel responsible for Bea's death," said Thea, "but while lying here on my bed of pain, I've been thinking about the whole greenhouse scene and it bothers me. Why was the *Cereus* torn away from the shelving? The opening bloom was low enough to be seen without climbing up a step-ladder." She finished the last of her tea but held the empty mug as if to warm both hands. "It's a nasty thought, but who most wanted to prevent Bea from making waves. Nobody spoke up during the dinner party, but I felt everyone was waiting for her to shuffle their cards. Do you really think her fall was an accident?"

Hannah licked lime mango chutney from her fingers. "I can think of at least five people whose lives she had the power to change for the worse. Maybe only four because, from what I hear, Grace has nothing to lose. She has plenty of money of her own. And Thea, remember one very important thing. You couldn't have known she was lying over there. It was late and Bea wore a dressing gown, but her slippers were rough soled moccasins. She shouldn't have slipped."

CHAPTER 11

Luther's diesel motor growled out through the harbor's green water toward Muscle Ridge Channel, and Clay watched the numbers change on the Fathometer's screen as it plotted the contours of the ocean floor. The weather had turned clear and calm, and Sunday or not, it was a day they needed to make up for the northeaster that had kept the boats three days in the harbor. Traps were set shallow this time of year when the lobsters began their crawl inshore to shed.

Luther hunched himself on the dry port rail, eating jelly doughnuts from a grease-spotted bag. Between swigs of coffee from his big chrome thermos, he watched the boy work the hauler.

Clay's fingers in his cotton dunkers were stiff with cold, but he knew he'd soon be sweating. He wasn't as strong as Luther, but the hydraulic lift made it easy to gaff the day-glo buoys. They were ugly, but no use chasing whitecaps. There were nasty days too—cold, rough and wet, even in mid-summer, when he stayed in deck and let Luther cope with the hauler.

He looped the pot warp through the sheave disc and let the engine shaft pull the kelp-ribboned lobster pot to the surface. He balanced it, dripping, on the rail, smiled at the four keepers, tossed back the shorts, and put the crabs in a separate pail to deliver to Mrs. Cobb. He got paid extra for this. The summer folk couldn't get enough fresh crab at $4.00 a pint. He'd tried picking it out himself and decided the summer people were getting a bargain.

They didn't talk much. The scavenging gulls, wheeling and screaming above them, discouraged conversation. On calm and foggy days when time stretched, they'd tune in the CB band and chuckle over the "chat time" gossip. The best thing was that, unlike his father, Luther never nagged, never criticized. If Clay goofed up, the lobsterman just reached across and put things right.

Today had been good. The uncanny gulls seemed to know when they'd reached the end of the string, and swept toward home, leaving them some quiet. Coming into the harbor, he'd wielded the banding pliers like a surgeon, and now, his work done, he rested his eyes on the cliff face beyond the boathouse beach.

Something was different. Low down was a dark opening and below it a pile of fallen rock that had tumbled down onto the pebbly shale. Last week's storm must have pounded that cliff face, probably worked away on a soft spot. He glanced at Luther, busy over the bait pails. He'd check it out later on his own. Maybe he'd bring Carrie, but then maybe not.

Back in the harbor, the final pot was waiting with the cold beers they'd left that morning tied to its toggles—their private celebration after the day's haul. He popped off the caps and handed one to Luther who drank half in one swallow, then wiped his mouth with his left sleeve and his nose with the other. The man fumbled in the pocket beneath his vinyl apron and tossed Clay a package of salted peanuts.

"Cleanse the breath," he mumbled.

After the beers, they munched the nuts and Clay reflected that it had been a quiet day. He was glad they'd not fouled any mussel nets. He understood Luther's anger and respected the lobsterman's undefined rights, but legally "undefined" was a questionable word. The cursing flood of threats Luther would suddenly let rip during his rare outbursts against the musselmen frightened Clay. He didn't understand enough of the argument. He'd overheard the musselmen's side from Doris and Stella. He'd decided that it was best to keep clear when adults fought.

His back and arms ached. He'd worked hard, and when they reached the dock Luther handed him the usual package to drop off at Doc's. Doc had lost his license to practice medicine and now ran the only video store within miles. Clay had never questioned the contents of the package. He sensed that Luther wanted it this way. Today he had pulled his weight, literally, as an equal partner. A little dizzy from the beer, he shook his head and shoved the bag of crabs they had kept aside for Mrs. Cobb under his bike rack. He felt lucky to have such a good summer job. He and Luther were a good working team.

Clay pumped hard up the steep hill from the town dock to where it joined the main street of the village. The Post Office, Strait's Market, garage-gas station, library, the Domestic Institute, fire station, Grange Hall, the Thistle Do Cafe (open 5 am to 8 pm), and the church. No traffic lights and only one stop sign. Ten miles further down the peninsula, the road ended at the ferry dock in Port Clyde.

Around the harbor, solid Victorian houses fronted neatly tended gardens and backed onto rough meadows that sloped down to the calm inner water. Carved wooden gingerbread trimmed their eaves and pendulous blued hydrangeas overgrew their foundations. They were kept freshly painted and some 'For Sale' signs appeared every summer. A hundred years ago, sensible Yankee efficiency had connected the sprawl of barns to the main house, making the winter care of livestock require fewer struggles through ice and snow. These barns were mostly empty now, housing a few goats, some sheep, a horse or two, and the occasional flutter of hens. Most men fished for a living.

Clay peddled past the side street that led to the abandoned stone quarry. It was the only warm water around and conquering the opaque green bottomless swimming hole was a rite of passage for the local kids. He remembered the day he and Carrie passed this test of nerves. They'd been coaxed out onto its high rocky edges by the taunts of those who had already jumped and threatened with the fate of those that had backed off. He remembered his own rigid fear the first time he had swung out on that rope, forced his hands to let go their grip, and dropped, for what seemed miles, past the jagged quarry face into the water.

The kids often retold horror stories about rotting bodies buried deep in its oozy bottom.

He headed his bike toward the market that was the social center of town. The sign above the door had changed over the years—from IGA to Sav-Mor and back again—but it was always run by, and called, Strait's. He liked Lennert Strait and his twin brother Everett. His mother often bragged to her posh Boston guests about the two old-time butchers who owned the store.

"We're so lucky," she'd gush, "to have, in this tiny village, such a superior selection of meats, homemade sausage, and wonderful fresh fish."

She never added that the fish was mostly mackerel and not a big seller, because anyone with a rod and some chum bait could catch more than they wanted in five minutes off the end of the town dock.

The Strait brothers were large, ruddy and habitually good-natured men, who greeted everyone by name in identical booming voices. Everett always shaved Clay a slice off the big wheel of rat cheese in the meat case. There was a crowd around the meat counter when he came in, and he saw Lennert scoop up Mrs. Southworth's new baby in his big hands. He placed the naked wee thing, limbs flailing, gently on clean brown paper laid on his meat scales and everyone laughed at the ritual banter and jokes.

Clay pushed through the regulars that crowded the narrow aisles with wire trolleys. He dug into the freezer for an Eskimo Pie and then remembered he'd brought no money. He'd meant to take Mrs. Cobb the crabs first and get paid. Damn. He wanted the Pie, but knew better than to charge junk food to his mother's account.

Arlean Strait was up front at the cash register, surrounded by home baked pies, leaden chocolate doughnuts, and the eternal supply of blueberry muffins. She'd been there since before he was born and was not always cheerful. He knew that the amount of torment caused by her current ailments determined her mood, and today she looked bad.

He couldn't believe his luck when he saw Carrie came into the store. She had spent the night at Lucy's and had stopped on her way home. He could borrow from her. Carrie always had money—mainly because it made her fingers bleed to spend it. Then he saw Arlean lean over and clutch his sister's hands.

He moved up to the register and overheard the final anguished words.

"Darlin', I'm so sorry. I thought you'd already been home. I wouldn't 'a dreamed of saying anything if I thought you'd not been told about your poor Gran."

He came closer, but wary when Arlean noticed him.

"Oh Clay honey, you'd both better both go right on home. There's been a terrible accident. And Carrie, you tell your Mom how upset I am over speaking out to you both before your family had the chance. I'm just miserable. Mrs. Swann was such a friend for so long."

Clay and Carrie both knew how Arlean thrived on miseries— other people's as much as her own. They looked at each other, frightened and eager to escape her consolation. In the sudden quiet, the entire store pretended not to listen.

Outside, as they got on their bikes, Carrie told Clay in a strange slow voice what little she'd understood from Arlean.

"Gran is dead," she said bluntly. "She fell and hit her head on something in the greenhouse last night. We'd better get home."

She pedaled off ahead of him. He was more worried and scared for his sister than over the terrible news of his grandmother. Carrie was a serious person, but he had never seen her this solemn. Gran was her favorite.

CHAPTER 12

Colin hiccoughed a polite goodnight to Emily and went unsteadily up to his room, cradling a bottle of Courvosier. The brandy had become a numbing solace.

Summer twilight lingered downstairs and Emily wandered through the house seeking a less destructive escape than whisky for herself. She needed a soothing place away from these eerie shadows, some spot to settle in and forget the past weekend's horrors. She wasn't cold, but in her sitting room she lit a fire for its comfort and curled into her reading chair. The book was a good mystery by Janet Smith, but she couldn't concentrate on the Seattle lawyer and the islands amid waters that sounded so much like Maine. Her nerves rebelled from too many cups of tea and the words wouldn't stay put on the page. She dropped the book into her lap and thought about Phil. He'd been unusually quiet during Bea's birthday dinner. Yet could she blame him for wanting to avoid embroilment in her family's undercurrents?

Perhaps she was being foolish not to marry him—acquiesce and become the rector's good wife. They might think her stubborn, but she didn't ever want to leave this wonderful house. Especially to set up in the dingy vicarage and be forced by social responsibilities to feign politeness amidst the village's gossipy boors. She was not one of those altruistic women that took stoic delight in conquering the unpleasant. She got up, pulled on a thick Guernsey cardigan, and headed down to the rectory. She needed Phil's comfort and company tonight.

Later, they lay stretched on the pillows on the wide sagging couch in front of the parlor fire. Emily curled against Phil's rangy body and traced a finger across gray-flecked eyebrows and along his hooked nose. Above the angular planes of his face, his dark eyes were steady and guileless.

"You look more like a woodsman than a minister," she said. "Especially on the Sundays when you let your ratty work shirt cuffs hang below the sleeves of your vestments."

"*Mea culpa*. I should check the mirror more often. I don't mean to neglect the trappings of the clergy, but sometimes they get away from me."

"Don't worry," she patted him. "Your congregation overlooks your lapses and adores you. All that disgusting competition by the ladies to mother and capture you for their daughters. Look how they show up every Sunday for your ritual dedication to their souls."

He grinned and kissed her nose. Emily looked around the frowsy room.

"Philip darling, what you need is a housekeeper."

"Not true, Em. I've got the dutiful Mrs. Pink."

Phil had taken on the church in the harbor three years ago after a drunk driver killed his wife and son on their way home from swim practice. He said he could not stay in the town where it had happened, and had found spiritual and emotional refuge here in this small Maine village. The rectory's rooms lacked a woman's touch, but he didn't notice. It was enough that Mrs. Pink, with all her allergic huffing and wheezing, dragged her vacuum and dusters around once a week to 'do' for him. She didn't consider the parsonage with its yard sale furnishings and threadbare carpets grand enough to bother wearing the trouser suit uniform that her friend Stella found so pretentious. When cleaning here, she rolled down her stockings, baring her swollen ankles below a loose wrapper, and got to work. The acrid odor from her menagerie of cats hung about her person, but only the lemon scent of diligent polishing remained when she left. Above all, the woman's ears were enormous. She was the village font of gossip.

Phil's charms were not lost on the village ladies—especially those burdened with marriageable daughters. They gathered outside church after services to woo him.

"Dear Reverend Vaughn," Mrs. Hooper would coo, fluttering her mother-of-pearl fan. "Can we count on you for supper and bridge on Tuesday?"

Dilys, her vacuous, but cardsharp daughter, would be marshaled as his partner.

Mrs. Smith would engage his arm, pull him aside and whisper, "Philip dear, I've been baking all day and saved a special treat for you. Could my Janie bring it by?"

Or, overheard in Mrs. Wattson's loud voice "Reverend V., some of the students from your hospice course at the hospital are coming for supper tonight and they'd be so pleased if you'd join us. My Sue Ellen's been cooking up a storm and she's done herself proud."

No stratagem was beyond them. And for a man whose idea of a 'roast' was a clove-studded Spam, Emily knew it was fine by him. He told her he accepted it all as an additional form of tithing.

She was glad for his health's sake that he seldom needed to cook. Tonight his meal for the two of them, one step above his biscuit-mix salmon pinwheels, was tuna melts preceded by canned pea soup. They had numbed their palates with large pre-dinner whiskeys.

"So far," she said, and snuggled against him, "without entering your kitchen sweepstakes, I've managed to keep ahead of your pack of seducers."

He raised a cynical eyebrow. "Don't be too sure, Emily. That old chestnut about the way to a man's heart—"

She cut him off. "I have better ways. I hear your heartbeat just fine, love, and you know that neither Dilys or Sue Ellen would permit any pre-nuptial soothing of your more needy hungers."

There were only the sounds of their slow breathing and the crackle of the fire. He pulled her closer and his voice became solemn.

"Em, why do you let me love you but refuse to take me seriously? Won't you trust me enough to marry me? And don't give me that line about how you couldn't live anywhere but up in Bea's house. There's a lot of bad karma in your family and I want you to get free of it."

She pulled away, but Phil wouldn't leave her be. He raised himself on an elbow.

"Emily love, I want to have you legally and regularly in the Biblical sense. Please think seriously about marriage? I know this place is a mess, but you can make it over any way you want. If you must, keep space of your own up at the big house. I'm liberal about lifestyles."

He tickled the corner of her mouth, trying for a smile. "I'll even take the 'My Boss is a Carpenter' bumper sticker off my car."

She smiled, but felt drained from the misery of the past days. She unwound from his arms and sat up, hunched on the edge of the couch.

"Phil, I can't make that decision right now. I know you're serious and your proposal deserves a serious answer. I just can't cope tonight; so soon after this awful accident. Please wait. MacNeill isn't through with us. No one murdered Bea. I'm sure she fell and bled to death from the blow to her temple before poor Thea found her."

"I'm sorry, he said. "It was callous of me to bring it up tonight. I understand Bea was like a sister to you, in spite of your battles, and I too find it hard to believe she's dead." He spoke softly into her hair. "Em, what's going to happen? You are right about MacNeill, he's sharp. I hope you are right about Bea."

She sighed, "I wish I knew what's next. Bea must have agreed to some changes. She said Graham and Hannah convinced her that, only by improving the greenhouse spaces, could they make a success of the nursery business. The business can't survive without her financial backing and if that fails—well, Hannah and Thea will leave." She straightened. "Phil, there's something the others don't know. Bea told me she bribed Robin to come back to the harbor by offering to give her the big house. She assured me that it would always be home for Colin and me, but tell me, what's to stop Robin from selling it out from under us?" She added angrily. "If Robin returns, it will be for more money—not a house in Maine where she was miserable."

"Wait a minute, Emily. Bea was too canny not to have arranged legal restrictions to protect you and Colin. None of you liked Robin—you helped raise her, and she sounds like a rotten kid—but did you really hate her? That is pretty strong."

"Phil, you are too kind. There were times when I did. Robin was twelve when her father died, and he'd pampered her from the day she was born. She was the classic spoiled brat. He left her too much unrestricted cash, and she spent it mostly on herself. She was unpopular with her peers. While dear papa doted on his daughter, he neglected, almost ignored, Ian and Colin, so, naturally, they resented Robin. Their little sister had a car at sixteen. At that age, Colin and Ian got bicycles! Bea needed and used my help raising her, but then overruled me on any kind of discipline. Believe me, we had big problems, wicked rows, over that." Emily gave a bitter laugh. "Naturally, to Robin, I came off as the nasty every time." She chewed her lip. "Maybe Bea was unconsciously getting back at me for standing up for my mother. She had no sympathy for Diana."

Phil looked puzzled.

"Never mind," she said and lay back on the cushions. "The friction between those sisters is another bitter story." She sighed. "Poor Bea tried too hard in the wrong way to make Robin happy and lost her. When Robin finally got way out of control, Bea threw up her hands and sent her away to a strict religious boarding school in Switzerland."

"That sounds like pre-ordained disaster," said Phil. She was not amused by his pun.

"Phil, it wasn't funny. Robin got into serious difficulties. She reverted to all that sixties stuff; hanging out with kooks in multi-colored vans, smoking and sniffing weird stuff. If Bea had left some of those early head-on decisions to me, we might have formed some new behavior patterns and weathered it. Instead, Robin slipped away from us and Bea blamed it on me for interfering."

Phil got up to stoke the dwindling fire.

"What's going on about the confusion over Stuart's late arrival?" he asked.

"I don't understand that. Stu doesn't make those kinds of mistakes, and we don't know what's going to happen until he reads Bea's will. I assume she wouldn't make any big changes before meeting him."

She sat up and rubbed her face. "We have to work something out to save the greenhouse business. If for some awful reason Bea cut us out, we need that income. I admit it's a horrid thought, and I hope it's my state of shock, but we might all get along better without her. Bea meddled so. She tried to manage everyone—irritating us, making complications." Emily hugged her knees. "God, what am I saying? My aunt is dead. But it's true, damn it! Bea was sometimes frightening and overbearing, but we let her have her way. We were all too greedy and eager for the generous handouts." She shuddered. "It was disgusting how we allowed her to control us; using all her airs of *noblesse oblige*. We deserve contempt."

For the first time since Bea's death, she felt tears sting her eyes.

"Oh Phil, I'm so mixed up. Tonight I don't know what I feel."

He kissed her and handed her his handkerchief.

"Hey, Niobe, lighten up. No lamentations. Let me remove your hair shirt. I promise you will feel better by morning." He started down her buttons. "Maybe sooner."

CHAPTER 13

"That's it. I've had it!"

Hannah blew a curl of hair out of her eyes and glared around her. Graham was right. The nursery office was a cramped, inefficient, time-wasting mess. All the painstaking records she'd made on her wildflower tissue culture trials were missing; buried under this clutter. They were filed someplace, but where?

Muttering her private string of four-letter expletives, she attacked shelves and drawers again, tossing outdated catalogs onto the floor. She found the missing folder jammed behind an outdated manual on polyploid production by X-ray mutation. Dead info. She chucked the manual into the trash basket, and for one regretful moment, clutched the tissue culture folder on which she had spent so many hours to her chest like a lost child. She scanned the pages then let them, too, slide into the dustbin.

All that wasted effort. Weeks of unmarketable results from over two hundred snippets of plants, genetically identical to their parents, proved what she'd guessed from the start: only sterile laboratory conditions produced controlled results.

"Damn." She cursed more than her lost time. Stuart must find the money to provide more space. Without it they'd have to concentrate on the undemanding *colchidine*. They were a sure bet. Everybody loved crocus. Consistent, true breeding polyploids would be the marketable reward. But that kind of propagation wasn't interesting or experimental, just profitable. Her eyes drifted to the box of nicotine sulfate smoke cones that might have killed Bea. She reached for one and read its warning label. If one acted in time, was there an antidote? She looked for the poison manual. Thea insisted that their reference shelf, with her Braille supplements, be kept strictly in order. The Braille edition was where it should be, but the standard poison reference was missing. When had she'd used it last?

"Thea, Hannah! Help!"

Clay's sobbing cries from outside the greenhouse brought her to her feet. Please God, she thought, not another disaster. The boy flung himself through the door and ran into her arms.

"Clay," she said calmly. "Catch your breath. What's happened?"

He tugged at her, pulling her toward the door. His arms and hands were smeared with dirt and blood, and he'd made a frightening mask of his pale face where he'd wiped away tears.

"No one's home at our house," he cried. "Come quick, please, please. It's Carrie. She's hurt and it's my fault. I took her down to the beach to explore a new cave, and it was a dumb idea. I saw this opening in the cliff beyond the boathouse while I was out with Luther on his boat. I only asked her to come with me to take her mind off Gran. She's been acting so gloomy. But I can't lift the stones off her and she's all bloody. Part of the roof caved in and fell on her. Please come help me."

Thea came from the storage room, still limping on her bandaged but healing foot. Hannah touched her arm.

"Stay here and call the doctor, tell him we'll need an ambulance. Colin's next door in the studio. Ask him to follow us down to the beach beyond the boat house."

Clay pulled away from her, arms flailing, and was out the door, already yards ahead and racing down through the field to the beach.

Carrie's body lay on the shallow cave floor, its entrance newly opened from the storm's pounding, just above the level of the beach. She was nearly buried under dirt and fallen rock. Clay had cleared her mouth and nose, but a large stone, too heavy for him to lift, pinned down one shoulder. She was unconscious, and Hannah knelt quickly to check her breathing. She realized was holding her own breath and let it out in relief as she heard soft, shallow puffs coming from Carrie's lips.

Together, she and Clay gingerly cleared away the dirt and stones, careful not to brush against the walls of the opening. The rear of the cave was blocked by collapsed rubble, and ominous splatterings of dislodged rocks clattered around them. Clay pulled off his t-shirt and gently wiped the blood on from Carrie's arm. His eyes were wide and anxious.

"We've got to get her out of here before more of the roof comes down."

"Wait Clay, we mustn't move her before the doctor comes. We could hurt her further." She helped him to his feet and hugged him. "Hold on, honey. They'll be here soon."

Once again, Thea's call to the emergency number brought Dr. Hastings, led by Colin. The doctor raised his brows at them before kneeling to Carrie, but his tone was gentle. "You folks getting ta' be my regulars."

They heard the ambulance lurching and bumping down the boathouse road. Trained hands took over and eased Carrie onto a carrying board. When Hannah insisted on accompanying them to the hospital, Colin, pacing nervously out of the way, looked guilty, but relieved.

"Hospitals make me sick," he admitted hopelessly. "I get woozy at the sight of bodies on stretchers. The smells and all those people in green pajamas rushing around—"

"Don't worry Colin," soothed Hannah. His face was as chalky as Clay's. She assuaged his ego. "It's an acceptable male weakness. Go back up with Clay and try to find Ian or Grace. Also, please stop by the greenhouse and tell Thea what's happened. She'll be anxious."

Hannah got into the ambulance beside the stretcher carrying Carrie's unconscious form, and the doors closed behind them.

Inside the cave, Colin put his arm around Clay's shoulder. "Come on, your sister's in good hands. We'll get you cleaned up and I'll fix us my famous chocolate restorative."

Clay watched his uncle look thoughtfully at the raw opening made by the storm in the face of the cliff, then back at the blocked passage.

"Clay," he said in a casual tone, "was the rear of the cave already closed by the rock fall when you and Carrie got here?"

Clay stared at his feet. He didn't want any more pain about his mess-ups. He already imagined his dad yelling at him. Jeez, why was he was always in trouble? If only once this summer he could do something that his father thought was great. Be good at some sport or something. Maybe if he kept his mouth shut about this place, nobody would poke around, and no one else would get hurt. He and Carrie had been about to explore that dark tunnel beyond the opening when it suddenly disappeared in front of them and the roof collapsed on her. What if they'd gotten through and been trapped on the other side? No one would have ever found them. They'd have rotted into skeletons!

"Clay?"

"Uh, I'm sorry, Uncle Colin," he mumbled. "I can't remember. There wasn't time to look around."

Halfway up the boathouse road, they saw Emily running towards them.

"I heard the ambulance coming through the village," she gasped. "I was in the garden and couldn't believe it when I saw it turn down our road. Thea said there's been an accident. That Carrie's was hurt." Emily forcibly slowed her breathing. "I promised her to get back quickly with some news. What's happened? Where is she?" Colin told her briefly of Carrie's rescue.

Emily saw Clay's pallor of shock and put her arm around his shoulder. "Come on, we'll have a wash and track down your parents."

"Don't hurry" said Clay grimly, "I'm going to be in deep youknowwhat soon enough."

She laughed and roughed his hair. "Don't worry, I'm sure Carrie will be fine, but you're a mess."

"We'll go up and make some lunch," said Colin. "First we'll stop by the greenhouse and get Thea."

An hour later, the five of them sat around the picnic table on Colin's sun porch finishing, by Clay's standards, the perfect meal. While they ate grilled ham and cheese sandwiches, pickles, chips, and chocolate frappes, Hannah phoned them from the Bay Hospital. Colin picked it up on the first ring

"Carrie's awake. She has a mild concussion, some deep gashes that needed stitches, and is on her way to the operating room to have her shoulder set. It's not broken, just dislocated. Please assure Clay she's going to be fine. Not even a cast, just a sling. Ian's here, and I'll stay until Carrie is settled back in her room."

Clay made flapping motions toward the phone and Colin handed him the receiver.

"Hannah, is my Dad going to kill me?"

"No problem, Clay," she said. "He's just glad that you weren't hurt too. It'll be okay."

Colin emptied the remains of the frappe into Clay's glass.

"We'll lie a little and tell your father that we three found that cave together," said Colin. "That it was my idea to explore. That's not really a fib because I do want to investigate further. There might be a passage beyond that cave-in, originating from somewhere in your house. Your father and I didn't grow up there, but we heard the tales of places along this part of the coast used by bootleggers during prohibition. Many houses had indoor access to secret tunnels leading down to the sea. Remember, Emily, the stories of the *Grey Ghost*? Right here in the harbor. Clay, your friend Luther Pollard's father told us how the faster lobster boats would signal and rendezvous with 'mother ships' out beyond the three-mile limit. On dark or foggy nights, cases of booze were off-loaded onto our beach and stored in a tunnel leading up to the house. Later, an unmarked van would arrive and complete the 'delivery.' I remember old Pollard boasting that his *Grey Ghost* could out-run any Customs Patrol boat. 'Like trying to catch a handful of farts!' Excuse me, ladies, but that was his colorful description."

Colin collected the last crumbs of chips with his fingertip. "I regret to speak ill of our ancestors Clay, but it sounds exactly like the kind of scheme our renegade grandfathers would have relished. Most of their escapades were either illegal, dangerous, or both."

"It was a hazardous game with stiff penalties," added Emily. "They weren't all so lucky."

"But that cave, opened up after all these years, could have historic importance," said Colin. He saw Emily look at him, perturbed.

"Colin, let your curiosity rest awhile. We've got enough going on with your art show and the Grange Hall Supper this weekend. There have been too many accidents, and I don't see Ian welcoming you right now to pound his walls for secret passages or rip up carpets looking for trap doors."

Colin regarded her absently, but made no commitment.

CHAPTER 14

MacNeill phoned Stuart the next morning and asked if he and Hannah would please come by the Police Station in Rockland.

"Nothing official, just to talk."

"Sure. I'll call Hannah."

The next morning, in Stu's old Chevy, they crept along Route 131 through an early pea-souper fog. Whenever the road wound inland, away from the ocean, the whirls of fog hung only in low places, and by the time they reached town, the sun shone bright and hot.

Hannah glanced at Stuart and guessed that his choice of the tan corduroy suit over a blue shirt and navy rep tie dotted with little red hockey players was natty enough to project a professional image in his role today as the Swann family's lawyer.

"Who was Bullwinkle's little buddy?" she asked.

"Sherman? Yeah Yeah, I remember, the one with the big glasses." He pushed the oversized horn rims back up his nose and gave her a look.

"Listen, I bought these thinking they would make me look judicious. It was a mistake, but I can't afford to chuck them. Don't smirk."

"I'm not smirking." His gesture reminded her of Clay. "You look fine. And definitely wise. You will be a youthful looking old man."

"You're very kind, and may I say that MacNeill will find *you* demurely innocent in that Nancy Drew outfit."

Hannah regarded her pleated shirtwaist dress, pleased that she had actually found a dress. Lemon yellow to combat the dank early morning, and certainly demure for her first-ever police visit. But perhaps he would see through her guise. Like a hatchet murderer appearing before the judge wearing a Peter Pan collar. She had contemplated her wild Ken Done tops with the red leather mini skirt that showed her long legs to advantage, but decided it was not suitable for a police occasion. She wasn't sure just what the occasion was going to be. She leaned over and switched off the radio to relieve them from the auditory assault of an operatic diva.

"It's too early for that kind of howling."

She became serious, anxious. "Why do you think the detective wants to see us?"

"I didn't ask and he didn't say."

"The family wants to accept Bea's death as an accident," said Hannah. She decided to keep her own doubts private. "Emily told me Detective MacNeill is an old chum of yours."

Stuart looked pensive. "We were good friends as kids and through high school," he answered. He smiled as if remembering good times. "I spent a lot of time at Mac's house. My dad wasn't easy to live with. He was self-absorbed, distant, even more so after mother died. I had hoped her death might draw us closer, but he retreated even farther into his own world. He had no interest in sports. We never did things together that most boys do with their dads, or even talked much. A game of chess or Chinese checkers after Christmas dinner was his big effort at togetherness. My father's law business was his life, and he was successful. Money was never a problem. He just never spent much. He had no hobbies." Stuart laughed, grimly. "No pleasures."

He shrugged and switched the radio on again. The diva had retreated to the wings, replaced by a love 'em and leave 'em cowboy wail. He kept the volume low.

"He gave me a lot of expensive stuff—sports equipment and lots of books. This car when I was sixteen. It embarrassed me, because most of my friends, especially Mac, didn't have much and made do with second-hand. Even clothes. But all the brand name stuff wasn't such a big thing then. At least in this town. Maybe it would have been different if I had brothers or sisters."

Hannah looked over at him but kept silent. She thought how often people opened up while they drove. She did herself. It's easier to talk about personal things when your hands and eyes are busy.

"I was fourteen when mom died," he went on. "After that, Mac's family gradually began to absorb me." Stuart smiled. "I'd go home with him after school and his mother and sisters would all be in the kitchen, cooking and teasing us. The MacNeills were gregarious—always getting up picnics and parties that included me. I remember the smells—frying chicken, cookies baking. Someone was usually swirling gooey frosting onto a cake." He paused, sheepish. "It was nice."

"Sounds like one of those perfect American TV families," she said, and saw him redden. "I'm sorry," she said quickly. "That was mean. The MacNeills sound wonderful. I was also an only child, but raised a happy kid. The Packwoods were a loving family. Most people aren't so lucky."

"Well, those were the good years. After high school Mac and I went our separate ways. But none of the ski trips, tennis rackets, or sports camps Dad paid for ever equaled my times with the MacNeill family." He grinned. "Mac and I were often rivals for the same pretty girls."

They drove without speaking along the by-pass stretch behind the huge cement factory. Beyond the sprawling gravel pit, she broke the silence.

"I have this worry that maybe things aren't as tidy as we think and your friend MacNeill may want some opinions from those outside the family. Innocent bystanders."

"You think he considers us innocent? It was in your greenhouse that Bea died. And Mac knows that, as her lawyer, I'm privy to her confidences and, if acted on, could trigger some unpleasant changes."

Hannah raised her eyes. "Do you have private information? Any hints?"

He didn't bother to answer, only reached over and flicked off the whine of pathos dredged from another hillbilly soul.

They pulled into the parking space behind the Sheriff's office. It was an unpretentious, square building built of last century's red brick. A neatly dressed man sat on a folding chair at the entrance to the lot. He held no begging can, and the placard at his feet simply read: 'Will work for food for my family. Can do anything.' A quiet protest against the state of Maine's twentieth century economy.

Inside the station, a large woman with improbable auburn hair held a phone receiver pressed to her ear. She cracked her gum, and wiggled her fingers at Stuart. Down an adjacent corridor were a few cells for the overnight DUI and bar brawlers, but anything serious was handled upstate. The room's junk food vending machines, the smell of overcooked coffee, worn linoleum tile, and varnished deal counters were all surrounded by walls of that dingy green particular to government agencies. MacNeill was waiting for them.

"Welcome to my private cubicle," he said and gestured them through a door at the end of the hallway. "Privacy is its only advantage."

Hannah found barely enough room for her knees between the metal desk and the two straight chairs facing it. On top of a gray file cabinet squeezed into a corner was an ailing philodendron. More than ailing, dead. Beside it was a tinted photograph of a determined looking young woman inscribed *"Love, Rosie."*

"I'll offer you coffee, but suggest you refuse."

"Detective MacNeill—" she began.

"Just Mac, please." He tapped a pencil on his Spartan desktop.

She looked around. "This room is probably more depressing than one of your cells."

"Yeah, well I don't spend much time here."

Behind his desk, a single window faced the cheerless brick wall of the courthouse next door. Aside from the dead plant and Rosie's picture, the only decoration was a girlie calendar advertising the services of a local garage. This month's coy cutie was panty-less, bending forward from the hips to offer a wrench to a grease monkey. The lecherous mechanic grinned up from his rolling cart, inches from her implanted breasts.

"Great stuff, that," said Mac. "The nucleus of my art collection. Not government regulation, but no one's complained. Lucille, out there at the front, says her lady doctor has a big photo of Burt Reynolds in a thong on the ceiling above her examining table."

Stuart sat forward and rested his corduroy arms on the desk. "Mac, why are we here?"

MacNeill tapped again with his pencil and kept his eyes down.

"The autopsy on Mrs. Swann showed massive cranial bleeding from the impact of her head hitting that bench corner. That alone probably killed her, before the clincher of nicotine sulfate smoke. But I'm curious about the circumstances. Personal curiosity. The overturned stepstool was not that high, and she needn't have used it at all." He raised his palms toward Stuart. "I don't want to cause trouble for the Swanns, or the rest of you, believe me, but after speaking to the family individually, I sense some odd undercurrents. Thea, uh Miss Morgan, was disturbed by the thought that Mrs. Swann's death was her fault. Maybe now, she's not so convinced that it was an accident. Don't misunderstand. No one has any proof, but I sense that the family is not satisfied that she slipped and fell."

Stuart shifted restlessly. Mac shrugged.

"Hey, relax. I didn't ask you here in an official capacity. I just want your unofficial impressions of this sad business." Mac stretched back and the springs of his swivel chair squealed in protest. He again gestured his apologies. "I'm sorry, but it seems the curse of policemen is interrogation. We have to torment people when they're most vulnerable, and suspicion becomes a reflex. You're their lawyer, Stu, and I know you can't betray confidences." He looked at Hannah. "I'm just asking for help. Off the record. As a friend."

"So," said Hannah, "do you consider us friends or suspects? I can't imagine any of the Swanns to be capable of such violence, but as a policeman, you know how oddly people can behave.

Who said 'All passions are possible beneath the surface when desperate'? If you think Bea's death wasn't an accident, if that's what you're leading up to, then you have to consider all of us, right?"

"What I don't understand," interrupted Stuart, "is why she fell? Bea was an agile woman, despite her years, and wearing non-slip moccasins. If she climbed up to get a closer look at the blossoms, maybe the stool tipped on the slick gravel and she lost her balance. She might have grasped at the vine and torn it from the shelving. Maybe it *was* an accident." He considered his knuckles. "But I'm not revealing any confidentiality when I say that everyone found some of Mrs. Swann's suggestions insensitive."

Hannah laughed. "Oh, yes. Thea and I have heard the complaints. When fed up with some member of the family, she would decide to rearrange their lives. We understand that Bea liked," she paused to consider her words, "playing the Olympian."

Stuart pushed up his glasses. "We planned to meet the day of the party to discuss her latest impulses. I was sure I could reason with her. Believe me, I've done it many times in the past. When she calms down, she can be persuaded." He turned to Hannah. "I will tell you it was her intent to divert funds for expanding the nursery business, but because of the mix-up on dates, no formal agreement was signed before she died."

"Explain to me this mix-up over the date of the party," said Mac.

Stuart groaned. "I showed up a day late for Bea's birthday dinner because my clerk, Jennie, told me that someone—she can't remember whether the voice was male or female—left a message on our answering machine to remind me to meet with Bea the afternoon before her drinks party and birthday dinner. No specific date was mentioned. Jennie checked with Colin on Bea's birthday and wrote it on my calendar. I made the mistake of assuming the party was on Sunday, her actual birthday. Neither of us checked on it before I left to fly west."

"Maybe someone deliberately wanted to put you off," said Mac. "A person who found Mrs. Swann's plans too threatening, and worried that this time you might not talk her out of it?"

"You mean someone planned that I not show up? That's absurd. But for argument's sake, I didn't show up and nothing was changed. So why kill her?"

Mac shrugged, as if the suggestion of murder was not his idea.

CHAPTER 15

The Lewisville Grange, a foursquare weathered white clapboard building built at the turn of the century, faced the ocean halfway to Port Clyde. White and red geraniums planted with trailing blue lobelia filled the window boxes on either side of the double doors. This was the meeting place for bean suppers, wedding receptions, or anything else that needed a public hall. Tonight it was set for the annual Grange Hall supper and art show.

All afternoon, aproned women streamed back and forth through the swinging doors between the kitchen and main room. The tables were crowded close as possible and laid with blue and white checked cloths. Each was centered with a circle of potted herbs from the Swann greenhouse, and a gold star under one of the folding chairs at every table would award its sitter the prize to take home. Blue and white paper napkins wrapped the cutlery, and clusters of votive candles twinkled in the twilit room. Already laid out on the serving tables up front were the breadbaskets, salads, and those desserts that could 'set.'

On the Grange's second floor, Graham Viero noted with quiet satisfaction that the art show was a success and most of his botanical entries displayed red "sold" circles. He saw that Colin was not so lucky, but loyal friends and their summer guests had mustered enough funds to protect him from embarrassment. Graham refilled his drink from his tagged bottle at the bar table and wandered toward Hannah. She was struggling in conversation with Colin's current lady companion. He pondered his partner's collection of parthenogenetic women friends and figured he chose these androgynous types to try and confuse people about his sexuality. They usually voiced eccentric philosophies, promoted with determined, serious inflection, and his guest tonight was no exception. Graham watched Hannah's composure fray under the onslaught of this stout, pugnacious woman who was introduced earlier as a 'poet manqué.' He caught Hannah's desperate eye and gallantly succumbed to her plea for rescue.

"Graham," she called. "Come meet ah, Madame—"

He was awestruck by the woman's costume. It would have enlivened a Soho loft party, but here, in the Grange hall, it merely stunned. The woman wore a beaded tunic of a chromatic nightmare that billowed over cropped black velvet pants. Below the tight band of these unflattering breeches, her calves bulged in mauve hose that drew the eye downwards to oversize red suede pumps.

"You must speak with Mr. Viero here," Hannah urged, drawing Graham in by the arm. "He handles the business side of our nursery which I leave in his capable hands." She smiled sweetly at this cunning and fled. The woman directed her energy toward Graham.

"You must devote a section of your next catalog to Japanese rock gardening," she said, stabbing at his chest with a long lacquered fingernail. "I will provide the rocks. The perfect rock is the focus, you know, the gathering up—the essence of Zen satori—unity of coherence—K'aiho!" She spat the syllables, spraying him with a guttural vigor that made him flinch. Her fixed intensity was alarming, but he controlled himself and silently cursed Hannah.

"An excellent idea, Madame. Maine has such a convenient source of rocks."

He saw that this inane response confused her and it gave him the moment to make a slight bow, smile and move away. He knew it amused Colin to produce these bizarre people for their shock value, but this Madame really was too much.

Across the room he saw Hannah fortify herself with a whisky. He considered doing the same when he saw a languid young man in pleated linen trousers drift toward the group surrounding

Colin. The man's silk shirt draped open at the neck and thin links of gold glinted in the light. Ribbons of smoke drifted from his nostrils as he gestured vaguely toward Colin's largest, unsold seascape. His stentorian voice penetrated the room.

"I think this work shows an intellectualized but totally transcendent interpretation of the sea's virility. The entire show is definitely worth a catalog."

Graham didn't agree and kept a safe distance from Colin's other invited oddballs. The party had gained noisy momentum. He refilled his drink and made his way across the room to where Hannah and Thea were talking to Livia Lewis. He liked the feisty young Aussie and hoped he had convinced her, during their lunch at Daily's, that they could work together.

"Hello Livvy. I see you've met our new greenhouse managers." He put a possessive arm around Hannah's shoulder. "Now, ladies, I don't know how it is in the wilds of Australia, but you can see how these get-togethers are the way neighbors in small, winter isolated towns, share and catch up on a winter's worth of gossip."

Mac and Rosie came up beside them, and when he gingerly introduced Thea to Rosie, both Graham and Hannah raised their brows over the future of that threesome.

The Strait brothers' joking voices boomed and their stout, wine-flushed wives responded with dutiful laughs. Arlean emptied a packet of herbal flakes into a glass of water and Len Strait hooted at her. "My Gawd, darlin', what's that to prevent? Prostate cancer?"

Graham saw Grace, back in control, wave away a plate of cheese and crackers, and in a dim corner Emily and Phil stood with their heads bent in conversation. He thought Phil would be good for Emily and hoped those two could get their lives together. The poor woman seemed emotionally unglued lately, as if Bea's death had set her adrift. Maybe Phil could pull her out of it.

Graham wove his way among the guests, nodding to the lobstermen he knew. Tonight they'd traded their sea boots for clean white socks and soft-soled Romeos. He listened to Angus

Laird, in his dour voice, explain to Livia why he'd never learned to swim. The petite blond who owned the Camden travel agency was promoting tonight's prize drawing for the Australia trip.

"Ma'am, if I went overboard wearing all that gear in that cold watah, why would I want to prolong my dyin' by tryin' to swim? Don't make a whole lot a sense, do it?"

Livia sobered at his grim logic. "Well then," she brightened and offered Angus a cheery smile, "I hope you've bought a winning ticket from us. If only to experience the joy of tropical bathing."

Angus looked dubious. "Ayah, the wife did," adding, morosely, "but I've never been a lucky man."

The lights flashed on and off, signaling the call to dinner and people moved downstairs. They entered the dining room with murmurs of appreciation The perspiring women serving behind the buffet tables dispensed as much cheerful banter as food, and the line moved slowly, further stalled by the consideration of too many tempting choices. Chowders, pasta and vegetable casseroles, honey mustard glazed hams, roast turkey, fried and barbecued chicken, ribs and the inevitable crock of beans. There were lemon-garnished platters of cold crab and lobster, baskets of home baked rolls and muffins, and salads—green, molded, and some better undescribed. Surrounding the coffee urns were frosted cakes, cookies, and every choice of pie. It was a night to ignore cholesterol and calories.

After a sharp exchange, Mac left Rosie to fend for herself and Hannah and Graham followed him, guiding Thea along the buffet table, describing the dishes. She explained her clockwise system and Mac carefully filled her plate.

"No garnishes," she laughed, "they're a menace."

Ahead of them, Grace, serving salads, convinced an anxious man that there was no more room on his plate and tonight he wouldn't starve and could come back for seconds. Graham and Hannah moved slowly down the line. Behind them, Emily served up a portion of lobster gratin that filled the last open spot on Stuart's plate.

"Away glutton!" she admonished.

When the shuffling for seats had quieted, Colin stood and rapped his glass with a spoon. Conversation hushed.

"I'll be brief and speak for us all when I ask God to bless us. We thank everyone for this extraordinary feast. It rivals the Captain's table on the QE II."

The room tittered in appreciation; and Graham thought they'd largely take his word on that.

"Livia Lewis," Colin continued, "the generous owner of the Lewis Travel Agency, tonight will draw the winning ticket for a journey to Australia for two lucky people. If the winner is a single person, he or she can choose a companion."

He held up a large wicker basket.

"Ms. Lewis, we can't stand the suspense. Come and draw for us now while we start on our dinner." He lowered the basket and with an unlit slender blue cigarette that matched his shirt, waved her toward him.

Livia rose with a schoolgirl giggle.

"Thank you Colin, I'm as honored and excited as you, but I insist on total impartiality!" She took the basket and walked to the next table, where Luther Pollard sat. "Will you, sir, do us the honor?"

Luther rose awkwardly. Redness flushed his stringy neck and suffused his face. "Er, ah" was all he could manage. Livia rescued him with a smile and a few blinks of her cornflower eyes. She held the basket above him, shuffling the paper bits inside. Luther closed his eyes and with great concentration reached up and slowly drew out a ticket. He handed it to Livia and sank back onto his seat. She held their suspense. "I hope we've picked someone who's here tonight." She read out the winning number and the room breathed again.

Then came groans of disappointment as people craned around the room, looking for an elated winner. No one came forward to claim the winning ticket.

"Damn," said Stuart, sitting next to Hannah. "I wonder who won. I wanted it for you so badly, Hannah. I thought I'd bought enough tickets to guarantee us a chance." He dropped the wad of losing stubs into his pocket and she reached over and pushed up his glasses.

"Stuart, you're very sweet to have bought all those tickets." She gave him a discreet kiss under his ear. "It would have been a lark. Maybe someday it will happen." He looked cheered by her nebulous "it."

Conversation rose again to its previous decibels and everyone concentrated on eating.

Hannah, sitting between Colin and Stuart, heard a familiar laugh from the table behind her. She turned and saw Thea's pleasure as Mac put his arm across her shoulder and hugged her towards him. Rosie, at the next table, looked daggers. My God, thought Hannah, maybe she won and is keeping it a secret. She'd seen the thick pack of tickets Thea had bought.

The serious eaters, already on their way to the buffet for seconds, stopped at their table to compliment her on the centerpieces and congratulate Colin and Graham on the success of their show. After a half dozen interruptions Hannah nudged Colin whose plate was still untouched.

"Eat your dinner before it congeals." The food was delicious and she had wolfed her own meal. She could hardly go back for seconds before he'd even started.

She knew Colin relished the attention, but he finally began on his plate of salad that seemed to be mostly white radish. Hannah was exceptionally fond of that Japanese daikon variety, with the creamy garlic dressing he'd ladled over it, and wondered how she'd missed it on the buffet.

"Going to powder my nose," she murmured to Stuart. She started to rise when she felt Colin's hard grasp on her arm. He looked at her strangely, making funny faces. For a moment, she thought he was being silly. She could barely understand his garbled words.

"Mouth's all numb, cold," he gagged. "Throat's on fire."

He clawed at his neck and the rest of the table watched in stunned silence, transfixed with horror as he tried to articulate his agony. Across from them, Colin's lady friend, with her own strange reaction to shock, began to giggle.

Livia's sensible voice jolted them.

"Someone call an ambulance, quickly."

Colin slumped forward onto his plate and Ian called out, "Is there a doctor here? My brother needs a doctor."

The room stilled and when no one responded, old Dr. Brown, who'd given up practice years ago, made his arthritic way through the crowd. A half-century habit of responding to emergencies summoned him.

His voice quavered. "I don't have my medical bag, but let me through."

Mac and Graham helped lay Colin gently on the floor, but couldn't make his rigid body comfortable. He pulled at his chest and Hannah knelt to loosen his collar. Nothing relieved the tortured breathing, and though his frantic eyes beseeched them, they were helpless.

The words "heart attack" ran through the room. Someone had called the emergency number and by the time they heard the keening wail of the ambulance, Colin had mercifully lost consciousness. Mac, down on one knee beside the still body, rose and carefully covered Colin's meal with his napkin. Hannah stood with her hand to her mouth.

"You sat beside him?" he quietly asked her. "Did you see anyone touch his plate?"

She shrugged helplessly then met his serious eye. "Not a heart attack?" she asked.

"I don't think so."

CHAPTER 16

Hannah twisted to regard her rear end's reflection in the bedroom mirror. Tight. Too tight. The black, all-purpose number was all she had suitable for Colin's church service. Maybe if she kept her coat on it would hide the strain over her backside. She would skip lunch for a week; both she and U. Joyce could suffer a little slimming.

Hannah didn't approve of funerals. She believed people attended them because of their guilt over remaining alive while someone else was being tucked under the lilies. For herself, she would insist on no ceremony. A quick cremation with her ashes tipped into the compost pile should be followed by a great party to regale the good times. No clerical maudlin, no eulogies, coffins, urns, flowers or gravesites. No guilt.

"My ashes shall fertilize my garden," she mused aloud.

"Hmm?" roused Thea. She was curled on the chaise in the same gray silk dress she'd worn to Bea's funeral; patiently waiting for her friend to get herself together.

Hannah frowned and shut the door on her jumbled closet. She would never manage *le tout ensemble*.

"My clothes," she announced, "are as mis-matched as the dishes in a summer rental." She admired Thea's color-coded wardrobe system that used different shaped tabs in hems or seams, and she envied how easily the blind girl found the right dress and accessories. This morning, however, in spite of her svelte appearance, Thea looked low.

"Hannah, this is going to be grim," she said. "I mean, Colin was poisoned, and people are thinking it's Swann murder number two. Right?" She unwound her legs and stood up. "Can we sit in the back of the church? I've got *le grand nervosa*."

The phone rang sharply, making them both jump. The voice on the line was tinny with the echoes of its satellite transmission, and the familiar accent gave Hannah an instant ache for home.

"Roit," the voice drawled in antipodal cockney. "This the Swann's? I'm trying to reach Mrs. Beatrice Swann. 'Ave I found her at home?"

Hannah automatically checked her watch and made the calculation. Nine hours earlier, but tomorrow. One a.m., Sydney time.

"Ah, I'm afraid Mrs. Swann is not available. Can I help you?"

"Roit, it's a bit of a tale. Has Robin arrived? I've been waiting to hear from her and should 'ave by now." Hannah guessed the caller.

"It's Keith Watkins," he said. There was a pause. "Her husband. I was thinking she'd be with her Ma'm and I want to know if she's arrived safe."

Hannah heard the familiar rise at the end of his words and again the pang of homesickness at hearing the cockney cadence of her countrymen. Then she focused on his last words. "Robin's husband?"

Thea looked up.

"Riot," came the relaxed drawl again. "Could you 'ave her call me? At the flat. Her visit was supposed to be a big surprise, comin' home after ten years to see her family and tell them about us. Knowing Roby, she might have taken a detour. But she should 'ave been there by now. I'm a bit off my bike, ya know?"

"Mr. Watkins, just when did Robin leave Australia?" Hannah tried not to speak over his echo. There was an expensive pause.

"The tart's not there then?"

"No, but—" Fragments of the conversation she'd overheard in the drive before Bea's dinner came back. She spoke quickly. "I'm sorry, Mr. Watkins, I'm not one of the family, I work here in the greenhouse. I'll have someone call you back tomorrow morning, your time. There's been some trouble here."

"She's not there?" he repeated. "What trouble—hasn't she arrived yet?"

His voice faded in and out and she held the receiver away as her ear was pierced by an inhuman celestial howl.

"I'm sorry, our connection is bad. We'll call you back in the morning." She copied the Sydney number he gave her and set the phone back on its cradle.

"You heard that?"

Thea nodded. "Mrs. Keith Watkins? Hmm, so it *was* Robin who Bea was waiting for that Saturday." She felt the raised face of her wristwatch. "We'd better leave for church, if you're ready. Lead me through this ordeal before I develop any excuse not to go."

Hannah thought it seemed too short a time since Bea's funeral had overflowed this church. The summer day was damp and cool, and during the service no one shed their coat. It was mercifully brief and afterward, the Swanns, amid clusters of Colin's friends, walked the short way down the road to the wooded graveyard above the ocean. A thin fog had drifted in and out all day and weakened the sun.

It was a quiet, mossy old place, and even with the mist, it wasn't mournful. New greening summer grass poked around the edges of the old granite headstones. Most of them tilted gently, yielding to the ground ebb of many years' winter frosts and thaws. Crusts of yellow lichen crept across the stones and etched delicate patterns on the worn granite.

Beyond them, offshore, the wind cleared the fog and raised white flecks on the ocean. But sheltered here at Colin's open grave, the damp air swirled gently around them, chilling their faces. Hannah remembered the day she and Carrie had brought a picnic here to make stone rubbings. The earlier ones bore those melancholy inscriptions common to most old graveyards whose plots held entire families lost to influenza, typhoid, and the woeful deaths of men and sons who never returned from the sea.

Hannah shivered. Probably no worse a way to die than from today's modern horrors, 'weapons of mass destruction' and all.

She tried to concentrate on Phil's words at the gravesite, but his litany sounded hollow and she lost it to the wind soughing high through the firs. She was angry because, unlike Bea, who offended, Colin had been innocuous. Who had hated him enough to plan such a horrible death? She shuddered and wrapped her coat tighter.

The stoic rank of Swanns, flanked by Emily, Thea and herself, stood together. Colin's friends from the village, the men in seldom worn suits, stayed beside their wives, a polite distance apart. The clique that comprised the other side of Colin's life huddled together with faces shuttered by dark glasses and elaborate scarves. Graham Viero stood alone, eyes hidden behind a low brimmed hat. She thought he looked like a bandit. There was a grimace, a tightness around his lips that almost appeared as a grin.

Phil ended the brief service, and when a handful of soil spattered onto the coffin, Carrie burst into audible sobs. Misshapen by the sling worn under her coat, she'd come home from the hospital, stitched, patched and impatient with her one-armed awkwardness. Grace embraced her two children, and Ian ushered them all away.

The groups of mourners broke apart and wandered down the grass toward their cars. Emily and Phil remained at the open grave and Hannah saw her suddenly sag onto his shoulder. He held her tightly against him for a moment, then he took hold of her arm and they followed the others out to the road.

Mac came up behind Hannah and Stu. He was wearing a dark jacket and gray flannels and only the tone of his voice and the grim facts of Colin's death reminded her that he was a policeman.

"Before you two leave, could we talk for a minute? Maybe somewhere over a cup of coffee?" It didn't sound like a question.

"I need more than coffee, Mac," said Stuart. "What's up?"

"Come back to the cottage," said Hannah. "We'll have drinks or coffee and make sandwiches." She held his arm. "Wait a minute," she said, and walked over to Graham, still standing alone. He looked stiff and miserable.

"You need a whisky, Graham. Come back with us."

At the cottage, the men shed their coats and ties. While Stuart fixed drinks, Hannah and Thea rummaged through the refrigerator and produced plates of sandwiches, sliced tomatoes, and the remains of a chocolate cake.

"Appetite must result from release of tension," apologized Thea. "I'm embarrassed to say that I felt awful this morning but now I'm famished."

The five of them relaxed with their drinks, and for a while, as they ate, let Colin's murder escape their minds. Mac brought them back to reality.

"The autopsy showed that Colin was poisoned by a toxic alkaloid called *aconitine*," he told them. "It's incredibly lethal. I did a little research." He nodded at the two women. "As botanists, I'm sure you know its scientific history, but I read that the stuff is known as the 'Queen Mother' of poisons. According to the books, it was the brew that those infamous witches and medieval sorcerers used to keep their reputations as agents of Satan."

"Oh yes," said Thea. "It's a classic vegetable poison and— unless you know what to look for—hard to detect. It has wonderful names: wolf's bane, monk's hood, devil's helmet. Gardeners love it because of its deep blue color. It grows well in the cool of Maine and we stock it in our nursery beds."

"I don't understand," said Mac, "why anyone would eat a plate of poisonous blue flowers without just a tad of suspicion."

"You don't eat the flowers," said Hannah. "Unfortunately, the leaves look like salad greens and, under dressing, the root could easily be mistaken for an icicle radish. The person who murdered Colin knew what they were doing. His deadly salad must have been prepared by someone who set it before him after he was seated. I love those sweet white radishes and if I'd seen another like it on the buffet, I would have grabbed it." She put her hand over Thea's. "Which makes the two of us, with our knowledge of plant poisons, look extremely suspect."

"But saved, I hope, by the question of motive," said Thea.

Hannah turned to Mac. "The funeral put it out of my mind, but I've had some interesting news. We had a phone call this morning from Australia. Things are getting rather thick." She related her conversation with Keith. "Considering Robin's inheritance," she asked, "does he join us as suspects?"

"Thea mentioned the call to me earlier, but he has a twelve thousand mile alibi," said Mac.

Unlike the rest of them, Graham ate little. When he smiled, no emotion reached his eyes.

"As a suspect, I probably rank number one," he said. "Stu will soon verify that Bea left a large portion of her money to Colin, and I know that Colin has left a good portion of that to me." His voice became wooden. "But I did not kill him."

Mac shifted in his chair beside Thea. She nudged him gently.

"Can I tell them?" she asked.

"Sure, this day could do with some good news."

Thea took a deep breath. "Hannah, I won the raffle prize trip to Australia."

Hannah grabbed Thea's shoulders and gave a cry. "I knew it!"

Emperor, slumped over Thea's feet; raised protective hackles and Hannah stroked the dog's head.

"When I saw you smiling after the draw, I tried to get to your table, but when the panic around Colin started, everything else was forgotten. Why didn't you speak out? My God, Thea, how wonderful, you'll love it!"

"Wait Hannah. I didn't speak up because I can't go."

"Nonsense, what a chance! You've got to go."

"No, I mean it. I want to stay here. I'm feeling comfortable for the first time since the accident, and I'm not ready to race around the world. Anyway, I wouldn't go without you and we both can't leave. Please Hannah, I want you to use the tickets, and believe me," she stifled Hannah's protest, "I'm not all that altruistic. Mac and I have decided that you must go, especially after Keith's phone call. We insist. If you took Stu, he could help you check up on Keith."

She had seen Thea and Mac talking in the pantry while fixing lunch, and she now caught Stu's raised brow. He finished a bite of sandwich and the dregs of his Bloody Mary before he spoke.

"Hey, I'm all for playing detective for Mac if Hannah is up for it. But before we take off, I can tell you that Bea's existing will, subject to probate, will stand. You now know, from Keith, that Robin was on her way here. Bea and I tracked her down in Sydney and arranged for her to come back, but the logistics and exact date of her arrival was a secret between them. I had no idea that Robin's homecoming was Bea's surprise for the birthday party." He paused. "Though knowing Bea's flair for the dramatic, I should have guessed."

Hannah related the bits of conversation she had overheard between Bea and Emily out on the driveway before the dinner party, and the changed table settings.

"We know now that Emily was sent to the airport to bring back Robin. Bea's mystery guest."

"Maybe meeting Robin was a surprise for Emily, too," said Stuart. "Bea liked her little secrets. More likely Bea simply made Em promise to tell no one, and when Robin didn't show, she probably thought 'good riddance.'"

He offered them all the last sliver of cake and, with no takers, ate it in one bite. "Tasty," he said.

"Lovingly homemade," said Hannah, "by Sylvia, one of Phil's parish 'cake' ladies. As for Stuart coming with me, well, business combined with pleasure, why not, and I'd like his company."

Stuart radiated a smile at her. He stretched back in his chair, took off his heavy glasses and rubbed the reddened bridge of his nose.

"Jennie and I still can't figure who left that message." He looked at Mac. "Was it a deliberate attempt to mislead us? Is there some connection between Bea's fall in the greenhouse and this last ugly death?" Mac didn't answer.

"I don't know where Robin is," Stu continued. "And Keith is right about her being irresponsible. Spoiling other people's plans never bothered her one bit. She probably chickened out from

the reunion with mom and is staying with some friend in Boston.
I suppose we should be more concerned, but the kid was a real
pain, and none of us liked her. When she ran off, I was away at
law school. I was five years older, but I'd hear about all the trouble
she caused her family. Her father doted on her and, despite my
dad's council, he gave her too much money while she was an
irresponsible kid. She ignored her brothers, but that was mutual.
They had never been close. And she was nasty and patronizing to
Emily. You can guess the results of Bea's unsubtle attempts at
control. Robin accused her mother of causing her dear daddy's
fatal coronary by nagging him to death. There was a lot of flack
when Bea sent her off to that Swiss convent school. You can't
believe some of the reasons the town gossips thought up."

"She wasn't there long," he added. "After one final long-
distance blow-up, she ran away. Finally Bea gave up trying to
track her down. Since then, Robin shows up once or twice at
Christmas, cajoles Bea, and begs for money. But then we lost
complete contact and, except for her mother, gladly wrote her off."

Mac set his empty beer mug on the floor. "What about this
marriage business?"

Stuart shrugged. "It's the first I've heard of it."

"I'll talk to Emily," Mac said. "Then I'll check with the
airlines. They keep passenger flight information on their
computers for months." He looked around at their uneasy faces.
"I understand how you feel. When our orderly lives start falling
apart, people get the 'it can't be happening to me' syndrome. I'm
used to it. It's part of my job, but that doesn't make it easier
when members of your family or personal friends become
suspects in homicide cases."

Silence followed his frankness. He had laid his professional
cards politely on the table, but now he pursued them further.

"I take it none of you have ever met Keith Watkins?"

Graham helped himself to another whisky. "He wasn't her
first lover," he said. "Robin was only seventeen when she ran
away from the Swiss school. That was about ten years ago. Colin
told me some of her escapades and, as Stuart said, she would

check in occasionally, begging some cash. Colin was especially bitter. He, more than Ian, resented their father's blatant favoritism. If Keith claims to be Robin's husband, then Bea's death gives him a very rich wife."

"Well, he's got to prove it, and we have yet to find this prodigal daughter," said Mac. "What we need is gumshoe work. That's why Thea came up with the idea that Hannah use those tickets to help us find her." He didn't look at Stuart, but stopped speaking to examine his trouser crease. "As you said, business with pleasure. Combine a trip back home for Hannah with helping us sound out this Keith Watkins. Our department can only do so much by fax, and there's no budget for any kind of across the world investigation. If you use your vacation to help with some inquiries, our police here will arrange the professional contacts in Sydney."

Thea insisted. "If Bea's allowed us the money for it, it will take some time to remodel the greenhouse space. Graham and I can cope with the rush of spring orders for the next two weeks. We promise to make no final design decisions until you get back."

"But Thea," Hannah protested, "you won that prize. Maybe Livia will give you the ticket's money's worth?"

"No, Hannah. No more excuses. You're going."

She was touched by Thea's generosity and then remembered a fact that the travel agency had not publicized. She wondered if she should even mention it.

"You are a generous sweetie, and if you really mean it, then I'd love to go. There's not going to be a lot of swimming, though, unless Keith is hanging out up north in Cairns. The travel agency forgot to mention that June here happens to be dead of winter in Sydney. It's nice," she added quickly, "very nice, and a lot warmer than Maine, but we won't be lying on the sand every noon in our Ozzie-cozzies."

Thea looked stunned. "My God, of course. I never thought about that." She brightened. "So then, you've no cause for guilt! I'm not giving up such a wonderful thing after all."

Hannah turned to Stuart. "Will you come with me? We can play Nick and Nora?"

CHAPTER 17

"Angel's goin' to heaven," Angela sang to herself, "'cause that's where angels belong." Her boyfriend Rick called her Angel. Not the ugly nasal 'Ange' whined by her mother and kids at school.

Angela felt all soft and floaty. Hemorrhaging might be a sweet way to die, but it wasn't her plan, and in that sharp remaining core of her mind, she knew she'd better make an effort pretty soon to stop this nice drifting away. She needed Rick to get her to the hospital. She'd pull herself together now, and think nice and clear. She felt like she'd drunk a six-pack.

Now first, where would Rick be? She squinted at the Big Ben on the bedside table. It was 4:30 in the afternoon.

"Geez," she said aloud. "I've been bleeding four bloody hours!" She giggled at the pun. The paper bag on the floor by the bed was full of crimson soaked maxi pads. The bath mat she'd finally wedged between her thighs felt warm and heavy. She didn't even want to look.

Rick would still be working at the video store. She'd call him so he could get her to the hospital before her mother got home from work. She smiled, pleased at how clearly she was thinking this out. A little slow maybe, but she was on top of it.

She pushed herself up in bed and felt a fresh gush of warmth between her thighs. "Geez," she repeated. If she'd been pregnant, she sure wasn't now. Rick had gotten the special pills and suppositories from Doc, and just like he'd promised, within a week she'd gotten her period.

"It might start a little heavy," Doc had warned, "but there's usually no problem. But no guarantee," he'd cautioned Rick. "In some cases it plain doesn't work, but it's a lot safer try this than havin' an illegal surgery."

Doc should know. Rumor had it that the reason he lost his medical license was because he botched one of those illegal abortions. He'd offered Rick and Angela a fantastic price for the baby if she'd go the nine months and hand it over to him for adoption. But no way. No one was going to know about this but her nearest and dearest. Angela had heard of Doc from a girlfriend who swore that he'd saved her future, and the same Doc turned out to be Rick's boss at the video store. Along with his porn films, she hated to think what other scams the sleazy creep had going.

Doc was a source of the magic RU 486. Easy and legal, if you lived in China or France or had enough money to get to California, but not in Maine. Rick had paid for the pills from his savings—big bucks too, but then Rick was a special guy.

"My fault, Angel, not yours," he'd told her. "But a baby now would wreck our lives, so if you want try the stuff, it will be worth it. And if your body's going to take the risk, the least I can do is pay."

But it seemed that Angela was one of those with what Doc had called 'a little bleeding problem.' Maybe, when she called the store, Doc might be there and could tell Rick what to do, but it wasn't likely. He owned the place and checked on it out once in a while, but left it up to Rick the others to manage the lottery franchise and film rentals. Rick had told her about the raunchy ones not listed in the catalog. With such sidelines, she could understand why Doc kept a low profile and paid Rick so well.

The abortion pills were a great idea, and she didn't blame him that they hadn't worked so easily for her. Doc had told them fair and square that there could be complications. But she wasn't going to die. No way. When she rolled over on one elbow, though, the room whirled and grew dim.

"Geez."

With all her concentration, she dialed the store's number.

"Please Rick," she prayed, "please be there."

CHAPTER 18

In the empty waiting room of the Penobscot Bay Hospital, Emily made herself another cup of tea and checked her watch again. It was keeping exactly the same time as the wall clock. She'd been waiting over an hour for Phil and had badgered them twice at the nursing station to see if he had left her a message. She rationalized that something important must be delaying him and reproached herself for her impatience. While he was comforting some poor dying soul, she waited here dying for a scotch and soda.

On the Formica table beside her, a cigarette butt floated in a Styrofoam cup of cold and whitened coffee. Brown rings stained the leaflet some joker had left beneath it, and its heading caught her eye: "These Selections of Videos Are Not Available to Miners". She mused over the under-age excavators who were going to miss out on 'Nurses with Tender Loving C—'s' or 'Stirrups Queen," which she doubted was a western. She stuffed the leaflet into her canvas carry-all. Phil would get a kick out of it. Or, even better, she'd slip it into his IN basket in the parish office and stir up that pious village woman who donated her spare time as his secretary.

Em stretched out her legs and wiggled her toes in the white orthopedic shoes. Her feet ached and her jaw muscles were stiff from hours of good-humored smiling. Usually she enjoyed her volunteer work as the hospital's "library lady." Her rolling cart was an oasis in the patient's boring routine and they welcomed anyone who offered time to talk. On her days in the hospital, she wheeled her trolley—shelved with books, cassette tapes, and magazines—over the same yards of familiar corridor, but today she had found too many rooms with patients overwhelmed by misery, bad temper, pain, or noxious combinations of them all.

She jammed her fists into the pockets of the gray and red striped coverall and lost control of her patience. "Seven goddamn o'clock! To hell with it." She'd leave him a message, go home, shower, and make her own drink. When Phil's weekly hospice classes coincided with her days on duty, they usually treated themselves to a dinner in town. Well, forget dinner.

She shrugged angrily into her coat and pushed open the lounge door just as Phil pulled on it from the other side. She fell awkwardly towards him and he barely kept her from pitching forward onto her face. His ungraceful rescue added to her bad humor.

She pulled away from him. "I've been waiting here since 5:30," she said coolly. "If you're not ready to leave, I'll go home alone." Then she remembered that they'd come that morning in one car.

"Emily," Phil said, "I'm sorry. I got caught up in the emergency room. Let's get out of here."

As usual, he squelched her ill temper by not joining the fight. They crossed the parking lot behind the hospital and the night air restored her.

"It's been a mean day," she offered. "I'm sorry I snapped." She kissed his cheek. "What kept you in the emergency room?"

"A young girl from the village," he said. "Not much older than Carrie. She was scared she was dying and needed to talk."

"A girl we know?"

"Yeah. And knowing how gossip flows here, everyone will hear soon enough. She's a nice kid from what the locals denigrate as a 'loose family.' Luckily, the boyfriend got her to the hospital in time. Just. He was sincerely anxious about the girl. Explained their plans for the future and insisted on paying all the bills."

"A botched abortion?"

"Not by an operation. I don't think so. I've become such a fixture around here that I overhear more than I should. And Em, I'm telling you more than I should. There was a sympathetic woman doctor on duty, and the girl admitted that she'd taken some pills, then two days later the 'prescribed' suppositories. They were supposed to have done the job, but in her case, overdid it. She'd lost enough blood to need a transfusion, but her pressure was so low that they couldn't raise a vein for the I. V. The kid was sobbing more about getting AIDS than bleeding to death."

"Poor child. I don't blame her."

"So, it's been a tough day for both of us. We need a good meal. Let's treat ourselves to a fancy dinner at Fletcher's."

The following morning Hannah sat in the same Pen-Bay Hospital lounge waiting for Carrie and Angela. She felt like the tool of a teenage conspiracy. Angela's mother thought that her daughter spent the night at Carrie's, and Hannah, weakened by Carrie's desperate appeal, had agreed to come and sign the hospital release forms and take her home.

Rick had left for work after spending most of the night by Angela's side in an outpatient recovery cubicle. While Hannah signed papers, Angela sat scrunched in the regulatory wheelchair, ready to escape the hospital's responsibility. Carrie watched the cheery nurse's aid settle her friend gingerly in the back seat of their car, then climbed in beside her. They drove the long, winding road from the hospital out to the highway before Hannah spoke.

"Okay, guys. My lips are sealed. *Omerta*, like the Mafia, but what's all this mumble about pills? Angela, did you try to abort yourself with some drug?"

"I'm fine now, Miss Packwood. Everything's okay." The two girls sat huddled together behind her.

"Angela," said Carrie gently. "It's not okay. What Doc did is against the law. You could have died. Rick could have been an accomplice to murder."

"Doc who?" asked Hannah. "Carrie, what are you talking about?"

"Shut up, Carrie," snapped Angela. "Doc didn't make me take that stuff. The other girl he gave it to didn't have any trouble. He fairly warned us. I was just one of the unlucky percent. And if Rick loses his job because of this—" Her voice quivered. "Well, he makes a lot of money from part-time work at Doc's, and we are saving to get married. He's not dropping me because of this business."

Angela started to cry and as Carrie comforted her friend, Hannah reminded herself that this was a sixteen-year-old who had just been through a hell of a night and perhaps now was not the time for heavy questions.

She parked in the drive behind Angela's house and they helped her upstairs and into bed where Angie devoured the lunch from the tray they prepared. Convinced of the girl's resiliency, Hannah set the portable TV on a chair beside the bed, and pulled the phone within reach.

Carrie hovered. "We won't leave unless you promise you'll call us if you feel funny."

Angela sank back on her pillows. "I promise. You both have been great. Thank you, Miss Packwood. Without you guys I hate to think of the flap I'd be in. My mother, well," she shrugged, "I guess she's over-strict because she had such a rough time herself. She'd be real hurt to find that all her years of scrimping for me had been trashed. She'd never kick me out, but she'd wouldn't understand about me and Rick either. Honestly, I feel fine. Just sleepy."

Angela winked at Carrie. "In fact I feel a lot better than after some of our keg parties."

Back in the car, Carrie picked the scab off a mosquito bite. "Who is this Doc?" Hannah asked.

Carrie continued to work the scab. "He's the man who owns the video store where Rick works," she said idly. "He used to be a real doctor, but I guess there was some trouble." The sore finally bled, and Hannah handed her a tissue.

"I bet. Like illegal abortions? Carrie, I'm serious, if this man is handing out drugs to young girls and you're involved—"

"But Angie needed it!"

"Carrie," said Hannah, trying to keep her voice reasonable, "I understand that Angie's worried about Rick's job, and of course I approve loyalty to your friend, but you're too young to be mixed up in something like this. If your parents knew about last night they'd have a fit." There was a long silence. Carrie sniffed and swiped her nose.

"Clay's even younger," she admitted grudgingly, and Hannah's stomach sank.

"How's Clay's involved?"

"I'm not sure what's going on," Carrie began. "Clay thinks there's something funny about the packages he delivers to Doc from Luther. He says they're too small and light to be money or lottery tickets. Angela told me that Doc has these special pills that Rick could get for her. They're RU—some number, from France—and they're much safer than an abortion using dirty knives or whatever." Carrie looked pale, but continued. "Angela's not the first one around here to get in trouble. The harbor's a small boring place; nothing to do but make out." Hannah winced.

"So when one of her girlfriends told her about how great it worked, well, she asked Rick if he could get Doc to help her, that's all." Carrie, unburdened, slumped back against the seat. "Please don't tell my mother."

Hannah leaned over and hugged her, careful of the tender shoulder.

"Don't worry," she reassured. "I promise you. The important thing is that Angela's going to be okay. Leave it to me. Stuart and I will be gone for the next two weeks on this trip down under, but MacNeill said he would help rescue Clay. I'm sure you've noticed how often Mac's been around here these past weeks."

Carrie managed a grin. "Uh'm yes, he's got a thing about Thea."

Then she sat up. "Oh Hannah, I forgot that you're leaving tomorrow! You probably have loads to do. Thanks for helping me and Angie, and trying to get Clay out of this mess with Luther and Doc."

"Don't worry," said Hannah. "MacNeill will sort it out. Go on down to the dock now. Out-sail those hunks."

CHAPTER 19

Grace parked in front of the greenhouse cottage and hauled two overflowing cartons from the trunk of her car. She set them heavily on the wooden bench by the front door, pushed it open and yoo-hooed into the entry. No answer. Good. She had hoped that Thea would be working in the greenhouse and Hannah out doing last-minute errands. She wanted no discussion about these humiliating bundles. No explanation for the sudden urge to clear her closets of all these un-worn, expensive clothes. They were small sizes that she'd bought with an honest dedication to diet, and too good to be chucked out. 'Sort through them,' she wrote, on a note taped to one of them. 'Keep anything useful and I'll take the rest to the next rummage sale.' She was miserable over this expensive proof of her lack of will power. How could she complain about Ian's spinelessness?

Thea was tired. She'd been repotting seedlings here in the greenhouse all afternoon. It was tedious work by feel, and her neck ached. She felt her watch. It was after six. She called to Emperor. On the evening walk back to the cottage, she wondered if he too was savoring the warm summer smells. Inside, she fed him and had poured herself a glass of wine when Hannah struggled in, huffing over some burden that dropped with a thump on the kitchen floor.

"Two big cartons were left on the porch by Grace," she explained, and then stopped. "Thea, it's gloomy in here!" she complained, then laughed. "Only you can afford to be a miser with light bulbs." She turned on a lamp and read aloud the woeful note. She pulled open the first box.

"Fabulous Christmas! My God, Grace has emptied her guilt closet!"

She held up a cashmere cardigan finely beaded with black jets. "Some of these things are elegant." She handed over and described the sweaters, silk blouses, and a fine-grained leather belt that Grace must have bought with great optimism. She felt sorry for the woman who had hoped to wear these lovely clothes. Folded at the bottom of the carton she recognized Carrie's spurned quilted robe, sprigged with the little red ladybugs, and shook it out.

"You're always freezing, Thea, and this is perfect for your chilly boudoir, especially since you can't see it." She explained its cutesy pattern. "A preppie's delight."

Thea pulled off her favorite ratty cardigan—her rice pudding sweater, she called it—and put on the robe, pushing her hands into its deep pockets. She struck a pose and drawled, "Miss Laura Ashley is eagah and waitin' here at the bottom of the stairs, Rhett honey." Her seductive pout changed to a frown as she pulled a folded card from the pocket of the robe and handed it to Hannah.

"Is this something Grace forgot?"

Hannah read it and was quiet so long that Thea repeated her question.

Hannah read aloud the card with its pairing of possible disasters.

"Rather nasty, hmm?"

She told Thea of the other strange verse that Graham had found in their mailbox the morning she had brought them their mail. She looked again at the card Thea had found.

"This must have put a bee in Grace's bonnet. I wonder why she never mentioned it?" Hannah looked at her watch.

"Talk to Grace first, if you want, but I'd show that card to Mac," she said as she began to place the clothes back in the cartons. "I've got to pack. I'm sorry to dump this on you and then leave for two weeks. We can sort these clothes out when I get back, but I don't see much for the rummage sale. Help yourself to whatever fits. Oh, and I have a favor to ask. Would you see if Mac could find out what's going on with Luther and the packages Clay delivers to Doc at the video store? Clay's only twelve, for God's sake, and if Luther's using him as some sort of drug mule . . . Anyway, I promised Carrie that Mac would look into it without making trouble for Angela or Clay."

She and Thea had discussed earlier Angela's arrangement with Doc and his dispensing RU-486, as well as Carrie's fear that Clay and Luther were involved.

Emperor padded over and stuck his head between Thea's knees for an after dinner scratch.

"Hannah," she said softly. "I like Mac. I've been too busy getting myself back together since the accident to try a serious relationship, but I feel comfortable with him." She paused and blushed. "What does he look like? I've asked him, but he turns all modest. Give me a quick description, then you can go up and pack while I make dinner."

Hannah smiled and refolded the scattered clothes. "Well, he's tall and slim, but not skinny. Blond hair—sort of shaggy." She pursed her lips. "Considering that the only barber in town also works at the Thomaston state prison, I wouldn't hold his haircut against him. Let's see, he has light eyes. He's not handsome, but he's good looking in a plain brown wrapper way, with a sexy face. You know, sort of sleepy. But in Rockland that morning after Carrie's accident, he had his sleeves rolled up, and he's got great, lean and muscular forearms—my particular turn on. Physically and mentally he's definitely a cut above the local boys."

"He's very perceptive, and gentle," said Thea. "Stu told me he isn't sure what's kept Mac tied to this small Maine town. He said he was at the top of their high school class and got a scholarship and graduated from Bowdoin. He left a high paying job in Chicago to come back here."

Hannah hoisted the carton and spoke over her shoulder as she started up the stairs. "He seems to hold more responsibility than most local detectives. Stu said that instead of bringing down someone from Augusta, the higher-ups gave him complete charge of the Swann investigation They must think he's very good at his job. And I sense he wants to stay here. I'd choose our coast of Maine over Chicago any day. You may have strong competition from that Rosie, though," she added. "That night at the Grange Hall, she eyed your every move." Then she laughed. "Go for it, Thea. I like him too."

CHAPTER 20

Their plane touched down in Honolulu at midnight, but Hannah and Stu were too numb to appreciate the sweet scented leis draped over their heads by welcoming wahines, or the soft twang of electric ukuleles amplified throughout the airport. In relief from hours of re-breathed airplane air, Hannah inhaled lungfuls of the moist, fresh-air miasma.

On the plane, a tour group of polyester-clad blue-heads and their wizened mates had exercised along the narrow aisles throughout the eternal night, knocking their elbows and ankles and jarring them from the semi-coma of travel sleep. The final leg of their flight would leave the island at two in the morning, then eleven more droning hours to Sydney. Her body rebelled at traveling halfway around the world in a day.

"I can't sit any longer and I'm too tired to stand," she said firmly. "I want to stretch out on the floor of this airport and sleep."

"Hey," said Stu with chastising cheer, "be proud of how civilized your home town is not to let planes land before six a.m. It gives us happy travelers yet another chance to be offered drinks, dinner and in-flight entertainment at three a.m."

Hannah glowered at him.

Endless hours later, the sudden exhilaration of coming home lifted her nadir of fatigue. The Agatha Christie paperback—appropriately titled *Death In the Air*—had slid from her lap, and she peered through the scratched Perspex as the jumbo jet's shadow crossed the red tile roofs of Botany Bay.

As the massive jet lumbered lower, she picked up her book and nudged Stu's arm.

"In this story, when Poirot flew to France in the thirties, they asked your weight. The aircraft flew so low you could open your window, and you got off for meals. I bet the pilots wore leather goggle helmets and white scarves."

"Ughmp."

She nudged him harder, annoyed that he could sleep. "Stu, I'm excited."

"It was the candy bar," he mumbled and opened an eye. "Your blood sugar's up."

A card on their meal trays had issued dire warnings to bring no airplane food into the country, and breakfast, if that's what it was, had included her favorite—a Violet Crumble candy bar. Stuart roused himself, ran his hand over his bristly chin, and smiled at her.

"You remind me of Dorothy and her glee at coming home to Kansas."

"It's funny," she said. "All through my teens I had this awful fantasy that my parents would die in some tragic accident, and my bosom classmate—naturally a rich American—would insist I come back to the States and her family adopt me. My dear parents were, still are, the best, but I wanted to escape from Sydney so badly, and the American girls who boarded at our school made their home lives sound wonderful."

"Well, you made it," said Stuart. "Without the tragedy. But compared to Sydney, I can't believe you find Elmore Harbor such a swinging place."

"Maine is wonderful, and if you want to get away, you can be in Boston or New York in a few hours. Australia was dull and boring fifteen years ago when I was a teenager. The next town, if you could afford to get there, was thousands of miles away."

He sighed and stretched as much as he could in the impossible seat.

"I'm glad you think our harbor is a good place to roost."

The cab wound them through the morning traffic from the airport and into the city across the soaring bridge. It was good to come home again to the blinding light. She had missed the palm trees, hibiscus, and the hot clash of bougainvillea that bloomed against sun-warmed walls even in mid-winter. The dark pines of Maine were half the world away.

When she left University, her parents moved south to a suburb of Melbourne, too far to visit in her short time here, but she would catch up by phone. Livia Lewis had arranged for them to stay in a private home whose owners were on leave in Hong Kong and glad to have responsible house sitters. While Stuart paid off the cab and hauled in their bags, Hannah made a quick tour. The Victorian house with its high-ceilinged rooms was in an up-market, well-tended neighborhood that overlooked a notch in Sydney Harbor called Neutral Bay. She stood for a minute at one of the tall windows in the lounge and watched the lazy ripple of the Royal Sydney Yacht Squadron flags. Later in the afternoon, the wind would stiffen, and fleets of sailboats would begin races across the bay.

She checked out the two large bedrooms, each with its own luxurious bath, and approved the streamlined kitchen and utility rooms. Everything was smartly furnished and immaculate.

"Fantastic!" she pronounced, and blessed Miss Lewis. She opened the fridge and read the note propped against a bottle of champagne.

'We hoped you'd look here first! Welcome home! Enjoy our flat and have a great vacation.'

She heard the front door shut and the thump of their bags dropped in the entrance hall.

"Champers, Stu!"

"Just let me stretch out a minute," he called.

She found him collapsed, soundly asleep in the nearest bedroom. She pulled the curtains against the morning sun, covered him with the duvet, and shut the door. Back in the kitchen, she found the proper flute and gently nudged up the cork from the bottle of champagne. She let the bubbles subside, toasted herself, and sank onto the oversized sectional sofa in the lounge. Twenty minutes later, at eight thirty in the morning, she too fell into tipsy oblivion.

The harsh, foreign burr of the phone jarred Stuart awake. "Christ what an awful sound," he muttered. He scowled at the digital clock on the bedside table. 5:15. Morning or evening? It could have been either.

"Hello," said a cheery voice. "Keith Watkins 'ere, this Mr. Hobart?"

"Um, yah, sorry, was having a nap." His mouth felt like a woolly sock. "It was a long trip."

"Too right mate, ya got the jetties." The cockney argot paused in brief sympathy, and then continued briskly. "My problem, see, is I've got this job coming up out back of Bourke and I'd like us to have a chat before I 'ave to leave. I was hoping you and your tart, sorry, ah, lady friend and me could meet and crack a tinnie. I'm over on the Rocks. You could have a scenic little chug over on one of the Ladies. It's the best way to see the harbor. Wake you up."

The twanging voice assaulting his ear did not penetrate the fog in his head.

"Hold on a minute, let me get Hannah."

He found her on the couch in the front room, curled around a champagne bottle. He jostled her gently into consciousness.

"Our friend Keith is on the phone and wants us to get together. Come talk to him. I don't speak Australian."

He removed the champagne bottle and guessed Hannah did not feel her best. She stumbled down the hall to Stu's room, shouldered the phone, and somehow managed a civil greeting. After a lengthy pause she mumbled, "Yes, I know it."

She hung up and snuggled under Stu's rumpled duvet. He pulled her to her feet and steered her to the opulent bathroom off the other bedroom. He pointed to her unpacked duffel, handed her a thick towel from the heated rod and turned on the shower. "Revival time."

CHAPTER 21

The Lady McKell, one of the little ferries that for a few dollars carried people to and fro around the Bay, picked them up from the stone landing below their back garden. The boatman cast off the mooring lines from the bollards and, with a diesel growl, the little passenger ferry churned out past the Governor's Mansion into Sydney Harbor.

Outside on the upper deck, wrapped against the mild winter wind, they did revive. On one side, the magnificent bridge soared above them, and across from it, the Opera House floated under its shell-like roof. They landed at Circular Quay, paid their fares, and walked around to the revitalized district known as the Rocks. Hannah explained how the touristy scramble of shops and pubs was once a warren of opium dens, dysentery filled hovels, and 'places of coarse revelry.'

"The latter still holds," she added.

They entered the *Three Brass Cats* under its swinging sign, and as their eyes adjusted to the dim, smoke-choked room, a young man stood and beckoned them over. Hannah wasn't sure what she'd expected. Wild hair and bulging pectorals under black leather? Pounds of gold chains? Keith Watkins was a tall, clean-shaven, rugged blond. Healthy looking. Not one's idea of a rock musician. Rounding up sheep on a Harley Davidson in the blistering outback looked more his line. They shook hands and squeezed around a little table. Keith ordered beers and exchanged the emptied nut bowl for a full one from the next table.

"I'd 'a stood you to a meal, but I'm a little short of the readies. Sort of sitting on the bones of my arse as it were." He laughed, showing perfect white teeth and Hannah could understand

Robin's interest. He was good looking, but he made her wary. Keith, with all his Aussie charm, didn't look you in the eye.

"You've not heard from Robin then?" asked Stu.

Keith looked up, no longer smiling. "Not a bloody word, pardon my lip, Hannah. I thought she might come back with you two. Before she left, she'd heard from her Ma'm. Wanting to make things up and smooth over past bad feelings." He grinned. "Maybe release a few quid."

He scooped up another handful of nuts. "As I said, we were down to flake and damper when Robin left. The band is taking some time off. I'm leaving for a stockman's job on a station up in Queensland and I wanted to reach her before I take off. Roby decided that, since I had to go Out Back, now was a good time for her to put on the little red shoes and tap two times." His eye's widened with sincerity. "I've no intention to white-ant her, no way. What's hers is hers, but I hoped we'd share a little until I'm back to regular work."

Hannah thought from the look of him that regular work might be riding the surf up at Curl Curl.

"About your marriage," insisted Stu, "when did it happen? There was no word from Robin and we'd expect to hear that kind of news."

Keith emptied the nut bowl into his palm and chewed. Hannah guessed that bar snacks were his regular dinner. Stuart ordered another round of beers.

"We did it this fall, in April," said Keith. "A civil service by a celebrant at the Botanical Garden. Rob and I aren't up for church. We filed the license, all-proper, with the Registrar, but decided to keep it quiet and have Robin break the news in person when she got home.

"Umm," said Stu. They'd check it out.

A frizzy haired waitress in a six-inch skirt cleared off their table, but when Stu offered to buy another round, Keith begged off.

"I'm bagging down with friends this last night in town. I'll call you when I hear from Roby."

His concern appeared genuine, but Hannah thought him uneasy and too eager to get away. Refusal of free beer seemed out of character, but maybe her instincts were wrong. Maybe he was a nice guy just in a hurry to get to his new job. She tried to forget her experiences with his type.

Later that evening, the wind softened and the clear winter night turned cool. On the ferry ride back to Neutral Bay, they huddled together on an outside bench under the bright stars of her familiar Southern Cross. The bag with the cartons of take-away Thai was warm against her leg.

Back at the flat, the expensive CD system let Handel soothe them. Hannah had found an array of candles for 'ambiance,' and while she sipped a tangy Shiraz, Stu struggled messily with his noodles.

"Hannah, it's like a Viennese wine grotto in here, I can't see what I'm eating."

"When were you in a Viennese wine grotto?"

"All part of my shady past," he muttered. "Tomorrow I'll check out Keith's marriage story, and we'll call Mac to see if he has found any trace of Robin."

She regarded him over her wineglass. "I noticed that you didn't mention to Keith that Bea was dead, making his new 'wife' a rather rich woman."

He gave up on the chopsticks and forked up the last of the noodles. "I'm still hungry."

"Pizza delivery here is guaranteed to arrive within twenty minutes or you get your money back. How can you eat so much? You must twitch it off."

"Come on, I haven't had a regular meal for two days." Hannah surveyed the empty cartons while Stuart patted his flat stomach and tossed the chopsticks and paper napkins into the carry bag. "While I'm checking on Keith tomorrow, you might rent us a car and find a food market. Bring back a nice roasted chicken—chooks you call them—some baking potatoes, veggies, rolls, and some chocolate cake. And find a wine shop." He appraised the empty wine bottle. "More of this Hunter Valley."

He looked up to find her eyeing him sharply.

"Well, I tried," he sighed. "So I'm traveling with a female 'ocker who didn't pack her apron. Luckily, my dear, I'm a crack shopper and excellent cook. You just lie here all day, Hannah, with a box of chocolates."

She ignored him and carried their debris into the kitchen. She returned with a carton of ice cream scavenged from the freezer and handed him a spoon. "I'm exhausted. You finish off this caramel nut swirl. Leave the mess to the cockroaches. They are giant-sized here. I'm going to crawl into that wonderful big bed."

"I'll clean up," he promised. "How can I resist using something called 'Fairy Washing Up Liquid'?"

She gave his cheek a soft kiss. "I'm still disoriented. We can start real life tomorrow."

CHAPTER 22

When the ugly burr of the telephone again ripped open his sleep, Stuart lifted an eyelid and saw the red digital numbers glowed seven. This time his body knew it was morning. The jetties had gone.

"Stuart, can you hear me? It's Mac." The detective's voice, transmitted across 12,000 miles, was strong and clear and Stuart came fully awake.

"Mac, I hear you. We talked to Keith last night and he's heard nothing from Robin. Any luck tracking her down?"

"No, and in spite of statistics saying that three quarters of the world's missing people are living happily somewhere, I'm worried. I talked with Emily about meeting Robin at the Rockland Airport and it's a strange story. Too long and expensive to explain over the phone, so I've faxed it to you at Sydney Police headquarters. I added my own thoughts and ask your discretion, since you're acting as our emissaries half way around the world and the circumstances are unusual. I feel I've involved you and Hannah more than I'd like. The police in Sydney sound easy and are ready to help. They're expecting you both."

"I'll call them this morning," said Stuart, "and I'll read your report before we meet with Keith again. I also want to validate their marriage legalities before he leaves for a job tomorrow somewhere in the outback. Hannah warns that the Ozzies are not fast-trackers, but we'll try and hustle them as much as we can."

"Thanks Stu. We appreciate it. It's hard working long distance with just the facts. I'm so used to operating on my impressions and instincts. Let me know your personal feelings about the guy. Anything. Send it on."

They showered and dressed for mid winter—a blinding sunny day that registered 22°C, which converted to around 70°F. Stuart thought of Maine in January. He stared in disgust at the thermometer hanging on a bracket outside the window. A hairy spider with a body the size of a golf ball hung crouched at its base. The fauna here were formidable.

He entered the kitchen whistling with uncontrolled enthusiasm. He found fresh ground beans in the freezer, started the coffee maker, and mixed up a jug of orange juice. He sliced thick slabs from a whole-wheat loaf for toast and set butter and marmalade on the table. He was loudly into Rigoletto's aria *La Donna Mobile* when he saw Hannah clinging to the kitchen door. She spoke weakly.

"Are you often like this in the morning?"

"*Ma petite femme du menage,* one must greet every day with *joi*."

He swept two chicken-shaped placemats onto the table and pulled out a chair. Hannah sank into it and lifted the mug of heady coffee he set in front of her.

"When I was a poor man with gourmet cravings," he went on, "I learned to cook. Sadly, now that I have a few bucks on which to live high, I subsist in a Maine village with no place to do so." He shrugged. "So I must produce my own taste sensations."

Hannah groaned softly.

"You needn't speak. I am dismayed to see that you're not a morning person. Just nod your head. Shirred eggs au gratin? A rasher? Toast? Crisp hashed potatoes with salsa verde? The pantry here is well provided, and I am your *sous chef.*"

Hannah remained comatose. "Just juice, toast and marmite. Thank you, Stuart, but I'm a slow starter. I've heard of your kind, but I've never met one in the morning."

"Marmite? I saw some in the fridge. I thought it was axle grease. Ah, well, just smile when you're able to function."

He admired her clean washed face and mussed hair but, with respect for her perilous grip on the day, concentrated his enthusiasm on his own breakfast. He watched her spread the smelly brown paste on her toast. He'd tasted it. Salted dung.

"I'll speak softly," he said after a few minutes, "so not to jar you. Why don't you just flop around here this morning. Sit on the patio in the sun while I rent us a car and lay in some groceries—snags, chooks, yabbies—see, I'm learning the lingo. Lammingtons, all those Aussie treats. There's a gas grill on the terrace and if this is mid winter, it's Down East heaven! Oh, Mac called."

"I heard," mumbled Hannah. "I'd forgotten how the phone bell here ruptures your ear."

"I called the Sydney Police, and they can see us this afternoon. Mac says he's faxed them an update on the investigation."

They took a cab to the car rental agency and Stuart let Hannah maneuver them over the Bay Bridge into the city. He was not ready to negotiate left side driving in Sydney's maniacal traffic. The lights here held on red forever, and he had time to admire the deliberation with which the woman driver of the car on his left applied magenta polish to the nails of an entire hand while waiting for the green. Then everyone raced between lights to make up for the standing time.

At the Municipal Police Department they were introduced to the genial detective Mac had contacted from Maine, and in spite of the rush of activity surrounding them, the man implied he had endless time available to help them with their inquiries. He also explained the intricacies of tracking down a marriage license, and wished them the best of it.

They followed a bouncy breasted secretary to an empty office. She handed them Mac's faxed report, left them, and returned shortly with two mugs of tea. With an expansive smile that showed wonderful white teeth, she ran her fingers through a tangled yard of crimped hair and, after apologizing for the chill of the day, left them alone.

Stuart grinned. "Have you noticed that brassieres are not an item here?" Hannah ignored him and sipped her tea while he turned his attention to the report.

"It's what we guessed," he said. "Bea planned that Robin should make her entrance during the cocktail party. She couldn't leave her guests, so she sent Emily to the Rockland airport to meet the plane from Boston. She knew of Robin's surprise return, but Bea had made her promise to keep it a secret. According to the flight records, a Robin Swann—" Stuart looked at her over the heavy rims, "—*nota bene,* not 'Mrs.' Watkins—boarded the plane in Boston. The Rockland airport terminal is only a single room and nobody at the counter recalls any young woman waiting around. Those small planes carry only a dozen people and most of them pick up their bags within minutes and leave. If the weather's good, the pilot unloads them on the ground outside the plane and you can walk directly to your car. All very informal."

Stuart took a drink from the mug. The tea was black and very strong. He shuddered. "What do they do, boil it in a can? This stuff would revive a corpse. Anyway, the airport staff remembered Emily. She told Mac she had to stop for gas and that made her late. By the time she arrived, all the passengers had left. She checked the cabstand and looked in the ladies room, then left word at the counter in case Robin turned up on a later flight. Mac says Emily thought the girl might have misunderstood about being met and taken a cab out to the harbor. There's always one waiting for pickups when a flight comes in. She told Mac that she expected to find Robin already at the party by the time she got back from the airport. Robin can be unpredictable. She might have opted to stay longer in Boston and sold her ticket to a stand-by at the gate. She still has friends there. Maybe she got cold feet about the surprise reunion scene with mother." He paused and took another sip of tea.

"Anyway, Emily said that by the time she got back, the cocktail party was breaking up. People were leaving and Bea was furious."

"Yes," Hannah recalled. "Bea was in a twit the whole night."

He folded the report. "Mac is following up on this, trying to find Robin, but there's not much to go on. No one's seen or heard from her since she left Boston, if she ever did."

"And the next morning Bea lay dead in the greenhouse," said Hannah grimly, "and we had worse things to cope with."

Stuart pushed the tea aside and stretched his length in the chair.

"Mac says Emily admitted that she didn't care whether Robin showed up or not. Still doesn't. He got her to open up about some things from the past she seldom talks about. Mac has a subtle and persuasive way. She spoke of her anguish over her mother Diana's death and being sent to live with the Swanns. Her futile efforts trying to help keep Bea and Robin from each other's throats. Colin and Ian weren't around much during those years. They'd been sent off to boarding school early, and by then were in college. She recalled the two brothers' jealously over Robin's being their father's pet and the recipient of all the goodies and big allowance. We remember her anger at being cast as the baddie whenever she tried to compensate for the worst of Bea's outrageous spoiling. There was no love lost between Robin and Emily, and I'm afraid we all sided with Emily. Still do. Robin was a selfish and impetuous brat." He shrugged. "I think most of us agree that, unless she's a changed woman, Robin's only come back for more cash and plans to return to Keith as soon as possible. Money and sex, the eternal ampersand. All the sentimental homecoming business that Bea has cooked up is one-sided claptrap."

Stuart stuffed the papers into his case and stood up. On the way out, they stopped by the police chief's office to thank him for his help.

"What I want now, here in its native land, is a cold Fosters," he said as they left the building. "I knew that Bea was considering big changes," he continued. "They were to be discussed at our bungled meeting. Robin was to have the big house, provided she stay in Maine. I was going to insist that it remains a home for Emily and Colin. Bea wasn't intentionally mean, but she didn't consider that Robin could sell the house out from under them. I wanted her to have time to think things out and make the legal provisions that would protect Colin and Emily and keep Robin in line. Bea also owns Ian's house and planned to deed that one over to Grace, suggesting she use it as a lever to secure Ian's good behavior." Stuart grinned. "Can you see Grace pointing to the door and casting Ian out into the snow when next he misbehaves?"

"Stuart, this is sad."

"I'm sorry Hannah. I'm being flippant. But to top all that, Bea planned to pressure Colin to give up his painting and find 'real' work, reducing his studio space, which she alludes to as his 'hobby' room, to enlarge the greenhouse."

Hannah shook her head. "Bea confided those plans to Graham when they first discussed improving our nursery business. He told me about them that day we had lunch at Daily's. He said that since you took over from your father, you've intervened to prevent Bea's worst manipulations. You say she means well, but she was pretty insensitive. Probably believed hers was a reasonable crusade to make them all better people."

"Well this time someone arranged that I didn't intervene. Someone who wanted her plans to be carried through. Before I could reason with her."

Hannah followed him out into Goulburn Street. "Bea's slip in the greenhouse seems like no accident now that Robin's disappeared and Colin's been poisoned. But why didn't our killer stop after Bea? What was the motive for killing Colin? Who's next? The family must be getting a little nervous."

"That's the frightening part," said Stu. "Murderers are not always logical or clear minded. And pathological vanity assures them they are too clever to be caught. I'm afraid Mac now considers you and me as peripheral family and is afraid that it's not only the Swann's who are in danger—or above suspicion."

"Mac's crazy," said Hannah. "What motives have Thea or I, or Graham? Or Emily, or Grace? Or you, for God's sake."

"As a lawyer, of course, I'm above suspicion." He smiled playfully and she pushed him toward the curb.

"Careful now. Mac considers the reasoning of all vengeful minds. As to motive," he ticked them off on his fingers. "Ian, on Bea's death, finally has money of his own. By Graham's own admission, he prospers greatly by Colin's death. As for Grace, Ian has become more than an embarrassment. She may appear a submissive lump, but her type can become driven and we've all seen her increasing anger at being publicly humiliated. That action out on the porch with Nan at the birthday cocktail party was remarked on by a lot of the guests. It's not pleasant to live in a village where people snigger behind your back. All the makings of the *crime passionelle.*"

"Stuart!" cried Hannah "You're being far-fetched and ghoulish."

"Believe me. I know of cases my criminal lawyer colleagues have tried that make these suspicions benign. Murdering one's family and friends is ghoulish stuff, but it's done all the time."

He continued ticking off possible motives. "If someone 'removed' you and Thea, the nursery operation—with all its costly investment—would shut down. Our friend Keith, if he really is Robin's husband, benefits financially. As to a collective motive for Bea's death, she controlled their purse strings and they all had reason to fear her wrath. Like Christie's *Orient Express* plot, yes? Even if Emily can manage to hold her own with Bea, she still dislikes and resents Robin. Especially, if she planned to come home and sell Em's beloved house out from under her."

"Enough!" cried Hannah.

"I'm sorry. Anyway, I've covered greed, self-preservation, vengeance, and general passion. That's all I can think of. No wait, I forgot the most important question. Who is psychologically capable?" He answered this theoretical question with another professional statistic. "*Any* person, who is sufficiently driven, can murder."

"Ah, I see you are now the family's professional shrink as well as lawyer."

He ignored her and continued to pontificate. "Don't make like a shrinking violet over my revelations, Hannah. It's not in character." He put his arm around her shoulders, easing her forward through the evening crowd, then suddenly bent and kissed her lightly on the cheek.

She stopped and looked up at him. "I am not a woman of emotional steel, Stuart," she said. "I do have a sensitive side."

He wasn't sure if she was serious, and decided to drop it. He patted his briefcase. "Mac included a copy of the invitation that you and Thea found in the pocket of Grace's robe. He has questioned the rest of them, but Graham said only Colin received anything similar."

"I was in the studio the morning it arrived," she said. "Both Graham and Colin thought it referred to Bea's birthday dinner and, when nothing happened, they assumed it was some crank's joke."

Stuart's high spirits deserted him. "I'm afraid even Carrie might come in to all this. Grace confided to me that she was sure her daughter had learned a bitter and embarrassing lesson, but recently Carrie and a friend played a nasty joke on a school mate they disliked by sending out intriguing invitations to a fictitious birthday party. Everyone arrived with gifts at the girl's house and, of course, there was no party. When Grace found out, she made Carrie apologize and provide a real pizza party using her own savings."

"I know Carrie's not involved in this, Stu. I read the card delivered to Grace. The one we found in the robe pocket, and it was mean. This was not a childish prank."

"I agree. Grace doesn't believe it either. I'm sure she'd never have mentioned it if she hadn't been so upset that morning after Bea's death."

"Let Mac work on it," said Hannah. "Remember that some of our time here is supposed to be a vacation."

He gave her a squeeze. "Absolutely. As soon as we finish up this business with Keith. I'll go over to the Botanical Gardens tomorrow and tackle the Marriage Celebrant's office. We might have some questions for Mr. Watkins before he takes off. I'd rather tackle him alone. I want you to keep out of it. He might get a little rough."

"Stuart, you are gallant, but I'm not that delicate, or a shrinking violet. Unpleasant or not, I wouldn't miss it for anything, and besides, you may need me to translate."

"Roit," he drawled.

They arranged to meet Keith at a coffee house on Hay Street in Paddington. Stuart steered Hannah, always hungry, past the tempting food shops where ethnic aromas of Greek, Thai, and Indian foods competed with the odors from steamy windows displaying racks of revolving spits of crispy brown chooks. The ready-roasted take-away chickens were more endemic here than beer. To offset the roasted birds, salad bars and health food kiosks were tucked between the cake and sweet shops.

"Stuart, I'm starving."

He gripped her arm firmly.

"No, no fast food," he said. "Tonight I promise you a good restaurant with white linen, fresh flowers, and ambiance candles."

"Stu, you're a dear, but let's save that celebration for when we're through with all this. After we've talked with Keith, let's bring home some more good takeaway and put our feet up on that comfy couch."

"You're right. Sounds good."

They found the coffee house across the road from the sprawling acres of Paddington's open market stalls where vendors sold everything from trained monkeys to all things edible, wearable, or portable. The bargains were questionable but the tourists were drawn thick as the native flies.

They settled in a booth and Hannah sipped espresso while Stuart and Keith leaned over schooners of beer.

"I spent the morning at the Registrar's," Stuart began without any preamble of small talk. "I think the marriage license you filed there was a false document. I don't know how you obtained the forms, but I think you forged the celebrant's signature, and you are liable for a stiff fine or imprisonment, maybe both."

Keith's face lost its affability and the heavy tankard stopped midway to his mouth. Stuart saw Hannah's surprised look and caught her eye to warn her from denying this invention.

"My question is," Stuart continued in a terse voice new to Hannah, "if we find Robin, she could deny the whole thing. Why did you risk it?"

Keith exploded. "It's not true, and she wouldn't deny it. We love each other and we *are* married. That's no forgery. What's your con, mate?"

Stuart ignored this. "More damaging to you, Keith, is that Robin's mother has suddenly and mysteriously died and left Robin a very rich woman. Now Robin has disappeared and you are claiming to be her husband."

Keith placed his beer carefully on the table. His tone was ugly. "I *am* her husband." He leaned toward Stuart. "And if her Ma'm's dead it's the first I've heard of it. Did you just *forget* to tell me when we met yesterday? I swear Robin's up there in the States somewhere. She gets high sometimes and does a walk off. You've got to find her." His elbow knocked his mug and he ignored the beer that slopped and ran across the table. "I told ya', I'm not out to fleece Robin. I got this job waiting for me on a station out in Cunnamulla. It's hard work in that heat, but good money and we'll make a go of it. She's promised to come back and we'll set up together as soon as she's made up with her Ma'm. We thought it would be a lark to introduce us as married, right? We didn't expect any legal eagle to fly out and grub around."

Stuart stared at him and Hannah thought she heard shades of John Wayne in his next menacing words.

"Keith, man, you seem to be only a minor rat, and I have no legal jurisdiction in this country. But I've met with your police here and they have agreed to help us look into Robin's disappearance. If she doesn't turn up, your scam might not seem such a joke."

"No scam, no joke," said Keith desperately. "You go back and find my wife, hear. I can't follow her, I've no cash, but I *saw* her get on that plane out of Sydney."

Stuart finished his beer and stood up. He took some bills from his wallet and tossed them on the table then helped Hannah on with her jacket.

"Good luck with your job, Keith. Let's hope you hear from Robin. Soon."

CHAPTER 23

On Saturday morning, Grace drove Thea and Carrie to the giant Rockland supermarket they had re-christened the Slop 'N Shop. When they returned to the cottage, she stayed to help unload the car then left them to sort out the groceries. As Carrie called out their contents, Thea punched out peel-off adhesive strips on the Braille cryotaper. They pressed the labels onto cans and boxes, and Thea shelved them in the pantry in her particular order. Organization was the first rule of her new life.

She was pleased at how two weeks alone had helped hone her capabilities. She missed Hannah's company, but she was proving her independence. Graham's time with her in the nursery office and long exploring walks with Emperor were healing relaxation. She had maneuvered competently around the greenhouse and managed alone in the cottage with only minor disasters, witnessed only by her dog.

The kettle whistled and Thea made tea. A surreptitious finger, bent down from the cup's rim, warned her when to stop pouring.

Carrie had become a dependable friend. Her injured shoulder prevented her from participating in much of the summer sailing, so instead of practicing racing drills on those afternoons, she sought out Thea's company and they worked together among the plants.

"Come sit, Carrie," she said. She sensed something was bothering the girl, because she loved shopping—even for groceries—and in the market that morning she'd been distracted.

Carrie brought over a box of gingersnaps to dunk. She poured milk into her mug and whirled her spoon as if, with enough vigor, she could dissolve her problem. Thea waited.

"I've got a friend who got in trouble. She's got a reputation for being kind of fast, but she's really nice. A lot nicer than some of the goody girls, only she's had some bad luck. Her boyfriend's great too. He's not going to drop her. They are going to get married."

Thea cradled her mug.

"Well, my friend got pregnant, and even though her boyfriend's a great guy, they can't get married yet. He's saving for college, and she's not about to drop out of high school and stay home with a baby. Rick, her boyfriend, got hold of this new abortion pill. The one from Europe that really works. And Angela knew if she took it she might need some days off while it was doing the job."

Carrie paused and Thea heard her take a swallow of tea. "But she had some problems with extra bleeding—Doc warned her this might happen—and she had to go to the hospital emergency room. Phil, you know, our minister, was there when they brought her in. He'd been sitting with somebody who was dying or something, but he came later and talked to her and she told him everything." She touched Thea's hand. "You know what a great guy Phil is, and I guess he comforted her like the Dad she never knew. She told him how scared she'd been about bleeding to death and maybe getting AIDS from the transfusion. She explained how Rick's boss at the video store got this stuff from somewhere, and, well—"

"Go on."

"But this is the weird part. Somehow, Clay's mixed up in it all and he doesn't even know it. Thea, Clay's a nerd. He might improve with age, but now he's only a kid. Can you imagine, he says that cat's crave earwax and feeds his to Ugly Joyce. Gross!"

Thea smiled. The derision in Carrie's voice did not hide the concern for her younger brother.

She answered seriously. "Carrie, I already know about Angela. Hannah told me the day they brought her home from the hospital. She knew I would not mention it and I haven't. We still don't understand Clay's part in this business."

"I'm not sure either," said Carrie. "Angela says Rick told her that when Clay brings Luther's package, it goes directly unopened to Doc. Last week, right after one of Clay's delivery, Rick had the pills for Angela."

Thea didn't see Carrie's eyes well up or her face crumple, but when she heard the sobs, she came around and cradled her head. She touched her fingers to Carrie's cheek, brushing away her tears.

"Don't cry, honey. We'll help get Clay out of trouble. Mac will find out what's going on. Is Angela okay?"

Carrie drew away and blew her nose on a paper napkin. "Angie's fine," she said and sniffed. "There won't be any baby and things will probably work out for them. That pill really did the job. Angie said she was just one of the unlucky few with complications."

Thea didn't think this was the time to delve into the maelstrom of teenage abortion ethics.

"But what about us, Thea?" Her voice sounded close to tears again. "Our family's a lot worse off than Angela. Clay's in this big trouble about working for Luther and delivering his packages to Doc, and then the stuff between Dad and his tennis friend Nan makes Mom so upset that she has started to eat all the time. Everyone's gossiping about the Swann murders. Oh, Thea, I miss Gran so much. We had such fun together."

At the fresh burst of tears, Emperor came padding over from under the stove and laid his chin on Carrie's knee.

CHAPTER 24

Mac stared at the dismal brick wall of the courthouse next door. The bleary coating of grime, even on sunny days, dimmed what little light filtered down between the buildings. Mac switched on his desk lamp and wrote *Windex*™ on the 'to do' pad.

Sitting across from his boss, Watty rested his elbows on the metal arms of the leatherette chair and let his fingers worry the sparse hairs sprouting along his upper lip. The attempted mustache looked like a plucked eyebrow. Mac considered comment. The addition was not a winner but hard to ignore because the new growth was a strange pale color in contrast to Watty's dark bushy hair. He would say nothing, maybe give it another week. His partner was short and wiry, but never cocky or abrasive—the twin faults of many small men—and Mac wished his effort at hirsute compensation every success.

He was grateful for Watty's tactful silence following the fiery blow up with Rosie over his increasing attention to Thea Morgan. Rosie was a close friend of Watty's wife, and he knew Watty had heard the whole story indicting Mac as a chief rat. Rosie's photograph, along with the dead philodendron, was gone from the top of the filing cabinet.

Mac hung a leg over the arm of his chair and with a pencil thrummed a jazz riff on the gray metal desktop. The routine of their regular police work had kept them busy for several days. Until now, they'd had no time to discuss the convolutions of the Swanns multiple murders. They worked best together by starting a verbal jigsaw puzzle, looking for shapes that would reveal the whole picture.

Watty stopped massaging his lip and, with his pen, checked down the row of skull and crossbones he had doodled along the margin of his notebook. He circled a skull.

"We've got one definite murder," he said. "Colin Swann was poisoned. Too bad it was a public affair and only a hundred people could have put the stuff in his food. Maybe ten, fifteen minutes passed before the poison dropped him. A lot of people stopped by his table to talk about the art show, but no one saw anyone monkey with his plate."

"Half the Swann household sat at his table," said Mac, "but it would have been pretty hard to doctor his food once they were seated. The ME said the toxicologist's report showed enough *aconitine* to kill him, but it wasn't the chopped up leaves or roots that were used as a salad—those were real icicle radishes. The poison was in the dressing. It was the only white radish salad prepared so it wouldn't get served to someone else by mistake. Thea says there are documented cases of parts of that plant being fatally mistaken for watercress or radishes, but for it to be dependably lethal you must boil the plant down and concentrate the toxin. Evidently, vegetable poisons are difficult to detect, but the report confirms that the concentrated liquid was in his salad dressing. It would have been hard to fool an experienced cook like Colin with plate of poisonous greens. No one recalls if Colin's salad was already at his place when he sat down, but his lady friend in the weirdo get-up says she remembers that he took off his jacket and hung it over the back of his chair when he went to talk to Ms Lewis about starting the auction The murderer knew where he'd be sitting."

"Yup. Both Grace and Emily took turns serving salads with the other ladies," said Watty, "as well as Doris and Stella, but those two old girls have helped out that family for years."

Mac chewed his pencil. "There's no motive there. But if we're to be unpleasantly professional, I guess we can't ignore Hannah and Thea's expert knowledge of the *modus operandi*. And don't forget, everyone had easy access to the reference books in the greenhouse office—poisons, insecticides, plant toxins, doses, their effects, all that handy information. And Hannah told us the poison manual was missing, then suddenly reappeared."

They were both silent for a moment. Watty circled another skull and said, "Was Mrs. Swann's fall in the greenhouse an accident?" He scratched his head and answered himself. "Nah, unlikely, but we don't have evidence. There's got to be some logic there. Somebody with a gripe or a greed. And where's this kid Robin?"

"In the Missing Persons mill. They're working on it."

Watty chafed at his lip. "The only one who seems to give a damn about her is the Aussie kid, Keith. His tale may be a bluff, but we can't prove they aren't married."

Mac riffled the papers in front of him. "We've got this report from Stuart. He says that Keith swears Robin left Sydney alive. Stu thought the guy was a bunco. He thought Keith started to sweat a little over the marriage story when he heard about Bea's death and Robin's inheritance, but he also thought Keith was telling the truth about seeing Robin get on the airplane."

"The airline records say she, or someone using her ticket, did arrive in Boston, and then Rockland," said Watty. "I don't see him arranging some fancy scheme using a stand-in, or stashing her body away in the outback."

"Too much trouble and the guy doesn't sound that bright."

"Hey man, when you got no money, nothing's too much trouble for some cash."

The phone rang and Mac relaxed at the sound of Thea's voice. Watty rose to leave, but Mac motioned him back.

"Yeah, sure, Thea," he spoke into the phone. "We'll check on it. The kid doesn't need any more grief. Could I come by later and take you out to dinner?" Then he remembered her unease eating out. "Forget that," he said quickly before she could make an excuse. "I'll bring out some crab cakes and a bottle of wine."

He hung up and turned to Watty. "Thea's had a teary session with Carrie. She's convinced Clay is connected with the delivery of Luther's mysterious packages to the video store—and ex-Doc

Scumbag's renewed abortion business. Another little item for your list."

Mac stretched in his squealing chair and cradled the back of his neck. He looked at his partner and a smile lit his face. "Maybe tonight I can combine business with pleasure."

"Yeah," said Watty, and wrote *WD 40*™ under *Windex*™.

CHAPTER 25

The wind had died early. Back in the harbor, Clay and Luther had hosed down the Sarah P, and she lay riding her anchor on the glassy green water. The air was strangely still. Most of the day had been rough and wet, and Clay was tired. He waved goodbye to Luther and pulled his bike from behind the bait shed at the head of the dock. He wanted to go straight home instead of riding all the way out to the video store with Luther's package. And he had to deliver the pail of crabs to Mrs. Cobb in the village. He needed the money. He stowed the crabs and his foul weather gear into his bike carrier. Thunderheads towered like nuclear explosions and were building up inland. Warm, sulfurous gusts blew across the harbor. It would be a wet ride back from town.

He dropped his bike on the Cobb's front lawn and pushed open the screen door. It squealed. Mr. Cobb was a meticulous handyman, but told Clay he liked its warning. "Announces them burglars," he would say.

The Cobbs sat at their kitchen table picking out crabmeat with practiced fingers. Mr. Cobb's face reminded Clay of a creased lunch bag. His jaw had folded into itself and Clay guessed it was because the old man only wore his false teeth to church on Sunday. He gave them a wave, then went over to weigh the day's catch on the counter scales. He entered the date and pounds in the spiral notebook beside it and went out to the glass louvered porch to stow the crabs in an old refrigerator. "Our Florida room," Mrs. Cobb called it, "where we retire after work." Clay wondered why she had filled the space with plastic ferns and fake flowers when she grew a super garden of real flowers out front.

Back in the kitchen, Mrs. Cobb paid him and offered iced tea, but Clay thanked her and refused. He wanted to stop at Strait's Market before the long ride out to Doc's. He was sticky and hot. He wanted an Eskimo Pie.

In front of the store, he dropped his bike against the ice machine. He saw that the parking lot was crowded with pickups. Big men idled against their trucks with arms crossed over their chests, and fingers dug into their armpits or hooked into pants' pockets. They sucked on toothpicks or beer bottles, or just tugged at the bills of their caps, but their negligent postures belied the tension. In the thick atmosphere that was more than the coming storm, he saw the men had grouped into baiting, unfriendly camps—musselmen and lobstermen.

Clay recognized some fellow lobstermen and a few of the musselmen who he knew represented their tough angry core. He debated skipping the ice cream. He didn't want to get mixed up in or even witness a fight. Naw, he chided himself, don't be a chicken-wimp. He'd be safe inside the store, and Mr. Strait would call the police if things got bad.

It was quiet in the market. Arlean was behind the register and looked grumpy, but that was normal. Lennert Strait leaned on the windowsill overlooking the parking area; keeping an eye on the scene. Vaughn Fleuve, a Canuck who spent his life fishing, or talking about it, shifted his bulk off the deep freeze so Clay could get out his ice cream.

"Going fishin' Len," Vaughn called to the butcher. "Ya wanna close up early and do some fresh water casting?"

"You're crazy," answered Lennert, without taking his eye from the window. "With this storm making up? 'Sides, the summer drought's brought the water so low there ain't any fish in the river anyway. This rain'll raise the water, maybe bring up some fish. Why don't ya wait 'til tomorra?"

"Cuz."

"Cuz why?"

"Didn't invite you for ketchin.' Said fishin'. Might not want to go tomarra.'"

The two friends' banter was a fixture of the village store, but Clay thought today's exchange half-hearted. An attempt to ease the tension building up outside.

When Clay came out, he saw the rivals had formed rough semi-circles in the parking lot. Between them on the gravel, lay a pile of bait-reeking mussel seines. Thunder rumbled as Gephert, the largest and loudest spokesman for the musselmen, kicked at the filthy pile.

"We found 'em," he said soft and threatening, "and a lot more of 'em, over at the town dump. Now just who dragged 'em up off the bottom and took 'em there?"

Clay was on his bike and away down the road before the first fist smacked against cheekbone. The wind gusted in the eerie green light, and a close crack of thunder echoed the ugly scene behind him. When the skies opened, he put his head down and pedaled against sheets of water. He was not even halfway to Doc's when an oncoming police car, its siren strobes flashing, wailed past him. He pulled over and turned to watch it disappear down the road. Probably headed to ward off the fight at Strait's. He pedaled back out onto the asphalt and was still looking behind him when his bike skidded on the oily wetness and he tumbled onto the graveled shoulder.

"Jeezus!" His glasses, useless in the rain anyway, flew off his face and his only thought was that, once again, he'd lost them. He scrambled frantically around his fallen bike and found them unbroken beside the front tire. His foul weather gear, which he should have been wearing, had flipped out of the carrier basket and was also wedged under the bike's front tire, along with Luther's package. But when Clay picked up the torn and sodden package, he forgot about the soaking rain. These were no lottery tickets or money. Instead, he saw a plastic, self-seal freezer bag filled with foil packets of capsules. Dope? Drugs?

He was suddenly very frightened. He stowed the stuff deep in his pocket, then turned his bike around. Forget Doc. He was going home.

CHAPTER 26

Thea and Mac scraped the last of the blueberry dump from their plates. They sat in front of the fire on cushions pulled from the sofa and listened to gusts of rain peck at the cottage windows and spatter down the leaky chimney. The sharp hissing of water hitting the coals of the fire made Mac recall the storm and the brutal scene he'd witnessed outside Strait's Market.

Thea felt for his hand. "What are you thinking?"

"About the fight outside Strait's this afternoon. Those fishermen went crazy. God, what a melee of bloody fists and broken bones. And when a crowd from the village hecklers gathered to take sides, it was like something from Brueghel. We fired our handguns over their heads. That broke up the factions and cooled some emotions, but I couldn't believe how quickly those peaceable, family men became atavistic hotheads."

Mac got up to pour them each a generous portion of the McCallums single malt he'd brought. He pressed the glass into Thea's palm, clinked it against his and kissed her.

"Cheers, Thea. I shouldn't load you with this unpleasantness," he said grimly, "but we haven't seen this much ugly action in the harbor for years."

"No, Mac, please, always talk to me. Remember, it's the only way I ever know what's going on."

He kissed her again; this time unhurried and sensually deliberate. They quickly moved together, impatient to remove encumbering clothing and then slowly, tactilely, aroused exquisite sensations in each other, oblivious to the dying fire.

When later, sated and content, Mac felt Thea shiver in his arms, he pulled the woolly afghan off the sofa and wrapped it around them.

He got up to rebuild the fire that had collapsed in on itself and wondered how he could ever have been enamored of Rosie. After their stormy breakup, Rosie's mother had rightly denounced him a no-good cad and bounder—her exact arcane words. Rosie's verbal tirade had been more explicit. He'd agreed with them both. He had hurt her and she was angry and he deserved all they'd said of him. But Thea entranced him and he must convince her that while her blindness might still burden her life, it didn't his. He nuzzled her chin with his nose and chuckled.

"What's funny?" she asked.

"Rosie's mother called me a churl."

"Possibly true," she considered. "But you have redeeming qualities."

She sat up and Mac brushed her silky hair forward to rub the back of her neck and shoulders with slow circular motions of his thumbs.

"I give a superior massage," he said. "Total body. Will you marry me?"

"No. Getting married for a back rub is not that good a deal. Much easier to hire a masseur."

"Masseuse?" he suggested and kissed along the base of her neck. Thea shivered and turned to face him.

"Mac be serious, we've got to get this Swann mess cleared up. It's afflicting us all, and Hannah and I have become the middle-monkeys for their grief. Emily's become depressed and angry and loses her temper over nothing. She yelled at Grace yesterday, then collapsed into tears. Grace is a nervous wreck and has gained five pounds. She's taken to caftans. Ian, as usual, manages to disappear with Nan for 'tennis' when things get grim. Carrie won't talk to her parents. Clay fears his father, but won't hear anything bad about Luther, whom he thinks is being someway threatened by Doc. Clay was innocent of the contents of the packages he helped Luther deliver to the video store. The boy was a soaking wreck when he collapsed in the greenhouse this afternoon after his bike accident in the storm. Hannah and I are becoming a regular hospice for the kids' disasters."

Thea's voice rose. She sounded perilously close to coming apart herself, and Mac pulled her against him under the blanket. She buried her head in his shoulder.

"The whole summer is an ongoing disaster," she said quietly. "I can't bear one more calamity."

"Hey, take it easy. Clay knows you've handed the evidence over to me and we'll handle it. We'll find the source of Doc's pills. Probably made through some offshore transfer. Like the old prohibition days. Clearing up the rest of the mess will take more time, but that's not your worry."

Thea got up and pulled on her slacks and blouse.

"But it is, Mac. The entire family's miserable, and when they use Hannah and me as their sounding boards . . . well, we want to help, but don't know what to say."

"Listen you're doing fine. And it's not so bad. I convinced the kids I'm their friend, not just a policeman, and they're relieved it's out of their hands. Grace told me how much she appreciates you. She's unhappy that the kids won't communicate with her, but with all the confusion over the deaths, she's afraid to push them. Her own life is in such a stew. Grace is a good listener, but her insecurities don't allow her the skill of subtle probing."

Thea leaned back and savored the last drops of the peaty whisky.

"Poor Grace," she said. "She can't cope. And Ian won't."

Mac poured himself another finger of malt. The logs spat and sang and Thea relaxed in the fire's renewed warmth.

"I'm glad that Hannah and Stuart come home tomorrow," she said drowsily. "I've missed her—but there have been nice compensations. You're a very nice churl." She found his face and raised her lips.

CHAPTER 27

After only one day back in Maine, Hannah's office overflowed with clutter. To top her welcome, U. Joyce greeted her with raucous purrs commensurate to his weight—plus the bonus gift of a dead rat the size of a meat loaf. He stretched, pleasurably elongated on her desktop and, after shuffling the mess of papers around to his comfort, raised his hind leg and gravely licked his large private machinery.

"Disgusting exhibitionist," chided Hannah. "But you've missed me haven't you, pussums?"

The cat ignored her affection and continued his lavage.

"Who's behind these dirty deeds, pussums?" He blinked his yellow eyes and assumed the inscrutable feline pose; paws curled inward under his chest. She lacked the will to attack the piles of paperwork. The long trip back had drained her of energy. Jetties. She raised her head at the sound of a gentle cough. Graham leaned around the half-closed door.

"You're so quiet, I didn't want to startle you. Do you have a minute?"

"Graham!" said Hannah, glad of any interruption. "I can't thank you and Thea enough. Everything's in better shape than before I left. Thea says there were no problems except the usual— too much new business."

"Yes, well, we handled it. But we missed your acerbic tongue. Thea's too nice. She's a remarkable woman. I have greater respect now for the accomplishments of anyone disabled, and I'll never again take my eyes for granted."

"Too right," said Hannah. "Thea's good nature can make you forget that she's blind. Life is a bit of a shit, right? She didn't deserve that accident."

"Speaking of 'too right,' how were the antipodes?"

"Bliss, even in mid-winter. We had so short a time, and Stu's determined to go back."

"As a duo?"

"Graham, Stu is a dear, but at this point in my life, I don't want a helpmate."

"Don't prickle," said Graham. "Romance is flourishing between Thea and Mac and I'm curious to know if it's infectious." He gazed at the ceiling. "I can visualize your double wedding written up in the Rockland Gazette. A complete description— including the spewing champagne punch fountain, the guest book passed by an organza'd toddler, and twelve bridesmaids posed in a rainbow of acetate."

"Seven bridesmaids," said Hannah. "The spectrum has seven colors."

Graham stopped bantering and his face sobered. "Other than work, it's been hell. The Swann family is going to pot."

"I'm sorry," said Hannah. "I know you must miss Colin terribly. We all do. What is going on? Have you talked to Mac?"

Graham recovered his composure "Actually he's on his way over. You, Thea and I are not members of this family, yet he seems to consider us involved. Which is reasonable since these murders, as they say in noir lingo, are most certainly an 'inside job.'

"I agree. It's unlikely any outsider broke into the greenhouse and pushed Bea off her stool—assuming it was no accident." Hannah gestured around her. "And unfortunately, the *Aconitum* derivative found concentrated in Colin's salad dressing strikes pretty close to our special province."

"The police have no evidence against either of you," Graham defended. "There were over a hundred people in that room. An enemy of Colin's might harbor motives we know nothing about. Some of his artistic companions are very strange."

"Tell me about it," said Hannah, recalling the Madam with the red suede shoes. She went over to the coffee machine and held up the pot.

"Cuppa?"

Graham viewed the tarry dregs. "Thanks, but I'll wait for Mac then make some fresh. What I came by for, Hannah, was to ask if you'd come over to the studio and look over Thea's and my scheme for the new greenhouse plans?"

She grinned. "And I shall just happen to be there when Mac arrives?" She'd been mollified by Graham's new humility, and bit her flippant tongue.

"I really don't know what he wants to discuss with me," he said, "but I would appreciate your being there." He looked at her archly. "You have such a direct ability to maneuver conversation. Maybe you can discover who the police suspect and what they're doing." He stroked the somnolent cat who responded by lengthening six inches. "Colin's will was generous, but it makes me unpleasantly suspect. I'm neither quick nor clever under the pressure of questioning."

Hannah saw him pull nervously at his mustache and reached to assure him.

"Graham," she said. "Mac does not come on like the Gestapo, but I'd be glad to come with you to the studio. I want to see what you've designed, and I'm fully aware that my coffee is gaggy."

While they waited for Mac, Hannah sat reading Graham's neatly drafted plans.

"I'm impressed," she called out. The heady aroma of good coffee came from the kitchen alcove. She was pleased to see how effectively he'd re-organized the space using the existing greenhouse foundation. With the addition of Colin's studio area there was now ample room for storage and supplies, a separate lab room for her experimental cultures, and an expansion of the cramped office. She recognized that Graham's professionally scaled drawings and elevations were adequate for any competent team of builders.

He came back with a coffeepot and two steaming mugs. She nodded appreciatively at the drawings. "Where did you learn your drafting skills? You've cut out the cost of an expensive middle man."

"It was a brief interest," he mused. "Then I found how long an apprenticeship was needed to become an accredited architect. And after all those years, if you're not exceptional, it's life in a sweatshop under some anal-egoist."

"Well, we're lucky," said Hannah. "You probably would have been one of the good ones. If we can hire Grevino as our contractor, these drawings are all he'll need. Someone said his crew rebuilt the village firehouse from the ground up without drawings."

"But with beer," Graham added. "After work, lots of beer."

They heard the crunch of tires on the gravel drive. Mac knocked perfunctorily at the open door of the studio and when he and Watty walked in, Hannah choked back comment at Watty's new facial garnish. Graham seemed not to notice. Mac grinned easily at her.

"Great to see you back. Thea says you found the trip worth those thousands of miles. She missed you."

"Too short a time for so long a journey, but definitely worth it."

She passed a plate of cranberry muffins that Graham had warmed for them. Watty took an appreciative mouthful, unearthed his ubiquitous notebook and uncapped his pen.

"We won't be long," said Mac, easing his long legs under the table. "Just a few questions. We talked to Grace about that unfriendly card she received before Mrs. Swann's birthday dinner and heard that you received something similar.

Graham had expected the question and removed the card from his pocket and tossed it toward him. Mac read it, then passed it to Watty.

"It was addressed to Colin," Graham explained, "and I found it, posted from the village, in our mailbox the day before the birthday dinner. We should have mentioned it before, but Colin was busy all day choosing pictures to hang at the Grange show and overseeing the preparations for the birthday dinner. We assumed that the threat of 'his last meal' meant some kind of poisoning at Bea's dinner party. When nothing happened, we passed it off as a vicious prank. We forgot about the Grange supper. With the grief and commotion over his mother's death, we didn't speak of it again." He paused to watch Watty scribble.

Hannah gestured with the coffeepot. "And someone finally did poison him. Do you think the same person wrote the earlier warning?"

Mac made no answer.

Later, outside in the squad car, Watty waved the card at Mac.

"This is loony. Nothing has happened to Grace Swann and she got a card the same day." He tucked it into his notebook and started the engine.

"I don't recall that Grace's message threatened murder," said Mac, but it certainly renewed all her demons."

"Well, whoever wrote them has to be someone pretty weird—and mean. Was it the same person who killed Colin? Nobody, as far as we know, threatened Mrs. Swann and we think her fall was no accident." He stroked thoughtfully at his patchy upper lip. "Do you think I can ever grow mine like that Graham fellow?" Mac turned away. Watty sighed.

"Watty, maybe our idea of a logical motive is different from the killer's. That family has some strange hang ups, and they're plenty of cases where people murder from improbable motives." They got in the squad car. "While we're out here in the harbor," continued Mac, "let's go talk to Emily. She phoned last night and left a message that Keith Watkins called from that Mulla Mulla place out in the bush. He wants to know if we've heard anything about Robin. Emily said she's starting to feel guilty about her indifference toward the girl and promised Keith she'd pressure us to track her down. Keith explained how he can't leave his job, and even if he could, he hasn't the money to get here."

Emily's front door was open and they called out her name. Mac reflected on the pleasant security of living in a place without locked—even closed—doors. Passing up another offer of coffee, they followed her into the kitchen where she made herself a cup of tea and laid out a plate of thick gooey brownies. These they did not refuse.

"Miss Parrish," Mac began.

"Just Emily, please. And thank you for coming by. I'm afraid I've been too callous about Robin. Of course we must do everything to find her."

"We're as puzzled as Keith. We're working on it, but it's taking time. Our trace through the Rockland Air Service shows her listed as a passenger on the flight up from Boston We will continue to check it out."

Emily bit into a brownie and played with the crumbs. "As I explained before, Robin wasn't waiting at the airport when I arrived, but I was late. The village pump in front of Strait's was closed, and I was down to fumes and stopped for gas. I thought she missed the message that someone would meet her plane in Rockland, or else she was just too impatient to wait around and took a cab out to the harbor. I left word with the girl at the counter to call us if she came in on a later flight. I tried to calm Bea when I got back. I explained that Robin probably decided to stay in Boston with friends, started partying, and missed her flight. If you knew my young cousin . . ." She trailed off and raised her eyes. "Bea was angry. She thrived on dramatics and planned on Robin's gala entrance. But she also knew her daughter's vagaries and I think, though disappointed, she wasn't entirely surprised."

Emily finished her tea and set the paper-thin china cup on its saucer. She frowned her disapproval. "I assumed the police would have made further progress by now. Gentlemen, where is she?"

Watty looked at Mac, then Emily. "Miss Parrish—I'm sorry, Emily," he said, "Did you or Mrs. Swann receive any kind of odd threat before the birthday dinner?"

"What kind of threat?"

Before he could answer, the phone rang and Emily picked up the kitchen extension. She looked at Mac and then passed him the phone.

"It's your headquarters. Would you like privacy in another room? There's a phone in the library."

"No problem," said Mac easily, and he reached for the receiver. He spoke his name then listened for a minute. He muttered, "Thanks, Everett," and hung up. "A little emergency. You'll have to excuse us, but I promise we'll get back to you soon with some answers about your cousin Robin."

"Great brownies, ma'am, thank you," said Watty.

Back in the squad car Watty stowed his notebook and pen. "Where to," he said. "What's up?"

"The dump. I think we've got a lead on Robin Swann."

CHAPTER 28

The road to the dump that curved away from the village beyond the church was not picturesque. While Watty concentrated on avoiding potholes, Mac stared out over the stony, unplanted fields. Most were blotched by old farm buildings edging close to collapse. Those folks who had chosen to stay had given up on the farms. They had cement-rooted themselves in mobile homes subsisting on the small piece of their original property that fronted the road. Chickens pecked away in the scruff of dirt yards and in one, a tethered goat with its sidebones showing rubbed itself against a rusting car body.

A line of purple bed sheets and grayish clothing flapped briskly in a side yard. Mac imagined a pale, lethargic woman lured outside from the TV soaps to let her wash snap dry in the wind. He had watched, with curious revulsion, these pale, obese women push their food carts along the aisles of the supermarket in Rockland. Some so grossly overweight that the massive lobes of their buttocks and breasts in elasticized knits moved with ponderous, independent motions. Upper arms the size of Easter hams rested on the open windows of pickups outside Dorman's Dairy out on Route 1, while tongues licked methodically around triple scoops of the rich homemade ice cream.

Even on these back roads, the summer 'For Sale' signs were already up, and Mac admired the optimism of these owners—waiting for that credulous tourist cruising Maine's offbeat roads and looking for the ultimate real estate coup. Since meeting Thea, he'd seriously considered his own economics. He and Rosie had never discussed it. She would use it up, wear it out, but might not do without. What would Thea want, or need? He didn't know. She'd made it clear last night that she was wary of commitments. He'd be patient.

The aura of the town dump preceded it. Not too bad, but a heady organic pong, and like all dumps near the sea, it was heralded by the din of squealing, wheeling gulls. Watty bumped in over the rutted entrance road and pulled up near a smoking ferment of garbage. Ulmer Nunkins, who organized the mounds of trash and managed the burn, leaned on his rake and waited while Mac rolled down his window.

"Sergeant Atwood called us about the suitcase you found, Ulmer."

"Thas' right." Nunkins was sober and dependable, but not a man of conversation. He carefully prodded the pungent pile in front of him with the long tines of his rake. He tossed on some pieces of wooden furniture to give it a boost of flame and, satisfied with the blaze, beckoned them to follow him. Mac got out and followed Ulmer along his alleys of sorted debris, leaving Watty to back the car onto safer ground.

"All this new recycling is driving me crazy," the old man muttered. "Smash it up and let it burn, I say. That was the good old way."

"Sergeant Atwood said that you thought the suitcase might belong to Miss Swann," Mac prompted. "He said you'd keep an eye on it 'til we got here."

"Thas' right," Ulmer nodded.

As Watty caught up with them, a gust of acrid smoke teared Mac's eyes and choked his words. He wiped his face with his sleeve and coughed. "Where did you find it?"

"Well, when Gephert come out here yest'day to fetch up those nets that the lobstermen dragged up and dumped—you know, the ones what caused the fight—he found this suitcase laying buried under the pile of 'em. Well, you know how we get a lotta pickers here." Ulmer spat expertly off the breeze. "Ayuh, I welcome 'em. Saves me more the burning. Anyway, this valise looks good quality and me and Gephert checks it over. Was a little damp from being under them seines, but no tags, no name, see?" Ulmer fell silent, as if so much talk had run him down.

"Ayuh?" Watty prodded.

"Ayuh," Ulmer repeated. He sucked in a deep breath and the inhale of pungent vapors seemed to give him new energy. "Not locked either," he continued, leading the officers to the galvanized shack he called his office. "So we open it up and it's empty. Well, Gep decides to take it home. Would ha' done so myself if I'd seen it first. One of the perks of the job." He grinned, exposing twisted yellow stubs. "You can't believe what some folks toss out." He turned grim. "'Ceptin' pets. When they leave off them little kitties and pups it makes you sick."

"I believe it," Mac sympathized.

"Well," Ulmer picked up, "as I said, it was empty, but before he shuts it up I notice this tear along the top the lining. The damp must'a loosened it see, 'cause it was sagging down, and inside we find this here diary. Not the little locked kind that kids keep their secrets in, more like a travel book. So we open it and there's the name in the front—Robin Swann, with some foreign address. Well, you know how gossip goes 'round. We all heard about that Swann girl who's gone missing. So Gep quick shoves the notebook back under the lining and closes the case. He tells me not to let anybody near it 'til you fellows come. So I called the station and here you are." Ulmer opened the door to his hut and pointed to the suitcase. "It's still in there—I checked."

Mac figured that, by now, its pages would surely be smeared with Ulmer and Gep's grubby prints.

"Gep says to tell you he'll be home after work if ya need to talk to him."

"Thanks Ulmer."

Watty checked his watch as they bumped out of the dump. "It's early yet. Gep won't get off work at the mussel factory for a couple of hours. What'll we do?"

"If we drive out to Long Cove we can talk to him at the plant it will save us a trip back later," said Mac. "Let's get some lunch in the village and take a look at Robin's journal."

Back in the harbor at the Thistle-Do Café, Emily and Phil were finishing their lunch when Mac and Watty came in. The screen door banged behind them, and Phil looked up and waved them over.

"Em's giving me grief over the rectory decor and dragging us out to that discount furniture place on the Route 1. Sure you guys won't insist that I come in for questioning?"

"Come on Phil," said Emily with determination. "If Robin and this new husband ever move into the big house, I'm moving out. And not into that squalor to which you're oblivious. You have no 'décor,' and if you can't afford new furniture, at least buy some paint and wallpaper."

"You tell him, Emily," said Mac. He winked at the clergyman. "You have to admit, Phil, your place is pretty sepulchral, even for a rectory. Go buy some duckie potholders and one of those clocks with the cat's tail pendulum."

"Thank you, gentlemen," said Emily and edged Phil toward the door.

Mac and Watty found an empty booth and stared at the chalkboard over the counter. Almost everything listed was deep fried except for the coleslaw and Nelly's famous pies. There were seven choices today, all baked this morning. Little Nelly, her daughter, who easily weighed in at one-ninety, stood waiting with her pencil poised.

"I don't fancy any more sweets, or coffee," apologized Watty. Little Nelly accepted this lapse with a shrug.

"Well," she offered, "Dad just brought in some fresh clams. How about a bowl of steamers, or deep fried?"

"Fantastic," Watty groaned with pleasure. "Steamers, a hot roll, melted butter, and a side order of slaw."

"Make it two," Mac added.

At the dump, Mac had gingerly removed the slim journal from the pocket lining of the suitcase and slipped it into a protective plastic bag. Now in the privacy of the high-backed booth, he opened it between them on the table. With gloved fingertips, he carefully turned the pages by their edges.

"It reads more like a travelogue than a journal. Start's out while she's with Keith on a road trip to Adelaide with the band." Mac skimmed to her last entry. "The writing's jerky. Probably wrote this on the plane. 'I'm on the penultimate leg,'" he read aloud quietly. "'It'll be good to get to Boston. I feel wiped from all the travel shit and miss the bastard. I'm not sure I can cope with my family *en masse* right away. Do I want to? Maybe I need some time to get myself together. We're landing. Only one more up and down. I need to be down for a while. I feel like a yo-yo. Too many uppers and downers.'"

Mac paused and slipped the book out of sight as Little Nelly put their steaming bowls in front of them. Watty eased the first clam from its shell and slipped the rubbery black neck off its siphon. He swirled the morsel through melted butter and dropped it in his mouth.

"Counting the flights ups and downs, it sounds like she got to Boston," he said, wiping his chin.

"And she arrived here with her suitcase," said Mac. "Dead or alive, she's got to be around somewhere."

He dipped a hunk of his roll into the cup of hot clam broth and got it to his mouth just before it disintegrated. They finished without talking and pushed aside their bowls of empty shells. Mac studied the chalked up listings and was tempted by the fresh raspberry pie. Then he remembered he hadn't run for the past two mornings.

"Considering the dwindling history of her family and the grim fate of her suitcase," Watty said, "she's here somewhere all right, but probably not alive."

CHAPTER 29

Carrie wiggled her toes in the loamy soil of the wide perennial bed edging the front drive of the big house. She snipped the heads off a spent mound of *Platycoden* with her secateurs and decided that deadheading, even to rejuvenate these beautiful blue balloon flowers, was the world's most boring job. She knew that inland, the day shone bright and sunny, but out here on the Neck, the fog bank that had canceled the day's sailing classes still hung solid and gray. At the squish of a slug between her toes, she shrieked and jumped backwards, wiping her foot in disgust on the damp grass.

Hannah and Thea, weeding their way down the drive, paid no attention. Carrie tossed down her clippers and hunched down on the gravel. Drudging outside in the garden is okay when you can work on your tan, but not on a blah day like this. She thought of her friend Lucy who was probably basking in the California sun, bronzed and wearing some wild thong bikini. She'd be lying on her towel under the gaze of a handsome blond surfer on a wonderful white sandy beach where you could actually swim without freezing to death. She checked her watch. No, right now she'd be sitting under a palm tree eating juicy mangos, fresh pineapple, and sucking up pina coladas for breakfast. And there'd be no slug juice sticking her tan toes together.

Here she was, stuck all summer on this clammy, cold Maine coast. She felt as dismal as the day and the sharp stones of the drive poking into her rear forced her up.

She began again to snip off the spent heads of the other early perennials. Prime them for a second coming, Hannah had commanded. Carrie daydreamed of the coming mysteries of boarding school this fall and the chance to escape her miserable family and make new friends. She'd miss Lucy, and of course they'd write all the time, but there'd certainly be some rich roommate who'd invite her to their family cabin on a mountain lake, or their western ranch, or winter skiing in Europe at their chalet and spring breaks in Florida, or maybe Bermuda!

Clay pierced her fantasies with his solo bicycle race up the driveway. She watched him wheelie over a bag of bark mulch and land his bike at an angle that spattered her with tar-specked gravel. He had ridden through the tacky new black top that the town used to re-surface the roads, always in the heat of summer. Her parents said they did it to spur solvent sales at the market.

Carrie didn't rise to a scathing reproof, merely gave him a piteous glance that her brother, slumped forward over his handlebars, ignored.

"It's a stupid day. Want to bike out to Doc's and rent a video?"

"You've got to be crazy. We're not supposed to go near that place, and you know it."

"Clay," piped Hannah rounding on him, "how nice of you to stop by. Why don't you help your diligent sister finish this bed and then I'll drive you both in to the video store and even pay for a film. Two films."

"It's idiot work, Clay," said his sister. "Even you could handle it."

"Eat a rock, Carrie."

Emily came out the front door and called from the porch. "I've been working at my desk all morning and watching you labor. The beds look marvelous." She stretched the muscles of her back. "I'll trade you ladies my paper work for some gardening." She came across the drive and looked down at the boy.

"Clay, what are you doing?"

Clay, squatting beside Thea, was neatly severing angleworms brought up by her freshly toweled earth.

"That," said Carrie, "is cruel and repulsive."

"It is not," said her brother with scientific authority. "I've just cloned them into twins."

"Clay, dear," said Emily. "While you pursue your powers of creation, may I borrow your bicycle to go in to the village library? Mine has a puncture."

Hannah turned from checking the health of a mass of white *rugosas*.

"I'm sure he'll let you, Emily." She gave Clay a wicked smile and patted his head. "Clay has come by to help us in the garden."

After Clay's quick lesson on the intricacies of multiple gears, Emily pedaled off on his superior bicycle. Hannah began thinning roses and Clay, bored by his annelid progeny, tried for her attention.

"Hannah, remember the day of Carrie's accident at the cave-in?"

"Um," she answered, picking a thorn from the soft palm of her hand. "Hold these while I cut."

"Well, remember?" Clay persisted, gingerly taking the spiky bundle. "Remember when Uncle Colin promised us at lunch that when Carrie got well we'd go over to our house and look for the passage leading down to the cliff? Instead of renting a movie, how about if you and me and Carrie go look for it now? It's mom's bridge day at the golf club and she won't be home for hours. Please—if I promise to help you weed first."

Thea eased up from her knees. "Go on, Hannah. We've done enough for today. You've been working non-stop since you got back from your trip and I want to go back to the cottage. Like Agatha's Hercule, I need be restored by an herbal tisane."

"Come on, Hannah," pleaded Clay.

"Clay, we can't go upsetting your house."

"This past spring, Hannah, I had a homework paper on colonial architecture," said Carrie. "Dad helped me find the original plans of our house and I showed them to Graham. He said there might be an entrance somewhere on the first floor leading to that tunnel. Even he got excited over those drawings." She laughed. "He acted like a kid with a treasure map. Let's go check it out!"

"Good idea," said Thea. "Clay, you're a great kid, but a rotten weeder. Why don't you three go over and look for secret passages. Go play Nancy Drew."

Hannah sent her a scowl, forgetting it would have no effect. "I always thought her competitor had better stories," she said. "Who was she? Jane somebody?"

"Judy Bolton," corrected Carrie. "She was way smarter than Nancy Drew."

"Do kids still read that stuff?" mused Hannah. "I'm impressed."

"What's amazing," said Carrie, "is that somebody still makes a fortune writing them. I liked the old ones better. When she wore frocks and drove a roadster."

Thea picked up the basket of gardening tools that she kept on a lengthy piece of twine tied to her belt. It tugged along behind her like a dory as she worked.

"Why don't you, Nancy and Judy, take Fearless Fosdick here and go play detective. I'll tell Graham where you're going. He'd probably love an excuse to explore it himself, and he'll have a chance to come to your rescue if you get into trouble." Thea frowned. "I'm sorry, I shouldn't even joke about another accident. Please be careful."

"Don't fret," said Hannah. "Believe me we'll be very careful. Grace and Ian would kill us if anything happened." She caught Thea's grimace and laughed.

"Not our day for the *mot juste* is it."

"Let's walk, Emp," called Thea. The black dog, lying off duty under the pink and white fountain of an *Abelia* bush, pricked up his ears and raised his head at the magic word to come and sit ready beside her. Thea took hold of his harness and went down the drive to the cottage.

"I've thought about it," said Clay, as the three of them entered his empty house. "If the smugglers had to cart their heavy cases of booze up from the beach, they'd want to come out somewhere downstairs here, close to the drive."

Carrie was as impatient as her brother. "We'll get the old house plans. They're rolled up in tubes at the back of the den closet."

They both darted off and Hannah was left waiting in the quiet cool of the entrance hall. She felt uneasy. Thea's sober warning reminded her that despite the kids' enthusiasm for this adventure, she was pretty sure Grace and Ian would not approve.

She followed the kids and entered the den just as Carrie backed out of the closet with her arms full of cardboard tubes. Hannah made space on the plank oak table and Clay weighted down the curling corners of the brittle drawings with books. They studied each page, but found no wall, closet, or chimney back that showed any unaccountable thickness. There was no clue of an underground passage that might lead to the sea.

Clay squinted at the squirrelly white lettering on the detailed pages.

"What are we looking for?"

"I wish we'd brought Graham with us," said Hannah. "This stuff is impossible to read."

She knew they were reluctant to give up, but the balloon of excitement was punctured. Carrie slowly rolled up the drawings and returned the tubes to the closet.

Clay remained stubborn. "There's got to be a way down to the beach from inside this house. Maybe we should start down there at that cave and work backward."

"No way," said Carrie. "I'm not messing up my other shoulder."

"No way too right," said Hannah. "But I wonder," she mused aloud. "We've only been looking at the walls. Smugglers weren't unknown in Australia, kids, and I remember some tales. There could be a trap door somewhere in the floor. It would have been easier to tunnel down than to excavate a wall passage."

She felt a little silly. The whole scene was truly one for Nancy Drew or Judy Bolton, but a look at their serious faces obliged her to continue their childish play.

"Let's check out the floors," said Carrie. She looked at Clay. "Have you ever seen a trapdoor anywhere?"

"Nah," he said and gestured around him. "These rugs have covered the floor since I was born!"

Hannah checked her watch. It was after two. "Right then. Let's take a fast look through the downstairs rooms. But," she held up a warning palm, "if we don't find anything today, promise me that neither of you will go near that cliff cave-in alone."

Carrie stared hard at her brother and raised her palm. "On our honor."

They started at the front of the house and, room by room, worked their way towards the kitchen. Wall-to-wall carpeting was not a choice of the Swanns and in most of the rooms it was fairly easy to tap for hollow sounds and check the alignment of floorboards. No luck. They'd progressed to the dining room where the three of them were gingerly moving the pedestal Sheridan table off the Chinese carpet when Emily pushed through the swing door from the pantry.

"What in the world are you doing?"

Concentrating on keeping the table and its leaves in one piece, they'd not heard her come in and, though startled by her astonished question, managed to set it down without damage. Hannah mustered her composure.

"Looking for trap doors."

"You've got to be kidding," said Emily. She shifted her load of library books to the other hip.

Hannah shrugged. "It's that kind of day."

Clay explained, still enthusiastic. "We're looking for the entrance up from the beach that the bootleggers used here during prohibition. The one we talked about at lunch after Carrie's accident."

"Well, I hate to spoil the fun," said Emily, "but your father never mentioned any such thing. We didn't live in this house then, but I'm sure they would have known about something that adventurous."

Clay looked disappointed.

"But keep at it," she encouraged. "Maybe these chimneys and walls hold secrets the ancestors didn't share. They weren't all such straight arrows, you know." She winked at Hannah behind the children's backs. "I brought over a book Grace reserved from the library. I'll leave it in the hall, and Clay, thank you very much—I left your super bike in the garage. Good luck guys."

They persevered after she left, but the dining room floor proved solidly impregnable. They rolled back the carpet and replaced the heavy table. The pantry and kitchen linoleum shone waxed and inviolate. They traipsed from the laundry room off the kitchen down into the huge garage that a hundred years ago quartered horses but was now reduced to sheltering a Volvo station wagon and Ian's sporty Peugeot.

At one end was a partitioned storeroom that originally held horse tack, but was now the repository for those household cast-offs no one ever discards.

Hannah checked her watch again.

"Kids, this is our last resort."

Clay unlatched the door and they peered in.

"I've never been in here," said Carrie. "I thought it would be full of rats and huge spiders."

To Hannah's surprise, aside from some filmy webs overhead and matted knots of spider eggs in the corners, it was very tidy. A burlap tarp used for the fall bundling of leaves to the compost pile was spread on the floor with an old push reel mower laid across it. Hannah thought that strange. The tractor mower was the only one she'd ever seen used. A frisson of nerves made her shiver. Carrie, the dramatist, pressed her hands to her chest and groaned with delight. "Sinister!"

Ignoring her theatrics, Clay pushed the mossy old lawnmower aside and flipped back the folds of burlap.

"Hey," he breathed. Under the tarp was a trap door. An iron-lifting ring was counter sunk into the wood, as were the two sliding bolts that secured it.

"My God," said Hannah. "Alfred Hitchcock wrote this script!"

Clay took charge. He slipped back the bolts and pulled on the ring. The door swung up easily and he rested it back against a vintage porch rocker. They looked cautiously at the short flight of wooden steps leading down into the dark.

"We need a flashlight," said Hannah.

Carrie ran back to the pantry and returned with a square business-like beacon from the storm emergency drawer.

"Me first," said Hannah, and took the light. At the bottom of the stairs, she flashed the beam ahead. It faltered and dimmed. Hannah shook it and it brightened.

"How old are these batteries, Carrie?"

They were in a narrow, earth carved passage that slanted gently downwards. It smelled musty and dank and Carrie and Clay followed close on her heels.

"I knew it," whispered Clay. "Pirates did use our house."

Carrie poked gingerly at the earth close over her head and became less enthusiastic. "Do we have to go far?"

The floor of the tunnel dropped away sharply, and Hannah guessed that by now they were down under the meadow, close to the cliff. She held her hand up.

"Wait here a minute," she said sharply. The sudden smell of putrefaction was awful and unmistakable.

"Something stinks," said Clay.

Hannah moved slowly around the bend in front of them and her light flashed long enough on the crumpled heap ahead to recognize a human body. Or what remained of one. Nauseated, she stumbled back where they waited. She focused her wavering light up the tunnel behind them.

"Back," she ordered. "It's not safe beyond that bend."

"What's that awful smell?" Carrie asked.

"It looked like a pile of dead rats," said Hannah. "Washed in by high tide."

No one argued about that.

"Water must have flooded up there during that storm before the cave-in shut it off," she explained. "It looks too risky to continue. We three know the passage is here, but it has to be our secret for a while. I can't be responsible for another accident."

She shone the faltering flashlight on the face of her watch. "Anyway it's getting late and if your mother had a bad day at the card table, she might come home early."

Carrie wrinkled her nose at the pervasive stench. She grabbed her brother's arm and pulled him back up the tunnel. The threat of parental fury made them eager to lead the way out. Hannah was close on their heels.

"We can come back another time," she said.

The outer garage doors were open as they came up through the trap door, and Clay was the first one to see Grace's station wagon parked out front in the drive.

"Oh my god. Mom's home!"

Hannah switched off the light.

"Hey kids, I think we're okay. Your mother didn't come in through the garage or she'd have seen the storage room open and the trapdoor up."

"Yah, she must have gone in through the front door," Clay added, "and doesn't know we're home yet."

Carrie breathed out her relief. "We're lucky!"

Hannah pushed them towards the kitchen door and nodded behind her at the tack room.

"Go inside. I'll shut up everything back there and leave it as we found it." After a guilty pause, she added, "I'm not setting you a good example, but we won't tell your parents just yet what we've been up to."

"Noooo problem," said Clay and they both hurried inside.

When the door had closed behind them, Hannah reluctantly went back to the tack room. She should find a better flashlight before she entered that tunnel again, but she might encounter Grace in the kitchen. I'll only be gone a minute, she reassured herself. Not wanting to think about what lay before her, but needing to be sure who she thought lay crumpled on the tunnel floor, she went quickly down the steps and back along the earthen passage.

Beyond the bend, the stench again repulsed her. The quavering light shone on the decayed bundle pushed up against the wall by the tides. She held her hand over her mouth. The tangle of long black hair didn't hide the decomposed head, chewed on by rats. Bloated by the gases of decaying flesh, the body had swollen. It must be Robin. She'd probably been here for weeks—since the night of Bea's birthday dinner. Fighting her rising nausea, Hannah glanced quickly at what remained of the girl's face. The eye sockets were empty and half her nose eaten away. Water rats, crabs, and God knows what else had done their grotesque work. Hannah thought if she stayed here one more minute she'd throw up. She had to get out.

Footsteps shuffled in the dirt behind her as the flashlight flickered out. A muffled voice called her name. She spun around in the dark.

"Graham?"

Had Thea called him to come find them after all? A blinding light shone in her eyes. She felt a crashing blow to the side of her head, and she collapsed onto the dirt.

CHAPTER 30

Thea fed Emp his dinner before pouring herself a glass of St. Emilion. Life is indeed too short to drink cheap wine. She slipped the first cassette of a Dick Francis thriller into her player, but when it ended and the smooth voiced Englishman instructed her to insert the next tape, she switched it off. She couldn't concentrate.

Where was Hannah? She felt the raised dots of her watch. It was only 6:30. She could be having a drink with Stuart somewhere, or running errands. Despite these reasonable possibilities, she was anxious. Hannah usually called if she was going to be late. Thea decided to phone Carrie and see if the kids had found any secret passages, then she would casually ask about Hannah. She picked up the phone, thought about it, then put the receiver down. It might cause alarm. She drank another glass of wine, too quickly, and in *vino veritas* admitted her lack of courage. She'd call Mac instead and dump her anxiety on him. As she reached for the phone it rang.

"Thea? It's Ian."

"Oh, my God. What's happened?"

There was a pause, then Ian's puzzled voice. "What do you mean? Nothing's happened here. What's wrong?"

"I'm sorry, Ian. Hannah isn't home yet, and I think about accidents. I guess I'm just nervous."

"Don't worry, you know her. She's probably out rushing around. I'm actually calling to invite you both to a little surprise party later tonight. It's our wedding anniversary and I'm sure Grace thinks I'm being my usual cloddish self because I've made no mention of it, but I've arranged for some cake and champagne and I'm asking you to join us and celebrate. I'm sorry to whisper but I'm here *sub rosa* in the den. I apologize that it's so impromptu, but it's a very informal surprise."

"Thank you Ian. That sounds lovely. As you say, Hannah will probably be home any minute." She paused. "But I was about to call Mac when you rang. We had plans for dinner." Why had she added this falsehood?

"By all means, bring Mac along—out of mufti, of course. We need cheering up, not reminders of these past weeks."

Mufti! Thea bit back an unlady-like reply that Ian interrupted.

"Come around back to the patio around eight"

In the kitchen, Grace slid a lasagna casserole into the microwave. Her bridge afternoon had included a filling lunch and tonight, with no appetite, she conceded that eating without appetite was one of her problems. She was angry, not hungry. She didn't expect that Ian would make anything special of their anniversary and a restaurant dinner was the last thing she wanted tonight, but he might have at least remembered the date. Brought her some flowers. She had forced about two words out of Carrie and Clay before they evaporated into their rooms, and the day's final misery was a desultory peck on the cheek by Ian before he closeted himself in the den. Setting up a tennis date with Nan? Her reward for sixteen years of marriage. She turned down the volume of the evening news and heard him murmuring on the phone. She didn't want to think about that.

Food, not drink, was her usual solace, but tonight she went to the bar off the pantry and poured herself a large whisky. She took a swallow and made a silent but resolute toast to herself. To the end of sweet sixteen. The insistent ding of the microwave brought her back to the kitchen.

The day's heavy fog had never lifted, and while they had canceled sailing class, it had cleared off to a fine evening and the kid's dance party tonight out at the Metcalf's barn was not dependent on the weather. She wondered why Carrie hadn't mentioned it when she came in. Her daughter didn't mind missing sailing drills, but she never missed parties. Communication had been terse these last weeks, but tonight over dinner both Clay and Carrie were impossible.

"What did you two do today?" She had tried to sound cheerful and motherly.

"Weeded," answered Carrie.

"Nothing," added Clay.

So much for conversation. Ian was oblivious and she wondered how much longer she could blame his emotional retreat from them on the shocks rending his family. She was angry with Ian and felt guilty for not insisting they openly discuss the tragedies disrupting their lives. But damn it, she was tired of being the guilty one. It was important they both talk with their children over the grief evoked by the deaths of Bea and Colin. Her tentative overtures to him had been rebuffed. She picked at a small plate of dressing-less salad while the rest of them helped themselves to lasagna and garlic bread.

"Go easy on the garlic, Carrie," she warned. "Your dancing partners tonight will swoon."

"Huh?" Carrie dropped the wedge of toasted bread on her plate. "Mom, I totally forgot. The dance party's tonight!" She turned to her brother. "Clay, you're invited too. Come on, you'll have fun," she insisted. "Lots of our friends will be there." She looked at her watch. "I've got to find some mouthwash and something to wear." She mumbled the required 'excuse me' and bolted from the kitchen.

"I don't want to go to that dumb party," said Clay sullenly. "I can't dance, so why should I go?"

Grace, with automatic gesture, felt Clay's brow. He didn't look well. Her son was a bottomless pit and he loved lasagna, but tonight he had only poked at his dinner. He pushed away his mother's hand. "I'm not sick. I just want to stay home and watch TV."

"But Carrie wants you to go with her." Grace silently questioned Carrie's unusual wish for Clay's companionship. "It was nice of her to invite you."

"She won't miss me. The minute she gets in with her friends she'll forget I'm around. And she's wrong. My friends wouldn't be caught dead there."

"Well, we won't insist, but you've been so droopy since the unpleasantness over Luther, and I know how boring this summer is for you now without fishing, but—" she looked across at Ian "—I expect your father's right. There are other jobs, mowing lawns, delivering papers."

"Mom, he's not right." Grace watched her son fight tears. "We're not in Boston. People here mow their own lawns and everybody stops at Strait's for their papers."

Ian looked up from his plate and spoke in a cold flat voice to his son.

"Listen to me, Clay. Luther Pollard, whom you call your friend, deceived you and used you as an accomplice in criminal behavior. He made you his crony in Doc's drug-running scheme and I want no more contact between you and him. Ever!"

"Dad," he pleaded. "You don't know that he's guilty. And even if he is, Doc only used him because he's simple. Luther would never knowingly trick me. They probably made it all sound okay when they asked him to deliver the stuff. If Luther didn't understand that he was doing anything wrong, then I was no accomplice."

Ian accepted his son's loyalty, but not his logic.

"Clay," he reasoned, lowering his voice. "Luther is not that 'simple,' as you call it. I think he knows perfectly well he is breaking the law for some extra cash and is aware that an illegal doctor is dispensing an illegal substance. Doc and his cohorts will be judged guilty, but until Luther's case is settled, you stay away from him, do you hear me? Clay?"

Clay lowered his head. "Yes, sir."

"Do what you want this evening," said his mother, "but be nice to Carrie."

Clay asked sullenly to be excused from the table. After he left, Grace looked at Ian and wondered why it's always the wife who does the patching. Ian folded his napkin.

"I'll take Carrie to the party. You go have a bubble bath or whatever, and when I get back, we'll drive down to Port Clyde for a drink."

Grace pondered this invitation. Ian seldom invited her anywhere. Especially for an after dinner drink. Maybe he'd not forgotten after all, and a bubble bath sounded wonderfully soothing.

CHAPTER 31

Stuart stared into the freezer compartment of his refrigerator and poked at the frost coated microwave entrees. A large Pussers rum had stirred his appetite, but neither the burrito-taco combo or the three hundred calorie chicken-de-lite left by some dieting girlfriend would taste any better than the boxes they came in. He shut the freezer door against a cloud of cold mist and leaned his head against it. Moments like these rankled, but he fought the surge of self-pity and resolved not to call Hannah. Then, he reasoned, why not? He'd propose a quiet, candlelit meal. No pushing her about the future—he'd cultivate patience. He finished his rum. He wanted her here, right now, and not just to cook.

He was about the call the greenhouse cottage when the phone rang. It was Ian with his invitation to the surprise party. Stuart wondered if the sudden attention to their wedding anniversary was enough to earn Grace's pardon for a year's bad conscience. Hannah must have been invited, too. He'd call her and suggest they have dinner together first. As he reached for it, the phone rang again. Jesus, it was a Ma Bell night. It was Mac.

"I'm on my way out to the Swanns," he said. "Thea phoned and said we've been invited to surprise Grace on their anniversary. She said Ian had called you, so why don't I pick you up? Save driving out in two cars." Mac sounded as if he had more on his mind than the party.

"Thanks, Mac. If I can't reach Hannah, I'll take you up on the ride. Probably save me from a DUI. On top of rum, champagne and cake was to be my dinner. You haven't heard from her have you?"

Mac paused. "Thea said she hadn't come home yet and hoped she was with you. She sounded upset because Hannah usually calls if she's out late."

So much for the romantic dinner. He thought of the last time he'd seen her. Two days ago. He remembered she had more or less told him to stay out of her hair until she got caught up with work. Her 'Don't Tread on Me' pennant was flying high.

Mac's voice was serious. "Look Stu, something fishy has come up involving Robin. I'm going to this party tonight strictly as Thea's guest, but I'd appreciate your moral support while I tactfully weasel some information. Ian's an arrogant ass when fending off peons, and I'm sure he places me well below the salt."

"Ignore him," said Stuart. "What about Hannah?"

"Thea's going to the Swann's party, but she wants to walk over on her own with her dog. If Hannah hasn't called, or shown up by then, I think we'd better get on it."

As soon as Mac hung up, Stuart phoned Thea.

"Stuart," she burst out, before he could speak. "Hannah's still not come home."

"I know, Mac just called me and if you're sure I can't bring you, then we'll meet you later at Ian's. If she isn't with you by then—well, we'll find her."

Stuart was waiting outside when Mac drove up in front of his apartment. He slid into the front seat and sniffed.

"When you said fishy, you meant it, what stinks?"

Mac nodded over his shoulder at the suitcase on the back seat. "I want to exchange some information. I need to know more about the Swanns. If I remember, your father was a close friend of the family, and confidante to more than their legal affairs. There's something in that family's past—"

"Mac, I can't volunteer client information." He heard himself sound pompous, but his lawyer's code of confidentiality was automatic.

"Off the cuff, Stuart," said Mac, shortly. "We're talking about possible multiple murders." He gestured at the back seat. "We found that empty suitcase buried under a pile of fishnets at the town dump and in its lining was Robin's travel journal. The suitcase was hers, and whoever stashed it was in a hurry and didn't notice the journal. Robin's been missing for weeks, but we're now sure that she did arrive. I'm afraid the odds against her still being alive are small, and tonight Hannah's disappeared. Given the Swann's track record, let's not pretend we aren't a little wary."

Stuart rammed his glasses painfully against the bridge of his nose. The call from Thea had recalled the Swann's hidden skeletons, and a real fear for Hannah emerged. The family's records in his father's files dated back to the great-grandfathers. He had meant to sort out all those brown edged papers, depositions and documents and read them more carefully, but hadn't gotten around to.

"I understand, Mac, but I don't know how much I can help you tonight. I inherited the Swann's legal work when Dad died but I haven't had time to go over the old paperwork. The old man kept everything and inferred that there were some past dealings that were better forgotten. Dad held his personal clients close to his chest, and it hasn't been easy trying to convince those older, but lucrative, farts that I'm not just Dad's kid. Aside from coping with Bea's schemes, I've been busy trying to bring the firm out of the dark ages.

Mac swung the car off Route 1 and up the hill onto 131.

"Stu, this case isn't easy for me. Watty and I are working alone on this, and we've been firmly told to keep the Swann's troubles off the front page. We've got three probable homicides and nothing but circumstantial evidence. Our head honcho in Augusta suggests we clear it up—fast, and with minimum damage to the mega tax paying Swanns. While there are still some of them left." He paused to focus on the road, then went on. "What we've got so far are mainly hunches based on speculation. Nothing that would stand up in court without one of those convenient television self-confessing scenes. I'm asking you, as an old buddy, for some necessary private information." He took a hand off the wheel and held up a defensive palm. "Never to be revealed, unless it pertains directly to the 'alleged perpetrator.'"

CHAPTER 32

Hannah rolled over in the blackness and shuddered. She decided she wasn't dead because dead people didn't throw up. Another convulsive retch lifted her head from the dirt and the sharp spasms of pain focused behind her eyes made death seem the better choice. Lie still, she resolved, rally the psyche. But she felt too weak to rally anything. She slid back into unconsciousness.

The shivering and the chattering of her teeth woke her again. She was cold but not so sick, and the throb in her head was a steady pain instead of a threat to mortality. The gritty dirt of the passage floor rubbed against her cheek, but to try sitting up might bring back the shooting stars of pain and unconsciousness. Without moving her body, she groped for the flashlight, sweeping with her arms as far as she could without raising her head. The flashlight was gone. Her hands fumbled on the messy heap of Robin's corpse. She jerked away, revolted by what she couldn't see. In the black tunnel, in her panic, she thought of Thea. How did she cope with the eternal darkness?

She must get out of here. By inches, she eased herself on to her knees, waiting as each wave of dizziness settled-like a sea diver warding off the bends. She began the slow crawl up the dirt incline, guiding herself along the wall with her fingertips until she felt the steps up to the trap door.

The air around her smelled stale and damp, and before she reached it, she sensed that the door was closed. She pushed gingerly upwards on it with her shoulder and saw stars. It was a futile effort because whoever shut it must have bolted it. Should she have crawled the opposite way down to the cliff entrance? No. She remembered that the cave-in on the day of Carrie's accident had been solidly blocked by the rock fall. Crouched on the steps, she again pressed her shoulders against the door above her with wasted effort, and reflected on the accurate description of 'trap' door.

Resigned to being captive in this dark hole, she gingerly probed the pulpy place under her hair. Would Nancy Drew cry? Probably. But never Judy Bolton. She giggled. Imminent dementia? Surely someone would come looking for her. Clay and Carrie know where I am and Thea will miss me, she reassured herself. Then she remembered she'd told the kids that she'd close the trap door before leaving. If they checked, they would assume she'd gone home. And Thea might think she was off with Stuart. How long could she last here? Something serious was wrong with her head, and she was freezing.

As Clay would say, no problem. A nice quiet way to die. Like people buried under avalanches, or huddled with twisted legs on an icy mountain ledge, blissfully freezing to death while waiting for rescue that would never come.

CHAPTER 33

Yellow light from the entry hall shone through the etched glass panels above Grace and Ian's front door. Mac dropped the brass whale knocker with a thud. A burst of laughter echoed from the patio behind the house.

"Let's go around," said Stuart. "Ian said they would be out back."

"Wait a minute," said Mac. He went back to the car and returned with Robin's suitcase.

"Hey," said Stuart, "you won't make waves right away, will you? You promised Thea, remember."

"Yes, but this is a police investigation and niceties might have to sacrificed." He leaned over and settled the suitcase in the bushes along the path. "Don't worry. I'll stow it here in the bushes and won't bring it out tonight if the timing's bad, but I'd like to see their reactions to our finding that case. You can sit there like a gent and eat cake."

"To hell with cake, I could eat a horse."

Ian had done well-after-dinner drinks, champagne on ice and a chocolate cake, complete with sixteen candles.

Phil accepted a frothy cappuccino from the tray that Emily passed. They sat in a relaxed circle in the dusk, their pale faces shadowed by the soft light from candles sunk in sand-filled shells.

Grace rose as the two men came onto the patio.

"Stuart," she said, then added with surprise, "and Mac, too. How nice of you both to come. I guess you know it's our anniversary and Ian has surprised me with cake and champagne.

Plus an elegant espresso machine! I'm about to go in for another round." She pointed to the laden picnic table. "Help yourself here to whatever."

"First," said Stu, giving Grace a hug, "congratulations to you both."

Graham fitted two more chairs into the shadowy circle, and Emily, gesturing toward the flickering centerpiece, offered them bug spray. "In this last burst of Indian summer, Citronella candles," she warned, "do not do the job."

Thea spoke anxiously. "Where's Hannah? We hoped she'd be with you." She sat rigidly; not eating or drinking. "Mac, I'm really worried," she said. "I left her a note at the cottage about the party but she hasn't called. We can't just sit here. What shall we do?"

Ian looked around at their uneasy faces and spoke in a tight voice. "I don't think our family can face another tragedy—are we being cursed?" He set down his coffee. "Thea's right. We've got to find Hannah, now."

Mac disregarded Ian's dramatic rhetoric. Instead, the crazy threats in the anonymous invitations flashed through his mind.

"Who saw Hannah last?" he asked.

"When she finished gardening this afternoon," answered Thea, "she came over here with Carrie and Clay to search for that fancied sea passage from the house down to the cliff that they were so eager to explore. Colin gave them the idea that bootleggers or smugglers had once used a tunnel like the one that caved in on Carrie."

Ian roared. "What! They knew to stay away from that cave-in. I forbid them—"

"Where are the kids?" Thea burst in. "Get them here right away. If there was some accident and Hannah's been hurt—"

Grace came from the kitchen with a fresh tray of coffees. She saw Ian was angry. He took the tray from Grace and slammed it down on the table, knocking the dainty china cups off their saucers.

"I'm tired of this unsettled business of mother's and Colin's deaths." He grabbed a handful of paper napkins and mopped at the puddle of spilled coffee. "And just where the hell *is* Robin? The whole damn mess is wrecking us all."

Grace pressed a napkin to her eyes and began to cry. Emily came over and cradled her shoulder like a child. "Grace, I'm so sorry, we've upset your lovely party."

Thea's voice was unusually cold. "I'm also sorry about the party, Grace, but I'm seriously concerned about Hannah. Could we please talk to Clay and Carrie?"

"Carrie's at a yacht club dance and Clay's upstairs in his room," said Ian. "They acted perfectly normal at dinner." He grunted and added, "Moody and sullen."

"They acted oddly," countered Grace.

"Goddamn it," said Ian. "That's become normal around here."

"Wait, please Ian," she said calmly. "Sit down. Neither Carrie nor Clay mentioned anything at dinner about finding a passage. Despite their fear of your monstrous rage if you knew about their explorations, they would have told us when they first came into the house if Hannah was hurt. They adore her."

"Grace," said Ian. "Do my children really see me as a monster?" He looked dazed, and slowly sat.

"The afternoon of Carrie's accident in the cave," said Emily, "after the ambulance took Carrie and Hannah to the hospital, Colin made us lunch. While we ate, he told stories about how rumrunners used secret passages along the coast during prohibition to unload their booze. He promised Clay they'd come over here and look around when Carrie recovered. When I brought over Grace's library book this afternoon they were searching the house. It was just a game."

Grace shivered in spite of the warm night. "I knew nothing about this."

Graham stood up. "It sounds like hokey pirate stuff, but I saw those old architectural drawings and knowing the history of this coast, it's very possible. Ian, do you remember if such a passage exists? Could she be trapped somewhere between the sea and the house?"

"For God's sake," said Mac. "Get Clay down here right away."

Clay, extricated from television, looked both nervous over the attention and fearful of reprisal. The circle of sober faces— and his father's steely eye—crushed any excitement. Grace handed him a plate with a large piece of cake and a fork.

"Clay," said Mac. "What happened this afternoon? Emily said that when she left, you were looking for some passage from the house down to the cliff."

"It wasn't in the house," answered Clay. "We found it under a tarp and an old lawnmower below that storage room in the back of the garage. There's a trapdoor in the floor with steps going down to a dirt tunnel." He finished his cake but kept his eyes on the plate.

"Go on," urged Mac.

"Hannah carried the big flashlight. It needs a new battery, and she went first. The path slopes down all the way, not steep, but we had to bend over. It was damp and creepy. Hannah went around a bend and came to this stinking pile of dead rats washed in by the storm tide. She said we couldn't go any farther. The cave-in is still blocking the far end, and it was really dark. She made us turn around and go back. Carrie was scared shi—uh, really scared—and the stink was awful. That's it. That was all." He shrugged away the anticlimax to their adventure.

"You all came back to the house," Mac asked. "Hannah too?"

Clay nodded. "She didn't come in with us. Mom's car was in the drive and Hannah didn't want us to get in trouble so she made us go inside and keep it our secret for a while. She made us promise not to go back alone. Boy, no chance."

"Did you see Hannah leave for the cottage?"

Clay looked at the cake.

"There's more, Clay, when you finish your story."

"No," he answered. "She told us that she would close down the trap door and leave everything the way we found it. What's the matter?"

Ian looked frightened. He came over and rested his hand on his son's shoulder.

"Hannah hasn't come home yet and we're all worried. I wish you had asked me about that tunnel before you decided to explore. Your uncle Colin and I discovered the trapdoor in the old tack room long ago when we were children. I don't know why he didn't tell you when you had lunch together. The cave-in that day wasn't the first rock-fall down there, and your grandfather forbid us ever to go near it. He faced his wife. "I'm sorry Grace. If I hadn't decided to clean out that room this spring they never would have found the trapdoor. For years it was safely buried under old trunks and furniture."

Clay started to cry. "I'm sorry, Dad. First Carrie getting hurt and now something's happened to Hannah. It's all my fault." He wiped his sleeve over his tears.

"No, Clay. It's not your fault." He sliced another piece of cake and put it on the boy's plate. "Take it upstairs now, and don't watch TV all night. And don't worry," he added gently, "We'll find Hannah."

As soon as the slider closed behind Clay, Thea reached for Emperor's harness and started for the garage.

"I'll come with you," said Phil. "But we need a good flashlight." He felt Emily's hand squeeze hard on his forearm.

"I saw that cave-in when Carrie was hurt—it looked forbidding even on that sunny day, and I'm not the adventurous type. I'd rather not go down there again." She stood rigid and Phil put his arm around her.

"No need to, Em. The best thing you and Grace could do is to stay here and finish off the champagne."

Mac spoke firmly. "You too, Thea, please stay here. The fewer of us in that tunnel the safer." Emily lifted the champagne bottle over their glasses. "I agree. We ladies will stay here and drink to that."

The men followed Ian inside and waited while he rummaged in the emergency drawer in the pantry, handing out flashlights.

"The big heavy duty one is missing," he said.

Out in the storage room, Mac pushed away the mower and pulled up the burlap tarp. The light shone on the trap door with its metal bolts shot tight through their hasps. Stuart ignored Mac's cautionary plea about fingerprints and slid back the bolts.

"We don't have time to find gloves. If Hannah's down there, someone locked her in." He hauled up on the ring, and sucked in his breath as their lights flashed over the crumpled body lying at the bottom of the steps.

"My God," gasped Phil, and ran back towards the kitchen. "I'll call 911."

Mac followed Stuart down the wooden steps. He knelt over Hannah and felt the faint pulse under her bloody temple. Stuart crouched silently beside him and reached toward her awkwardly twisted ankle.

"Don't touch her," snapped Mac, then added more gently, "She's unconscious and its best to let the medics lift her out."

Graham took off his jacket and carefully laid it over her body. "It can't hurt to keep her warm."

Mac stood and flashed his light over the walls and dirt floor. As he started down the narrow incline leading toward the sea, the putrid stench hit him. When he rounded the bend where Hannah must have stopped the children, his light caught the hideous bundle and he nearly retched. How in God's name had she managed to get Clay and Carrie back up the passage without revealing what she'd seen? He touched the decomposed body with the toe of his shoe. The ME won't like this one, he thought.

Mac's legs felt unsteady on his return up the passage. Phil was back from phoning for the ambulance and Mac saw them all hunched in a vigil over Hannah's body. He tried to compose himself.

They heard the rising wail of the ambulance siren hee-haw down the compound road.

"Someone tell them to bring down two stretchers—and a body bag," Mac said. "I've found Robin—or what's left of her."

CHAPTER 34

At Pen Bay Hospital early the next morning, Mac stood with Watty in front of the nurse's station waiting for the starchy bosomed beauty to notice him. He produced a gentle cough and she raised large lavender eyes from her clipboard. She smiled up at him and exhaled a soft, "Yesss?"

"Hannah Packwood," he said. "I need to speak to her. Very briefly," he added and smiled back, showing his police department shield above the edge of the counter.

Her tiny white cap was perched on a halo of auburn curls and, although her lips pursed in momentary disapproval, they quickly resumed rosebud proportions.

"I'm so sorry, but Mr. Hobart is with her," she purred on a quick southern breath. "He just badgered 'til the doctor gave in and fixed to let him see her."

Mac waited for her to flutter her lashes, but she didn't. Instead she checked over his shoulder that the corridor was empty, and whispered, "She's just out of ICU. Poor girl, such a terrible thing and all. If you can find out anything, anything that would help find the awful person who attacked her, well—. But it'd be much better if you came back later."

"Miss—" he checked the nameplate pinned to the seraphim's breast, "Kendall. By later this morning we'll be a lot farther away from nabbing the alleged perpetrator."

She smiled and the lovely eyes shaded to blue.

"Come on," she drawled. "I thought y'all only talked like that on TV." She stretched "y'all" into a four-syllable word.

Miss Kendall examined her watch, gave him another sweet smile and conceded. "I'll let you see her for a few minutes, but you act sensible, hear?" She attempted severity. "And you must leave the minute you see her flaggin'. I'll come checkin' on you."

"My solemn promise," he said and touched his heart. What, he wondered, had brought this luscious Georgia peach to Maine?

They followed Miss Kendall down the hushed, waxed corridor. Both policemen had great respect for Pen Bay. If you were sick enough to leave home, this was the place to be. It held an excellent medical reputation without suffering the impersonal red tape innate to most hospital bureaucracies. The staff was cheerful, dependable, and—in the form of Miss Kendall—restorative.

The nurse nodded an okay as Mac and Watty identified themselves to the police guard outside Hannah's room. She peeked on tiptoes through a small window in the door, tapped softly, and pushed it open. Stuart looked up from the chair he'd pulled close to the raised rails of the bed.

Mac's first thought was that everything was too white. Hannah's head was bound in a white wrap, and her body made a small, mummy-like mound under the taut white covers. Even her face, that a week ago had been summer-tanned, looked bleached. Her left arm was strapped to a brace, and a slow drip through transparent tubes fed a needle taped inside her elbow. Stu sat silently beside the trolley of hanging bottles and cradled her free hand in his. Miss Kendall gently shooed him out, but on his way to the door he stopped and spoke softly to Mac. "I need to talk to you when you're through here. I'll wait outside."

Only one of Hannah's eyes showed below the bandage wrapping her temples, but it recognized him and she encouraged him with a small smile.

"Thanks for finding me, Mac. I'm lucky you're Thea's friend." Her words were thick and almost inaudible, and with his finger to his lip, he motioned her not to speak.

"The nurse will give us only a few minutes and she warned us severely against causing you to wilt. Hannah, I have a gut feeling about who's behind all this, but no evidence. Did you see anyone before you were hit? Just a yes or no or a name will do, Hannah. We'll hear the whole story when you're stronger."

Hannah raised her free hand but it fell back limply of its own weight.

"Graham," she said, but at Mac's shocked expression she shook her head. She winced in pain and both Watty and Mac winced in sympathy.

"It's okay," she said. "My mouth is dry and my tongue feels huge and fuzzy from something they gave me, but it doesn't hurt to talk if I don't move my head." She jiggled the plastic drip. "Thanks to all these nice drugs."

Slowly and cotton-mouthed, she explained. "I hoped—thought—it was Graham, and that he'd come to help me. I'd made sure that the kids were back in the house. It was getting late and Thea said she'd send him over if I didn't show up. She said it as a joke, but after Carrie's accident, I hoped she meant it."

"Did you think it was Graham?"

"A voice called my name, but it was raspy and unfamiliar. When I turned around, whoever it was shone a light in my eyes and blinded me. And then—whack."

Despite her denial of hurting, Hannah looked spent and Mac touched his fingers to her cheek.

"Hey, no more now. We'll sort it out later. You rest and get well."

"Mac," she said sadly. "What about Robin? What happened?"

Only Miss Kendall's brisk entry rescued him from an unpleasant answer.

Outside the hospital, Stuart was waiting for Mac and Watty. They stood by the open doors of the police car while it released the trapped summer heat.

"I think Hannah guessed who attacked her," said Mac, "but didn't see or hear enough to be sure and doesn't want to think about it while the drugs keep her fuzzy." He nodded over his shoulder. "At least she's safe in there. Absolutely no boxes of poisoned chocs or explosive gift baskets—nothing is to be delivered or brought in. And no more visitors. That's official. A broken ankle and a busted head." He stared absently beyond them at the sea rescue helicopter waiting on its circular landing pad. "She wasn't meant to be found for a long time. Not until too late."

"She's lucky we did find her," said Stuart. "The doctor said a few more hours and who knows. The result of that kind of bleeding into the brain can be fatal. Our murderer is a real hit artist. According to the coroner's report, it's what killed Beatrice Swann. Mrs. Swann died of cerebral hemorrhage before the gas hit her."

Mac looked back at the mellow brick of the low, rambling hospital shimmering in the heat. It did not look like a fortress. He hoped that Hannah would be as safe as he promised. He slid into his seat as Watty started the engine and switched on the air-conditioning. Stuart leaned over to stop the rising glass of Mac's window.

"Can we can assume that Hannah was attacked because she interfered with the murderer's original scheme?"

"It looks that way," said Mac. "But who can guess what happens when a killer's plan goes wrong."

"Logically—but allowing that murderers aren't always logical—Ian's next in line," said Stuart. "If he hasn't figured that out, someone ought to warn him."

Mac adjusted the blast of cold air coming from the louvered vent. "I need to think this through, and we've got desk work piled up back at the station. I'll call Ian tonight or early tomorrow before he leaves for work, warn him to be careful."

A breath of rotten fish wafted from behind him and he slammed his hand against the dashboard. "Christ! The suitcase. We left it in the bushes at the Swanns!"

Watty looked nervously at his watch. "It's an hour out there and back."

"Hell, no one saw us with it," said Mac. "It was dark and I pushed it behind some shrubbery before we went around back. I'm sorry, Watty. Because of the search and commotion over Hannah, I forgot all about it. Even if Robin bought the case in Australia, I hoped one of them would verify that the handwriting in the diary was hers."

"It's well hidden in the bushes," said Stuart. "Leave it. One of us can go out and get it in the morning. We've been up all night and I don't know about you, but I'm beat."

Watty combed his bristling mustache with his fingertips. "Mac, I'll go out and get it if you say," he offered, "but Jessie and the kids are waiting. I sort of promised I'd get off early and take them to the river for a last summer swim. If I call this late and put them off, on a hot day like this, well, I'm a dead man."

"It can wait until tomorrow," said Mac.

That night at the station, the late duty officer swore as the phone rang for the third time. He slammed down the cardboard cover of the pizza box. Pepperoni, garlic and green pepper with extra cheese. He hated cold pizza, except for breakfast.

The voice on the line was tinny with distance. "Sydney Police here. Calling direct because our Fax is down and we know you're waiting for information on the Swann case. Can you connect me or get word to Detective MacNeill? A young lady came in this morning. Up from Geelong, south of Melbourne. Very pregnant, very frightened. Says she's Keith Watkin's wife and her Dad's going to kill them both if we don't find him and bring him back to support her. She says Keith told her he had gone to the U. S. to interview for a big music job and would send for her when he had work," the Sydney officer chuckled. "She doesn't believe him, rightly so. The fellow sounds a real 'ocker. We're tracking him."

CHAPTER 35

Mac was at his desk by eight the next morning. He wanted to catch Ian before he left the harbor for Camden. Ian would no doubt find an excuse not to meet him at the Swann's offices. It would not be expedient for a police officer to pass by his phalanx of curious secretaries or the discrete but questioning eyes of associates. Maybe this evening, in the privacy of his home, he'd cooperate and cough up some answers. Besides, he had to go out there after work and drag that damn suitcase out of the bushes.

While he waited for Watty to bring their coffee from the canteen, Betty, the dispatcher, buzzed him. He could almost smell the Juicy Fruit through the phone.

"A man called Phil rang up real early," she said through the wad tucked temporarily between her gums. "He wants you to call the rectory office over in Elmore Harbor as soon as you get in. Said you'd know who he was."

"Thanks Betty." He hung up and loosened his tie. The office held yesterday's stale heat and he envied Watty's picnic last night on the river with his family. As he reached for the phone, it rang beneath his hand.

"Me again," said Betty. "A Mrs. Grace Swann is on the line. She says she'll only talk to you personally and she sounds real upset."

"Thanks, Betty."

"Detective MacNeill."

Grace sounded jumpy. "I'm sorry to bother you at work, Mac, and I won't keep you . . ."

"No bother, Grace, what's up? You and the kids okay?"

"Oh, I'm not calling about us, we're fine. Everyone's horrified, of course, over that vicious attack on Hannah, but I'm calling about Ian. I'm worried because there's something odd going on. About his car, I mean."

While Grace stammered on, Mac accepted a plastic cup of coffee from Watty and poured it into his ceramic mug. It was already lukewarm.

"I realize that Ian's the last one, direct Swann I mean," said Grace. "I'm sorry. It's just an ominous feeling I have, and it's certainly not fair to blame something so dreadful on a person without any proof. It's my own suspicion, of course, but I'm sure I would have noticed if his headlights had been on all night. Ian left the car in the drive, you see, after he brought Carrie home from the party. I was up several times during the night—all that champagne I guess—" He heard her nervous giggle, then she went on. "They would have shone into our bedroom window. And then when Mrs. Pink's car broke down this morning, Emily brought her here from the village and offered to take Ian to work. She said she had an early errand in Camden. So what could I say when Ian was shouting at me in front of everyone?"

Grace's voice rose. She was babbling now and when her voice faltered, he interrupted.

"Grace," he said calmly. "I share your concern over Ian, and it's important that I come out and talk to him this morning before he goes anywhere. Now, take your time and slowly go over again this business about the cars." He heard Grace take a deep, composing breath, then begin again. "Ian's car. He left it out front on the drive last night. Well, it wouldn't start this morning, so he was in a rage. He insisted on taking my car and ordered me to call the garage mechanic from the village to come out and fix his. But I also had an early meeting and argued that my commitments were just as important as his. We had rather a row over it. I'm afraid neither of us are in the best of tempers early in the morning, especially since I've been trying to be less of a doormat." She sounded unsure.

"I understand, go on."

"Then Emily showed up with Mrs. Pink. It's my day for Mrs. Pink to clean. Emily said she had spent the night with Phil, and she'd had a bout of food poisoning during the night, but it was out of her system and she thought fresh air would do her good. She was on her way to the village for the paper when she came upon Mrs. Pink. The woman had run out of gas—she drives without her glasses you know, deadly—she can't see the road much less the gas gauge. Emily offered to get her own car and give Mrs. Pink a lift here."

Mac tried to sort out the multiple car situation. He uttered a non-committal, 'Uh huh,' and urged Grace to continue.

"Well, Ian and I stopped quarreling. We were all standing out in the drive. Emily had arrived with Mrs. Pink. You can't have an argument in front of that woman without the whole village buzzing over your imminent divorce. Then Emily reached through the open window of Ian's car. She said that he had left his lights on and maybe didn't notice when he came out this morning because of the bright sunshine. She said that they were probably on all night and had run down the battery. He doesn't have the newer model that turns them off automatically after you stop the engine," Grace added in irritation. "Ian knew that he should have replaced that battery ages ago, but didn't bother to take the time. He ignores these inconvenient problems until they become momentous and then blames someone else. Well, he stormed and swore that he had not left the lights on, and, as I told you, I honestly think I would have noticed if he had. He said he had meant to go out later and put the car in the garage, but because of the upset over finding Hannah, he forgot."

Mac interrupted again. "Grace, please have everyone wait until I get out there. Tell Emily and Ian that it's very important that I talk to them. Tell them I'm on my way. And don't call the mechanic yet."

For a moment the line was silent, then Grace sounded anxious. "Oh dear. I can't. Ian and Emily, I mean. They've left. As I said, the reason for our row was Ian's appointment in Camden, and he was simply furious. So when Emily told him to calm down and offered him a lift, he rushed off with her."

"Mac." Betty poked her head around his door. She looked grim and the bulge of gum was gone. "Miss Packwood's holding on the other line. She's calling from the hospital and sounds real upset too. Says she has to talk to you."

Mac punched the blinking button. "Hannah? Hold on a minute." He retrieved the waiting Grace.

"Grace. Relax now. We'll get to Ian and straighten this out. I'll call you back as soon as I can." He punched Hannah's line.

"Oh, Mac," she was almost crying. "Maybe I'm still thinking on drugs, but I made them let me call you. I can't stop seeing Robin's body in that passage and remembering some bits and pieces. She was acting strangely. I remember their voices in the drive, after the drinks party before Bea's birthday dinner."

"Who was acting strangely?"

"Emily. Then she was gone so long fetching Robin from the airport. What if she did meet her and brought her back? Robin would have wanted to wash up after the trip and change her clothes for the party. Because of the surprise, Emily might have taken her over to Ian's. Maybe after they drove into the garage Emily just—" She left the sentence unfinished. "She was strong and fit and Robin's small. She could have knocked her out with something heavy and dragged Robin's body down into that passage. She could have bolted Robin in—trapped her, just like me." He heard a sobbing intake of breath. "I hope I'm wrong. Em is my friend." He heard her quavery, humorless laugh and the prophetic echo of Grace's words. "Please look out for Ian, he's the only one left."

Mac dialed the rectory office and Phil's prim secretary, answered after one ring.

"He left early for his hospice clinic at Pen Bay Hospital, Detective MacNeill, but asked that you be sure and phone him there right away." Mac copied down the clinic's number.

He called out to Watty, who came around the corner from his own cubicle. After a quick recount of his conversations, he motioned for his partner to pick up the extension.

"I'm returning Phil's call and it'll save time if you hear it first hand."

Watty picked up the phone as Phil came on the line. He sounded exhausted.

"It's Mac, Phil," he said. "I'm at the station, what's up?"

"We've got to stop her, Mac." There were background voices and Phil's tone was urgent and low, as if shielding his conversation from curious ears. "I'm worried that Emily needs help. Something's wrong. I know she's been depressed these past weeks, living up in that big house alone. She's been coming to the rectory most nights for dinner, and after coffee last night, she suddenly got edgy and started going on about the drop-off above the quarry along the bypass. How perfect it would be. She wouldn't say what it was perfect for, but I thought she might be talking about suicide. I couldn't hold her attention and she wouldn't explain. Suddenly she rushed into the bathroom and was violently sick. She seemed better when she came out, and she joked about it being the normal reaction to my poisonous cooking. Then she started to shiver and shake and began retching again. We'd eaten the same food and I wasn't sick. All I could think of was Colin's poisoning that night at the Grange Hall. She looked awful, but she calmed down and insisted it was the summer plague going around the harbor. She wanted to go home, but I insisted that she stay with me and I bullied her into bed. I tried to stay awake and sit up with her, but I'd gone fishing at five that morning and we'd had a hefty brandy with our coffee. I couldn't keep my eyes open. I fell asleep on the couch."

"Go on," said Mac.

"I woke up about three a.m. Emily was up and wandering around; disoriented and holding her stomach. I remembered a bottle of paregoric left in the medicine cabinet, mixed a dose and made her drink it. I should have given her the stuff earlier because after a while she said she felt fine. She seemed exhausted and wouldn't talk, but she looked better. She said she just wanted to rest and I rationalized that maybe it was food poisoning after all. I left at six to get to the hospital in time for my clinic, and when

I checked on her, she mumbled that she'd be okay. That she'd stay in bed and sleep it off." He paused and Mac could hear the anxiety rise again in his voice.

"I've been calling the rectory all morning but there's no answer. Maybe she's sleeping too soundly to hear the phone, but we've had some odd conversations lately, and I think she's got more problems than a stomach bug. Mac, I'm worried that she needs some help. Especially after her ramblings last night about the drop-off by the quarry. A few others have used that quarry pit to end their problems. Can you help?"

"Phil," said Mac, "you are right to be worried."

Mac braced his feet against the floor as Watty peeled the squad car out of the parking lot behind the courthouse. The police siren scattered the morning traffic along the narrow road that by-passed the main route through town, and the flashing strobes revolving on the roof out-glared the August sun.

They were heading toward the granite chasm quarried out by the sprawling cement factory that coated the south of town with its dust. Gulls squealed and circled above the stinking, disused pits that now served as garbage and waste fills. Mac pictured the ragged snags of stone that jutted from its steep sides and the low cement buttress that barely separated it from road level.

In the front seat of Emily's old Saab, Ian was fussing among the papers in his briefcase when she made a sharp right turn, without stopping, onto Route l.

"For Christ's sake, Emily, you went through the stoplight! You're driving like a maniac! Please slow down."

She paid him no attention. She turned sharply again onto the Rockland by-pass that was the short cut behind town to Camden, throwing him against the passenger door. She smiled to herself, recalling the idiot officer who had given her a speeding ticket here this spring. Then she frowned. If he'd arrested her and given her refuge, she'd be secure in some genteel prison and saved from all this trouble. Now the summer was gone, and with it, all of them.

Like the scavenger gulls that cawed and wheeled in the stinking haze ahead of them, she and Ian would fly and scream to their end. She giggled like a young girl. But she was no longer that young girl, and thought sadly of her lost baby. Only it would be grown up now. She'd discovered the secret they had hidden from her. Last spring, when she delivered Bea's tax returns to Stu, she had found and read those papers in the old lawyer's files. Stuart's father, that stuffy old man, and Bea had stolen her baby from her. They stole it from her. And they gave it away.

Ian rescued his falling briefcase and glared at Emily. The verbal outrage he was going to let loose froze in his throat. He watched her arms stretch rigid and her knuckles turn white on the steering wheel. Her body pressed against the back of her seat and her foot jammed the accelerator to the floor. He spoke calmly.

"Emily, for God's sake. Slow down. What the hell?"

Comprehension compounded his horror. He saw her eyes widen, and a grimace contort her face. She was mad. She planned to kill them both. Quickly he lifted the solid case from his lap and smashed its sharp corner into the side of her head. With the smooth coordination of a past athlete, he released his seat belt, kicked her right foot off the gas pedal and grabbed the steering wheel. But they'd gained too much speed and he couldn't reach the brake pedal. The car was out of control. His weight crushed her body against the door and pressing the horn, he tried to steer the hurtling car away from the low curve of concrete coming toward them. She fought and bit him like an animal as they careened back and forth across the narrow road. She kicked savagely at his ankle as he tried to work his foot onto the brake. He stared with sickening fear at the road ahead, and realized there was more chance of meeting an oncoming car than going over the edge.

Emily stiffened against him and uttered a chilling howl. Her hands left the steering wheel to cover her face and she slumped sideways like a limp child. He grabbed the wheel and pulled hard to the right, avoiding by inches a truck rounding the bend ahead of them. Its driver flayed the air with his horn and in its receding echo the Saab lost its momentum and slowed to a stop up a steep grassy lawn two feet from a small, neat sign that read: FOR SALE—SEWING MACHINE $75.00.

Dry-mouthed and unable to move, Ian began shaking. He heard the sirens, and in moments the flashing cruiser hemmed them in. Mac and Watty slammed their doors and raced toward him.

"Man," said Mac as they helped him out. "We were behind you. You are some lucky guy."

"And some driver," added Watty swiping his dripping face with his sleeve.

Ian couldn't speak. A young woman ran from the house and stood wadding up her apron. Ian's knees buckled. And he sank to the grass.

The ambulance arrived and the attendants lifted Emily's unconscious body onto the stretcher. The squawking radio inside the patrol car was the only sound. The circling strobes still revolved brighter than the day.

CHAPTER 36

It was Clay's thirteenth birthday and they had gathered to celebrate, for the last time that summer, on Ian and Grace's patio above the ocean. The September cookout in his honor was a tradition that marked the bitter end of summer, and his parents resolved to put the brutal events of the past weeks behind them and make Clay's birthday a happy one. Grace recalled the morning Hannah had delivered the mail with the ugly card, the day it had all started.

Cool nights and a subtle impotence in the midday sun foreshadowed fall but had perked up the lobelia and alyssum overflowing the terra cotta pots. Long trumpets of white *nicotiana* sweetened the evening air. Above them, a gentle breeze stirred the pines and kept the last of the mosquitoes away. Smoke billowed from the grill where Ian jostled and sauced chicken pieces and steaks.

Twirling the end of a carrot stick in some green-flecked diet dip she had concocted, Grace saw Carrie crunch, reserve comment, and turn to regard her young brother. "Nice specs Clay."

He grinned and adjusted the steel rims of the Austrian Carrera frames, a gift from his father. Clay had not made his anticipated summer fortune because of the embargo placed on Luther's boat and had accepted Ian's peace offering a little warily.

They all accepted the new Ian warily. After his near fatal drive along the quarry road, he'd surfaced as a 'born again' father—and husband. Nan and most of the other summer guests had departed for less troubled and more glamorous climes, and Grace and the rest of them viewed Ian's determined efforts to win back their support with approval—but justified skepticism.

Grace saw that Clay was happy that Carrie was happy. He'd surprised her with a batch of her favorite cookies to take away to school tomorrow. "You'll think those black bits are raisins," he said when he handed her the carefully taped package, "but they're dead flies."

Lucy had returned from California, and Grace had watched her daughter and best friend lug their beach towels and picnic coolers to escape to their favorite seclusion. They would lie on the flat sun warmed granite, reunited and immersed in the gossip of conquests and devastations. Grace imagined Carrie's account of her romantic diversions would pale in comparison with Lucy's beach boy intrigues. She'd told Lucy that sailing was a combination of total boredom and physical discomfort.

When not with Lucy, she'd worked most days with Hannah and Thea, cleaning out the old greenhouse.

"Mom. I'll miss them more than anyone."

Grace tried not to be hurt, because while they worked, Carrie said that their talks helped purge her of the summer's havoc.

Tonight, everyone's culinary contributions were laid out on a long trestle picnic table. Hannah, rid of the alarming head bandages and hobbled only by her crutches and a hinged ankle cast, admired the artistic ribbons of basil that she'd snipped over a platter of Ox-heart tomatoes.

"Garden tomatoes must be cosseted in Maine, and this old-fashioned variety breeds true from seed saved year to year," she announced. "I brought them from home. And they are far better tasting than most of the new touted hybrids.

"A classic Maine gustable!" called a voice behind them. Graham dramatically uncovered and presented on his raised palm, a magnificent blueberry pie. Thirteen candles were tucked into its lattice crust.

"I baked it myself."

"Hmm." Grace smiled. "In that crinkly aluminum pan?"

"I only said baked."

"Like Vaughn's 'fishin' not ketchin'," said Clay, reaching between them for a handful of chips. "No problem. I'll eat anybody's blueberry pie."

Ian served Grace from the grill, and they touched and spoke without their habitual antagonism. They would both try harder to pull the family back together, thought Grace.

Carrie heaped her own plate with everything. "My last home cooked meal," she lamented.

Grace had gone with her to visit the new school where the student guide warned them of the mysterious and unspeakable food that would appear the day after the parents left. The excitement of shopping and packing with her daughter, the anticipation of a new stage in life, palled before the solemn fact that Carrie was actually leaving home. Tomorrow. Her throat closed and her eyes welled.

They laid their plates aside, and Ian began the ceremony, easing the cork from a bottle of champagne. He caught the overflowing bubbles in the proper glass and presented it to Clay. "Welcome to pubescence," he toasted, "may this thirteenth year be your luckiest."

"And a happier year for us all," added Stuart.

In the kitchen, Doris and Stella nattered at each other. Traditionally in charge of Clay's birthday cake, they produced at his request every year a dark marvel of fudge icing surrounding thinner, less important layers of chocolate cake.

Applause greeted their presentation and, in one fierce gust, Clay extinguished the candles.

"Champagne ladies?" asked Ian. Doris and Stella tittered as he filled their glasses. Clay opened his presents and Grace helped everyone to seconds.

"You'll be home for Christmas before you can believe it," comforted Hannah, as Carrie hugged and kissed them good-bye.

Carrie sniffed. "How can I be homesick when I haven't even left home yet?"

"I remember my first time away," said Hannah. "And if any snotty upper classmates intimidate you, just imagine them in their underwear."

They all laughed and Carrie left them to attach herself to the telephone for one final marathon with Lucy. While Doris and Stella cleared plates and dishes, Clay collected his gifts and repeated polite thanks before disappearing for a last orgy of television.

Beyond the harbor, the sun layered orange and crimson bands that underlined thin lines of tomorrow's fair-weather clouds. They sat relaxed in sated somnolence as the twilight paled away. August's frantic racket of cicadas no longer competed with conversation, but had slowed by chill to a lethargic, rhythmic rasp. The peaceful evening's quiet was broken by the squitter and plop of frogs in the lily pond. Grace thought of Bea and wondered if any of them sensed ghosts among them of that earlier birthday dinner.

As if reading her mind, Ian broke the silence.

"She tried to kill me," he said in disbelief. He sounded vacant and ran his hand over his face. "After the way we all treated her when she first came here as a kid, I can understand Emily's bitter revenge. All that hatred she kept hidden for so long under that civil facade. The deception over the baby must have been the last straw."

He looked across at his wife. Grace could tell by the anguish in his voice how difficult it was for him to recognize and admit any blame or responsibility. He would have to learn, she thought.

"I'm alive because of Phil and Grace, and you, MacNeill." He turned toward Mac with none of his previous disdain. "Thank you for your discretion while scuffling around our family skeletons." He laughed but his face stayed solemn. "I probably don't deserve your discretion—or being alive. You'll have to accept me as one of the family's major warts."

Grace broke their embarrassed silence.

"Stuart," she asked. "How did Emily find out about her baby?"

"From Dad's files. She came in to town this April to deliver the tax returns I'd prepared for Bea, and I left her alone with coffee in Dad's old office while I hassled some problem with a client on the phone. While I was gone, she poked through his file cabinets and found the hospital records. Dad had used his power of attorney to release the baby. Not only did she discover that it wasn't stillborn as they'd told her, but that Bea, with my father's help, took the law into their own hands and gave the baby away for voluntary adoption. No names were on the papers, only the docket number. It was handled without money, and probably illegally. Just an anonymous infant given to close friends who couldn't have children. Dad and Bea both decided that because her husband was dying of heart disease and Robin was still a toddler, it was not a good time to bring a seventeen year old's illegitimate child into the house. Colin was eleven and Ian, you were almost nine. Emily was disgraced and humiliated. She had lost her father and mother, been seduced by an older man. Though she never would tell us by whom, I guessed it was the last of Diana's lovers. Even while lying about ill, she was an attractive woman to so many men. Emily was told she should be glad that she had produced a stillborn baby. Bea comforted and protected her, promised to keep her secret, but at the same time exploited her as Robin's unpaid nanny."

The light was gone and the evening cooled. Stuart shifted in his chair. His voice in the darkness, unfolding Bea's tragic story, held them silent and united in compassion.

"Bea blamed her sister, Diana, as an unfit mother to Emily. She'd insisted it was Diana who was responsible for Em's 'disgrace.' I still wonder if Diana really did drift into a natural death. Was that a dramatic invention Bea chose to cover up for Diana's suicide? We'll never know, but Bea, too, may have aided that. Sleeping pills, abetted by a convenient carafe of brandy always on Diana's night table. When Emily's pregnancy became too obvious and she was sent home from her proper Boston school, Bea convinced her that it was despair over Em's disgraceful condition had caused her mother's death."

"My mother was an evil manipulator," said Ian.

Stuart poured himself more brandy. "I feel guilty over Emily's mistreatment by my father. I didn't know about the adoption until I found the papers she'd hurriedly returned to his files. Dad never mentioned any of this to me. Could I have stopped her final rage if I'd known earlier?" He looked plaintively at Mac. "I don't know. Dad was a taciturn duffer. I can imagine how easy it was for Bea to swear him to silence. After he died, I was so bogged down trying to rejuvenate the practice that I didn't take time to sort through those old files as I should have. I've no excuse. We didn't help Emily."

"I never knew about her baby," said Ian. He sounded confused. "Colin and I were away at prep school and then college while Robin was growing up. We came home for summers to the big house and I remember it was always filled with guests. Mother had so many amusing friends, eager to escape from the city. Emily was just someone in the background. Like an old-maid Cinderella sister, she was always there whenever we came home. Running and fetching for Bea."

"What a stifled life," said Hannah. "Yet she was kind and sympathetic to Thea and me. She acted so normal and—funny. Stuart, can you imagine her feelings that morning after that discovery in your father's office?"

"She was a good actress," he said. "When I came back and handed her Bea's tax work, she was waiting there, cool and calm."

Phil shivered. "I watched her change. Toward the end of summer, when she first began to need more of me, I was flattered and hopeful because Emily wasn't the dependent type. That night at the rectory, before she went after Ian, she was sick and psychotic, and I didn't know how to react." The grief in his voice was painful.

"They've shown leniency," said Mac. "She'll spend the rest of her days at an excellent psychiatric institution. If there is such a thing."

"She murdered three people," said Graham coldly. "The woman methodically planned the cold-blooded annihilation of the entire Swann family. Hannah hoped I was coming to rescue her from that sea passage, but it was Emily who followed her. And left her to die. She'd hidden Robin there, either dead or dying, after picking her up at the airport, and guessed that Hannah had found her body. She also knew about the tunnel from family stories."

Graham continued his dispassionate recital. "And that night, after the birthday dinner, she followed Bea down to the greenhouse. We all heard Thea's plan to come back alone later and light the smokers, and she hoped Bea's body would wait unseen in that dim corner. She was lucky that Thea did not bring the dog." He leaned towards them across the table, and added grimly, "A lot of murderers are lucky. Then she went after Colin. Hannah said they were missing their toxicology manual. Emily must have taken it."

They sat in the cold flicker of candlelight, pervaded by Emily's mad storm of revenge.

"She sent us those venomous cards," said Grace, "and must have left the message that made Stuart miss the party. She must have worried that he might interfere with her plans." Grace sighed and went on, "We both shared the ugly effects of dysfunctional childhoods, and I can understand her sick anger. Emily focused on destroying the family that stole her baby and made her a lifelong drudge." Grace reached for the champagne bottle on the flagstones beside her chair and emptied it into her glass. "As for her madness, well," she gave an unlady-like snort. "There's a genetic weirdness that's bound to surface in families when you consider our Bostonian inbreeding. God help our children." She raised her emptied glass. "Time won't heal this summer, but it might deaden it."

Thea roused her sleeping dog.

"Can I offer a ride to your cottage?" asked Mac.

"Thanks," she said. "But I need to walk."

They all needed time to accept the judgment of criminal insanity, to remember the real Emily, not the automaton she was now.

Mac retrieved Robin's battered suitcase from the shrubbery and tossed it into the back of his car before sliding into the driver's seat next to Stuart.

"Whether driven by genes or revenge, Graham's right," he said. "Emily killed three people, and tried for five. I spoke of leniency, for Phil's sake, but I don't share your guilty sympathy. Ian and Hannah are damn lucky to be alive." He paused and gave Stuart a sharp look. "And speaking of guilt, don't burden yourself with your father's. I bet he and Bea thought they were doing the right thing. Jesus, think what a miserable person Hannah might be now if she'd grown up torn between the seventeen-year-old Emily and Bea instead of the decent, loving Packwoods?"

He started the car. "Are you going to tell Hannah that her mother tried to murder her?"

"No," said Stuart. "Emily never knew that Hannah was the baby they took from her." He stretched his seat belt into its catch. "Emily lost control of her emotional baggage the night she murdered Bea. Here was her Aunt, organizing a happy reunion with her daughter—something Emily would never know. No, the truth can be too cruel. Lawyer's and policemen keep a lot of secrets. As far as Hannah's concerned, the Packwoods are her parents. We'll let sleeping dogs lie."

Mac grinned. "Unusually kind logic from a lawyer. But you're right. I hope Hannah never knows."

EPILOGUE

September's full moon had drawn the tide to an ebb that allowed Grace and Hannah to ford the sand bar between the harbor and Southern Island. The noon sun shone hot enough to make them sweat under the foul weather gear they wore for berry picking. Hot enough to make the shallow water with its skirts of mussel-weighted sea wrack inviting. Crossing the narrow spit was worth the effort. Out here, the unravaged patches grew the sweetest and ripest blackberries. Thick as thumbs.

Protected by their yellow vinyl, Hannah waded into the middle of the briars and began dropping berries into the coffee can that hung round her neck on a piece of clothesline. It was an invention that left both hands free.

"There's nothing like bramble jelly on your toast in winter," she said. "A taste of summer when you need it most."

"And there's something soothing about jelly-making," agreed Grace. "All those hot jars and purple stains. I love that sweet boiling down smell and sieving out the seeds."

"Not all the seeds," said Hannah. "You need a little busywork for your tongue. Her hair caught in an overhead wand of thorns and Grace untangled it. They picked and talked, emptying their filled neck cans into bigger pails.

"We'll take some jelly to Emily," she said. "Even if she won't recognize us."

There was a relaxed friendship between them. Hannah sensed a new contentment within Grace. She had ceased to anguish over every real and imagined slight. Without constant anxiety, she didn't need the solace of eating. Her friend was slimmer.

Hannah stopped picking and arched her neck toward the cloudless sky. "What a lovely end-of-summer day."

Then, more prudently, she eyed the rapidly incoming tide. "We'd better hurry."

They hauled the over-full pails down to the beach and sat on the shale to tie their sneakers around their necks. The shallow waves, already breaking over the sandbar, would cool their feet crossing back to the mainland.

Hannah, Thea, Stuart and Mac arrived at the Thomaston Cafe on the last night before it closed for winter. By seven it was too dark and cold to sit outside on the deck, and in the nearly empty dining room, the four of them had their choice of tables. Stuart pulled a chair out for Hannah and looked closely at her face.

"You look like you've been in a cat fight."

"Berry picking," she answered. "It was the only part of me not covered."

"Our kitchen smells like a blackberry bouquet," said Thea.

The waitress brought their drinks and Hannah eyed the paltry dram that barely covered the bottom of her glass.

"My God! A Scotsman spills that much in the pouring. Stu, could I have a triple? And please, no ice. Anyone who puts ice in malt whisky would put catsup on caviar."

"You're a very expensive date," he said, and turned to Mac. "She insists that she likes me, so why is she so mean?"

"She's not mean, just spiky." Mac leaned across the table and patted Hannah's hand. "Learn to trust men more. Especially Stuart here. He's a good fellow."

"Mac, you don't have to tout Stu. He's an excellent example of the species. Just too eager to settle down. I'm not ready for kitchen and cradle." She sipped her scotch and remembered wistful girls back home, entrapped too soon by babies and clothes patterns.

Thea laughed. "You're both impatient men. The type that paints dead flies into the corners of windowsills."

"No worse than women who call a cab and abandon their car if they have a flat," Said Mac.

Hannah frowned. "Now who's being mean? I am not competent around motors. I don't 'do' cars."

"Emily did," said Mac sadly. "She removed the rotor from Ian's distributor cap to disable his car. The garage mechanic discovered it when he came out with the new battery."

They finished their drinks and the waitress arrived with a platter of sautéed Cajun shrimp.

"Some good came of the whole summer fiasco," said Mac. He ticked off his long, sinewy fingers. "You'll get your new greenhouse. Luther was not sent to jail, but given severe restrictions—he's glad to be back working, but strictly as a fisherman. Doc was arrested, and on the basis of his record, he'll be gone for a while. And that boyfriend of Angela's is going to manage the video store. Rick's a smart kid."

Mac brushed Thea's cheek with his fingers. "And, if you'll marry me, we'll live happily ever after."

Hannah put down her fork and stared at him. "Mac, that's the most hopeless public proposal I've ever heard."

"Maybe not entirely hopeless," said Thea. Mac solemnly raised his wineglass.

"To hope."

BVG